Eye of the Dawn
by
Ernest Pick
ISBN: 978-1-9996623-9-4

All Rights Reserved.
No reproduction, copy or transmission of this publication may be made without written permission. No paragraph or section of this publication may be reproduced, copied or transmitted save with written permission or in accordance with the provisions of the Copyright Act 1956 (as amended).
Copyright 2018 Ernest Pick
The right of Ernest Pick to be identified as the author of this work has been asserted in accordance with the Copyright Designs and Patents Act 1988.
A copy of this book is deposited with the British Library.

Published by

i2i
PUBLISHING

i2i Publishing
Manchester. UK
www.i2ipublishing.co.uk

Prologue

Her father, Simone knows, works for the French government stationed in Germany. Even as a teenager, and despite her father's effort to protect her, Simone realises that something is wrong. When she and her father walk to the grocery, he grasps her arm tightly. Too tightly. Something is definitely wrong. Nervously looking over his shoulder, his lips are clenched tight. Upsetting. The street they take to the grocery is not the one she has travelled before. A circuitous route. At the grocery he stops, bends down on one knee to kiss her on the cheek, telling her not to be scared. This makes her more afraid.

A few days later, Simone is on the steps leading from the house to the driveway as her father slips by her. Looking unusually relaxed, he is not wearing a tie this morning. He unlocks their Peugeot with his key and opens the front door. From the glove compartment, he pulls out a map which he unfolds and studies earnestly. Simone wraps a scarf about her head against the rising wind. She can see her father turning in the driver's seat, reaching out his hand to wave goodbye. She waves back. Dad is lighting a cigarette, smoke curling about his face, then looks forward to turn his key in the ignition.

Suddenly an eruption, followed by an ear shattering crescendo, cut through the violet sky, enflaming it. A fireball has exploded from the underbelly of the car. The blast is fierce, cataclysmic. It not only rips apart the vehicle but launches fiery shards into the air through a nearby shop window. Glass fragments splinter, showering myriad slivers into the streets. Her father's car is stripped of paint, of metal, leather, fabric, of life. Nothing remains, she believes, but cannot quite process it. All physical presence of the man has disintegrated. Simone's eyes are wide open, her mouth whistling in shock. She is still cradling the residual sight of her father waving to her, a minute smile playing across his face as he bends forward to start the car. A fading image of the lit cigarette in his lips, smoke curling upwards. The event plays out slowly as if time were frozen, even reversed, so that the young girl may witness again and again in all its terrifying, intimate and bloody detail her father shedding his body.

1.   An Interview

Simone crosses the street at Buford highway, her heels tapping rhythmically, reflecting the quickening beat of her heart. Anticipating what is to come somewhat nervously. Despite the coolness of the morning, a small drop of perspiration forms on her brow. She dabs it away with an embroidered handkerchief. As she lifts her head, she takes in the full sweep of the Baptist church. It is built in a half circle with gray-painted brick. Centrally positioned, a clock tower rises high above massive front portals. In front of the church, Simone slows, smooths her outfit and takes in a deep breath. For her interview, she has chosen carefully. She wears a cream hounds tooth suit with metallic buttons. Not extravagant, yet not dull. A black pillbox with a short veil covers her hair. Simone is a slender woman of medium height with black hair, eyes which ordinarily shine blue, but when alarmed or surprised, recede into obscurity. Despite the accelerating of her heart, she works at remaining calm as she enters the building. Long, deep breaths.

She has been instructed to open the heavy, oak door to the left, to walk by the west wing of the church towards the rear. There she will see a short mauve corridor with three adjacent doors. Pass by the first two. For one moment, stand motionless in front of the third. Smile for the pinhole camera just below the ceiling. The third door is unmarked. Do not knock. Turn the handle and enter. Inside, a small antechamber with an unadorned pine bench and two mahogany chairs. As instructed, she enters and sits. Notices no decorations on the walls nor on the door in front of her. Five minutes pass. Endlessly. She would like to smoke but refrains. There are no ashtrays in this room. There is, in fact, nothing in this room to divert her attention. She fidgets with her purse. Settles back nervously in the chair, lifts her watch up. She has arrived exactly on time. She wishes there were a mirror in the room so that she could check the sweep of her hair.

Suddenly the door swings open. A round man sporting red suspenders, with spectacles drooping over his nose peers down and smiles, taking in her entire shape. She arises. He says something to her which she does not catch. Does not shake her hand. He turns and waves her into his office.

Simone sees two chairs, begins to lower herself in one. He motions her to sit in the other, the one directly in front of him. She complies. The man says his name is Anderson. A man of some fifty years with a pink face, sparse brown hair, and silver spectacles which cradle onto the bridge of his nose. A face swollen by time. She imagines that once Anderson may have been good looking. He has bright, debonair eyes behind the lenses, lips that curl easily into an agreeable grin. His gaze is strong, effective. This is not a man washed out by his duties, she thinks.

He sits behind his desk, picks up a file and opens it. His lips move without sound. Simone looks around. There is a photo of FDR on the wall. But something seriously amiss, something lacking in this office. No greenery, no plants to enliven this gray space. Not even photos of Anderson's family. A sterile room. Clearly meant to be devoid of distraction. There is a typewriter to one side of the desk. An Olivetti, she thinks. He looks up, catches her expression:

"We like to keep things simple here," he offers with a wan smile. "So how did you hear about us?" he prompts, throwing off the first question easily.

"Everyone has heard about the OSS," she responds carefully.

"I doubt that truly," Anderson replies, but he is not scowling. "Did you bring the file?"

Simone reaches into her purse and pulls out a folded brace of papers which she hands across the desk.

He takes the sheaf and nods approval. Opens the dossier.

"You speak French," he says. "Nice. How good is your French?"

"Fluent," she responds. My father was French."

"Ah, was," Anderson repeats sadly, and shakes his head softly. "Was."

"Yes, he died a few years ago."

"And you also know German?" his head lifting.

"Perfectly," Simone replies. "My mother was Austrian."

"So," Anderson says, "with these languages, particularly the German, you have useful skills."

Simone feels she must explain her language capabilities further. "My parents had a strict rule," she says. "My father would only speak French to me, and my mother German. If I answered in English, they pretended not to understand."

"Interesting," Anderson comments. "But how was growing up in such a climate for you?"

"I hated it."

Anderson looks up quickly, chuckles, a flicker of amusement quickly passing into oblivion.

She shifts in her seat, not out of nervousness, but out of eagerness to advance the interview.

"Still, my language skills could be helpful to you," she goes on. She does not smile when she speaks, No emoting. She maintains level speech patterns, intonations. Her diction is direct. No soaring similes. She gets to the point. Modulations are infrequent except when necessary to mark a point. Anderson likes this about Simone, although he wonders about this slip of a woman who succeeds in managing herself so completely.

"You consider yourself a patriot?" he asks, his eyes rising above the glasses.

"Just someone who would like to serve her country," she responds evenly. "I don't approve of madmen," she adds.

"You have filled out each segment?" he asks pointing to the paper in front of him.

"Yes."

"Swell. We shall examine all carefully. And then we'll get back to you."

"Do you need my phone number?"

He guffaws. "Surely we have that. Our agency prides itself in knowing a great deal about most people, including Simone Valois."

"I get that my question is superfluous," she says ruefully, chiding herself for asking it.

Anderson arises, fingers his red suspenders. "I have nothing else to add at this time. Go out the same way you came in. Try not to appear thoughtful. Look like you are coming out of a grocery store. Think about oatmeal or French toast, if you prefer. You may encounter one or two men at the end of the street who will study you with interest. Ignore them. They don't belong to us although we naturally are aware of them. If they contact you, feel free to engage them. Tell them everything you know. Since you know nothing, it will matter not in the slightest."

Simone bristles at the idea of knowing nothing, but she holds her tongue. Arises. Reaches over to shake hands with Anderson. He touches her hand and sits.

"Good day," she offers.

Exiting, she expects him to reply, but he remains silent. She leaves through the vestry and onto the path that borders the church. The path is cratered with uneven bits of concrete which time and the elements have unearthed into irregular, even jagged patterns. As soon as she reaches the sidewalk, she makes out two men in black standing under a lamppost. They are looking in her direction. She stops, then veers towards them deliberately, even provocatively. They continue to study her, but do not approach. Nor do they shy away. She shrugs. Walks back towards the bus station. Wipes a bead of sweat away from an eye. After a few steps, she halts, pretends to straighten her hose, and looks backwards towards the two men. They have not moved, although they continue to stare in her direction. She wonders how well she did in this very brief interview. Thinks she handled everything well. She did not want to show emotion for fear it would be interpreted as a weakness.

Now, Simone is walking steadily if not rapidly towards the bus station on Buford Avenue. She reaches the structure erected to shield passengers from both rain and sun, a green, metallic stall, and sits back on the bench. In a moment, her bus arrives, braking with a shudder. It is a snub-nosed green bus with little windows by each seat. The driver opens the front door with a hydraulic racket, takes her change, issues a ticket, but does not talk. The bus chugs along Buford Avenue, turns towards Peachtree. In some fifteen minutes, Simone yanks on the string that signals her stop, and descends. She is thinking about Anderson and realises that he has virtually said nothing to her about what he does, what his organisation expects and, if she is hired, what she may be asked to do. Frustrating. But Simone acquired patience in her early years and settles back into the shell which is the bedrock of her strength.

By the little house which now belongs to her, she searches in her purse for the key. Before she has located it, her fumbling is interrupted by two men who have come up behind her, their shadows looming on the wall of the house. She turns. The men from the church!

Unsure as to whether she should be alarmed or not. Breathing heavily again.

"Something I can do for you, gentlemen?" she asks steadily as she faces them. For the first time, she can see that they are wearing collars. Priests!

"Are you Catholic priests?" she asks

"We are men of God," he responds after a short pause. "If you wouldn't mind, we would like to speak with you." He is a tall, narrow faced man with scant facial hair.

"And what is this about?"

"We saw you enter the Baptist church earlier. The side entrance," he continues. "We know the church is a staging area for OSS to recruit people." This is said by the shorter of the two men. He has a slightly bulging midriff, his body pear-like.

"I am Father Michael, and this is my colleague, Father Paul. We don't mean to alarm you."

Father Paul is gangly, tall with a long, craning neck, and a pock-marked face. His eyes tend to drift from one direction to the other. Unnerving her.

"I am not frightened," Simone responds raising her eyes steadily. "Not in the slightest."

"Then you will speak to us?"

"Yes, of course." Pauses only a second. She is certain these men are innocuous and that she has read the situation well. Besides, Anderson knows these men, "Come into the house."

"Swell. You do know that we are not Baptist," the men say looking at each other, and beginning to unwind.

Simone unlocks the door. The two men find themselves in a parlor, beige walls replete with copies of art nouveau paintings. Their eyes roam to a plush red velvet sofa, several straightchairs, and a coffee table in front of a chimney.

"Cozy," Father Paul says. "Nicely decorated room," he compliments. They settle back on the sofa.

"Can I get you some water?" Even as she speaks these words, she is processing rapidly. Clear that if she has assessed the situation properly, these men pose no danger. Maybe they expect to change her thinking. In that case, she might have some fun with them or, at the very least, gain experience jousting with them.

"We expect that you have interviewed for a position with the government agency," Father Michael begins.

Nervy! she thinks. That question is out of bounds! "What possible interest would you have in what I do or don't do?" Simone ripostes sharply.

Father Paul stands briefly, tugs at his belt, cranes his neck, then edges back down.

"OSS is a spy organisation. You know this. An organisation which the government has created to thwart the popular movement of Germany. Yet, Germany wishes only to create a purer state."

"Really!" Simone replies before she can check herself. She is stuck on the word 'purer'.

"We would like to tell you our side of this story, if you don't mind."

"Go on," Simone says restraining a natural impulse to do battle and sinks onto one of the chairs.

Father Paul clears his throat. "It's not an accident that we are here today," he begins. Simone smiles at the naiveté of the sentence. The priest continues. "America is almost certainly going to war with Germany," he says, his eyes widening. "But military response is clearly a blunder. Our leader is interested only in the purification of his own people. Why should anyone find fault in this?" He trains his eyes now on Simone.

She for her part, has decided to play naïve, cool, detached. She shrugs the question away as if it requires no response.

"Go on, Father Paul," his colleague prompts.

"Yes, indeed," he says looking at Simone directly. "Have you read the Fuhrer's work?"

She shakes her head.

Father Paul reaches into his cassock and pulls out a volume which he hands to her. "A copy of the abridged Mein Kampf," he says. A very well-read copy, Simone judges.

"Now why would I want to do that?" she asks.

"Your mind isn't closed, is it?" Father Paul asks.

"I'll look at it," Simone says.

"Read it carefully, my dear. Will you?"

"Heavy reading," she says, fingering the book.

"In it," Father Paul continues, "you learn how the Bolsheviks seek to homogenize all economic activity.

Money for everybody," he scoffs. "Everyone the same. Crazy, isn't it?" he asks craning his neck.

"Total folly," she agrees.

"So, if you follow this, we ought to homogenize the Bolsheviks," he says with a short laugh. And then, he continues, his neck moving almost snake-like towards Simone, "Remains then but one common enemy to keep in check."

"Just one?" she asks innocently.

"Yes, my dear," he says smoothly realising that she is a novice to these ideas. "Jews. For Jews gobble up everything in their path. Gobble everything," he repeats smacking his lips. "The Fuhrer shows them for the menace they always were and how, in our time, they seek to control the banks and, perhaps, even take over the government. You know of course they lost the first world war for Germany. They will be dealt with severely."

"Severely?"

"Yes. Possessions confiscated. Power eliminated. They must be kept at a distance from money. Banks of course, but also stock exchanges, for with their insidious ways, they manipulate all of these centers of financial power."

"Not because they are smart?" Simone asks with an innocent cadence to her question.

"Ha," Father Michael laughs. "This is precisely what they would have you believe. An old wives' tale! The devil is a pretty smart cookie, you know." Father Michael has his hands inside his cassock rumpling the fabric in a rhythmic motion.

"All right", Simone responds, making a circular motion with her left hand. "So, what is all of this to me?"

Father Michael gets up, his hands out of his robe, and for a moment faces the chimney. Now he turns with a serious look on his face. "We are talking to clever and useful people, especially young people. That is our mission."

"So, you think I should not get involved with the OSS."

"Exactly."

"But I am interested, very interested in spycraft," Simone says, baiting them further while rising. "If the OSS accepts me, I may well accept their offer."

"Then you have failed to grasp what we have told you," Father Paul remarks, his tone acrid, his head lowering. "If you have the gift of espionage, and nowadays so few women qualify, then you should be working for us, not the Americans. If your gifts include cryptography or possibly some other aspect of intelligence, then why would you waste it on a system which ultimately will be overcome by Germany?"

"I didn't say that I had a political reason for joining the OSS. I just enjoy the idea of spying. But I want to spy for the side that most closely corresponds to my innermost values."

"Interesting," Father Paul responds. Then hesitates. "And these would be?"

Rather than answer their questions, Simone notices that Father Paul is reaching into his cassock to pull out a camera. He trains it on her, but she shields her face. She decides instantaneously to take control of this moment.

"You don't have my permission to do this," she says, turning away from the camera.

"We like to keep a record of the people we interview," Father Paul responds, somewhat taken aback.

"Perfectly innocent," Father Michael chimes in.

"Please do as I ask," Simone insists. Father Paul replaces the camera into his cassock. "I don't see why two men of God who should be praying for all human beings, are discriminating one group over others. Is this what God wants?"

"It is for the benefit of mankind," Father Michael responds quickly. "True, we pray for all men, but we are realistic these days. And our vision leads us to an indisputable fact. There are groups that strive against the interests of legitimate power. Jew and Russians. We believe that the Fuehrer is on the right path towards limiting their influence.

Simone shrugs, then replies in a gentler tone. "Gentlemen, I am considering your words. I do think your ideas are different, a little peculiar you must admit, but there is something persuasive. I will read your book. How then do I get in touch with you?"

The priests are now both standing, beaming. "Don't concern yourself with this. We know where you live, and, in time, we will return to chat."

After the priests leave, Simone flops down heavily onto the red sofa. She is angry, irritated that she has had to listen to such raw sewage. No way in hell I would ever work for the Third Reich, she says to herself. Pours herself a gin and tonic and begins to drink. These so-called pure race people haven't done their research. Had they done so, they would know that I am Jewish on one side of my family. Better scrutiny on their part is in order, she sneers.

After a while, she relaxes and visualises the silly side of this exchange. First, what are these men doing? Priests are supposedly devoted to peace. How did two men, allegedly of God, get addicted to Adolf Hitler and his gang? Their goal is a distinct betrayal of their country. Even a betrayal of God. How do these men live with that? Their accent shows that both were born in the south. They were raised here, yet their all-consuming passion is to undermine America.

Simone is giggling. They look foolish, sound foolish, and pose no threat to anyone with their sanctimonious analysis. I should forget them as quickly as I met them, she says to herself.

Next to the red sofa, a telephone. Simone dials her sister's number.

"Lazy girl," she begins, as Grace answers the phone. "I can tell that you are still sleeping."

Protesting, Grace yawns audibly and turns fitfully in the bed. "What do you want? You never call unless you want something."

"Yes, I do want something. To have lunch if you can rouse yourself from the bed."

Giggle. "Probably," Grace answers, "but the super says there is no hot water this morning. Maybe I won't shower."

"Not sure that I can have lunch with a dirty you," Simone laughs.

"Not saying what I plan to wash, if anything," Grace muses.

"At the Adolpho at 12:30," Simone prompts.

"Fattening Italian food," Grace complains. "I love it. I'll be there."

Grace is Simone's older sister. Two inches taller and a couple of waist sizes wider, and yet immediately identifiable as a Valois. She has the imperious family nose, typically a fraction too large, especially on the female side of the family. Eyes that predominate and turn dark under stress. Brown, thick hair. A smile that mimics her sister as well as her mother. Fun loving, smiling comes easier to Grace than to Simone. Grace is more playful, less distraught by the intrigues, and complications of this earth. Simone tends to take the daily annoyances that hound everyone more seriously. Grace works as a stenographer in the appeals court in Norcross. Simone has been searching for the right fit for her talents and inclinations. More than a year elapsed before she had convinced herself that spycraft would suit her abilities and interests perfectly.

"So, you went to your interview?" Grace asked.

"I did."

"They took you, didn't they?"

"I hope they will," her sister replies.

A waitress in a black blouse and white apron approaches.

"They would be fools not to," Grace says, blowing her nose. "But you are also a fool for wanting to join a group of people you know nothing about. What in fact do these people do? Follow one another around with guns in their pockets?"

Simone shrugs. "I know they are gearing up for the war effort. They will need people in cryptography, to establish codes, break them, to work in the field."

Grace snickers. "You're a little thing. If they send you onto foreign soil, someone will break your scrawny neck before 24 hours are up."

"I appreciate the faith you have in me," Simone reposts with her own snicker. "My neck may be scrawny, but my brain is bigger."

"You know we're about to get into it with the Germans," Grace muses lowering her voice. "Have you been watching the trailers at the movies of their soldiers? They all look like overgrown thugs."

Simone giggles. "You talk as if I'm going to be sent to the front lines to fight Nazis hand to hand. I really doubt that."

"I just care for you," Grace says, reaching over to touch her sister's hand. "I don't want to lose my one and only sister to murderous hooligans. Although it might be fun to be taken captive by a couple of lean, strong men," she considers, wetting her lips.

Simone looks over at her with amusement. "For the moment, "Simone says simply, "I haven't even been accepted, much less assigned"

The waiting is agonising. Waiting for news, any news. Simone chides herself for not requiring Anderson to specify a date by which she would learn her fate. Days elide. A week later, there is a knock at her door.

Anderson! Simone says to herself, looking through the spy hole in the door.

"You have news for me?" she asks too quickly, the door knob still in hand.

Dressed this day with a jacket, a foursquare in his pocket. As he moves, Simone makes out the red tinge of his suspenders. He smiles.

"I don't do business on a landing. Let me in." She feels foolish now and quickly leads Anderson towards a chair in the kitchen.

"I wanted to come by to tell you the verdict myself. First, he says, settling in. "I myself considered you an eminently qualified candidate. Young, intelligent, gifted in languages. Just what we need. At least that is what I thought. And yet, the office that evaluates transcripts has decided against offering you a place with us." His eyes lift to train on Simone's face which begins to blanche as she hears his voice decline into alow growl.

"My God," Simone answers. "I did not expect that." She fumbles for words here, woun ded to the quick. Can you tell me why I was rejected?"

"Yes," Anderson replies. "Of course, you would ask. The committee that evaluates candidates liked you as a candidate, but they always do their homework, as you might imagine. They unearthed an essay you had written for one of your university courses. The essay concerned forms of government, for and against. It is not that your work was considered subversive, but that your thinking is askew and incomplete."

"I hardly remember that essay at all," Simone responds shaking her head.

"You make the point convincingly, I might add, that all governments are more or less evil, more or less good. True, you find that some exceed the boundaries, but you don't value our own country, single it out for any particular praise. Surely, you could find instances in which America looked better than a banana republic. That was a mistake," he goes on chiding her.

"But that is only because I was focusing on other countries like Russia, Poland and Austria in the piece," Simone protests. "I have nothing against America or our government. To the contrary, our country is one of the very few that truly seems to care about its people. "Look," she adds. "I'm not used to rejection, especially now when I see myself as someone willing to work for and even die for her country."

"Not very clear in this essay, Anderson sighs. He rises. "I wanted to give you the news in person."

"But," she fumbles again for words, stung by the rejection. "I think you are making a big mistake. Nobody would be more active, more devoted than I. Nobody would be more committed than I to risk everything for this country."

"Sorry, my dear. It's not up to me. I do wish you all the best." And with that, Anderson pats Simone on the shoulder, and leaves.

2. Simone Acts on an Epiphany

For several weeks, a frustrated and even angry Simone rarely leaves the house. Brimming with unused energy and now bitter, she cannot comprehend that this agency has rejected her, an agency about to enter a warzone clearly in need of linguists. Just doesn't make sense, she repeats to herself.

Grace is equally shocked by the verdict.

"Tell those fools that the other side would jump to hire you," she shouts into the phone.

Calming herself at long last, Simone must decide on the path that will govern her future. What kind of work am I suitable for? she asks herself. Nothing momentous, even agreeable, occurs to her. She won't be a baker, cook or seamstress, the sorts of jobs that are now available to women. Demeaning work to be disparaged. Too pissed off for that, she snorts.

Night after night, unable to find the solace of repose, she paces the floor. Somewhere in the back of her mind, she knows there is a way out of this dilemma, but she has no means of reaching it. The more she focuses, the less productive the result. After several more days of preoccupation and white nights, she collapses into a deep and still sleep. After twelve hours, she awakens to the phone ringing. Grace!

"Can't talk to you right now," Simone yawns. "I'm still sleeping."

"Ha! You can't fool me," Grace bellows. "Tell me what's happening with you."

"Not a damn thing," Simone replies. "Let's talk tomorrow. Please!"

Grace relents, hangs up. But it is then that Simone recalls what her sister angrily shouted several days earlier. She said that I was good enough to work for either side, she remembers. And it is with these words in the forefront of her mind, she leaps to her feet with an idea, an incongruous idea, yet the only idea that may jolt her out of her lassitude.

"I'm going to join the other side," she shouts gleefully. "OSS doesn't want me? We'll see about that."

So, she picks up the phone and calls her sister at work. "I've got a plan. An epiphany. Don't interrupt, Grace. Just listen. I know this sounds nuts, but there is reason underlining my madness."

"Simone, dear," Grace begins. "Maybe you need to think this over more carefully. You're crazy! Forget what I said. You can't be working for the Nazis. It goes against everything you truly believe in, everything I believe in. Our parents are rolling in their graves just hearing you think this way. If you do this, I will have to question our sisterhood."

Simone giggles. "Don't be daft, girl," she whistles. "The other side is only a stepping stone for me."

Momentary silence on the other end. "You might as well jump out of a plane without a parachute," Grace continues, "fool that you are. You could wind up hurt or even dead if you do this. Please remember you have someone here who loves you. That person may even be me."

But Simone is adamant. That afternoon she retreads the road to the Baptist Church. Once there, descending the steps from the bus, she can make out the cassock of one of the priests, and she walks purposefully in his direction. Between her and the priest, a hummingbird hovers in midair, his wings a blur. Nature's way of intervening? she thinks for a split second, but then blots it out.

She spies Father Michael who is apparently standing guard. Guarding what or whom? Probably anybody that comes in or out of the wrong door of the Baptist Church.

"Hello, Father," Simone approaches, offering her hand. Father Michael turns a complete circle to ascertain that nobody is watching before taking her hand. "What are you doing here, Miss Valois?"

"I have read the book by Herr Hitler. To my surprise, I found it engrossing," she continues without guile. "Clearly, the Fuhrer has grasped our problems."

"Really?" Father Michael responds, his tone suspicious. "When we spoke some time ago, you surely had not understood the Hitler doctrine. Or were sympathetic to his point of view."

"Ah, Father, my mistake", Simone says softly, cringing slightly. "I judged too soon."

"What happened to your OSS application?" Her face turns dour. "Got turned down, didn't you?"

"I failed," she admits with the hint of a smile. "But this is all to the good. Maybe even God's plan for me. After I considered your words, I would not have taken a position there had they offered it. I made a terrible mistake by applying there. In fact, I would like you to consider me for your group."

Father Michael is processing. After a moment, he says: "All right. If this is your wish, then you will need to meet with one of our directors from the Embassy. Can you do this sometime in the next few days?"

"I can."

"I will be in touch with the arrangements. You may need to leave home at a moment's notice," he adds.

"I will be ready," Simone replies.

Father Michael speaks curtly back to her. "I hope this is not a mistake on our part. If so, you may pay consequences. Severe consequences."

"Father, you can trust me," Simone parries in a soft and sincere voice.

"Father Paul will be delighted by your turnabout," Father Michael exclaims. "He actually had faith in you. I wasn't so sure, but Father Paul is an acute analyst of the souls of men. And women too, I see now."

Three days pass. A Friday evening, Simone has completed a dinner of pork chops and beet salad, is downing the remainder of a glass of red wine, when the ring of her phone startles her.

Father Paul. "Simone," he begins, "I need you to leave in the next hour for the Henry Grady Hotel. Do you know where it is?"

"I do," Simone replies. She reaches for a pen on the nightstand and begins to write.

"Be there at eight o'clock. There will be a dance taking place in the hotel ballroom. You will enter the ballroom exactly at eight wearing a red dress."

Simone interrupts. "I don't have a red dress."

Pause. "Do you have any red article of clothing?"

"I have a pillbox hat which is red and topped with a red feather."

"Wear that hat," Father Paul continues. "When you enter the ballroom, look to the left. There are benches lining the wall. Sit on one of these. The man you are meeting is in his thirties. Wears a pencil thin moustache. A brown, tweed business suit." Pause. "Got this?"

"Yes. Someone from the consulate?"

Father Paul continues. "Don't interrupt. He will say the following words: 'The moon is rather large tonight'. You will respond. 'Yes, but not larger than last night.' Then the man will ask you to dance. You do dance, don't you?"

Hesitation. "I do dance," Simone replies, "but I can't jitterbug very well. Waltzes are more up my alley."

"Very conventional," Father Paul reacts jokingly. "I took you for a more modern woman."

"But I'll try anything," Simone interjects.

"That is good," Father Paul responds. "You may be asked to do exactly that, but to do it in the name of the cause. We must all make sacrifices on behalf of the movement. Even jitterbug. You get my drift?"

"I did say I would try anything," Simone answers, without deciphering the meaning behind Father Paul's tone.

Simone takes a shower without washing her hair for fear that it will not dry in time. Dresses carefully. She decides to wear her cream colored suit. This time with the red pillbox hat she has on a shelf in the rear of her closet. She sets it on her head at a jaunty angle. Lights a Chesterfield but snuffs it out half smoked. Opens the window to let in fresh air. Sucks it in deeply into her lungs. Satisfied, closes the window. This is my chance, she repeats to herself. My chance!

In the streetcar that whisks her downtown, she does not prepare for her meeting. First, she does not know whether it amounts to an audition. Or is it simply a way one of their agents can look me over from top to bottom to make an assessment?

She feels her muscles tightening before the uncertainty of the event. Happily, she has a procedure to deal with nerves. From late childhood in front of a situation which makes her tense, Simone has learned to adjust by relaxing her muscles, breathing deeply, unwinding even in face of the threat. In this situation, beyond an early queasiness gathering in her esophagus which she works to put at bay, she feels more focused. Excited! Yes, she recognises that she is on point. Ready to do battle. But battle as a woman does battle. She needs no billy clubs, pistols, armaments. She trusts in intelligence and intuition. Welcomes the art of war as a woman may wage it. And as she is processing that thought, the trolley stops with a piercing, grinding noise before the hotel.

She steps down gingerly. Adjusts one foot daintily to fit completely into a shoe. Checks her watch. Five to eight. Perfect. Walks quietly on marble floors through swinging glass-etched doors, the reception area, and towards the ballroom where, even at this distance, she can hear the music formed by a rather large band. Playing Gershwin songs. 'Lady Be Good'. Yes, Simone likes that one.

There are perhaps a hundred or more people on the floor either dancing or sitting on benches and at tables off to one side. As instructed, she heads left. Settles next to a woman fingering her hose, straightening it.

"First time here, hon?" the woman says to her without looking up. She is a blond with stringy hair and large breasts, and her breath smells of stale cigarettes.

"Yes. What am I supposed to do?"

"Just wait for some prince to kiss your hand and whisk you onto the floor of paradise."

"Is that all I have to do? Simone smiles. "Just await whisking?"

"We all serve by waiting," the woman replies with the hint of a smile.

In a moment, a prince wearing a jaunty suit too big for him sidles over to the woman and leads her by the hand to the dance floor.

It's a foxtrot. Never learned to dance well to that. Simone watches, grimacing.

Before the foxtrot is finished, a good-looking man in his thirties with a pencil-thin moustache has sauntered over to her. Sits by her side.

"The moon is rather large tonight," he says without turning to her.

"You can see the moon? From here?" she asks him skeptically.

"Is that all you have to say?" he turns to her, scowling.

"But not larger than yesterday's," she says quickly, scarcely flustered.

The man grunts "Close enough, Simone. It would be better if you didn't try to make a joke out of these signals. Someday you may regret playing around."

"Sorry," she answers, pretending contrition, but grinning slightly. She has decided nobody is going to make a stereotype out of her.

"Let's dance," the man grins, leading her onto the dance floor as a waltz begins. An Irving Berlin tune. As they sail around the floor, on the bandstand, a young woman in a yellow rayon dress takes to the microphone and croons:

> *I Love to dance the dreamy waltz*
> *Of long ago*
> *When grand-mama and grand-papa*
> *Were girl and beau*
> *While gliding o'er the ballroom floor*

To the waltz of long ago

Played by a band of some fourteen musicians all dressed in white, save for black bow-ties. Trumpets, trombones, a sax, guitars, and basses. The singer launches into a second verse. The dancer is whisking Simone around the floor. The man can gyrate, the room twirling around her in a miasma of flashing colors, sounds, and contorted, if happy, faces. The music slows, and he motions her towards swinging doors. Simone is taking his measure. Not quite as tall as she is with heels, but jauntily appealing. Still, something about his voice cautions her. An acidity disturbs. She looks up, wiping the miasma of flashing colors out of her eyes to study him. Dressed to the nines. Cultured in a manner she has not yet encountered. Not sure what to make of him.

"What's your name?" she asks.

"Let's go," he replies, grabbing his fedora from a rack, taking her by the hand before she can protest, leading her rapidly through the lobby to the elevators.

"Five," he says curtly to an operator, a young man in a pale gold uniform wearing white gloves. A large woman in an evening dress enters the elevator. "Nine," she says. The boy repeats her number. The large woman speaks.

"I bet you have your ups and downs," and guffaws. The boy does not respond, nor does he emit a grin. The elevator stops, the operator smoothly sliding open the metal gate.

"Where are we going?"

"To my room," the man says in the corridor. "Problem for you?"

"You could at least tell me your name," she says, stopping in mid-stride.

"David."
"David what?"
"David Johnson."
"Your real name? How do I know that you are what you pretend you are?" she asks.

David looks at her as if she is demented. He does not answer. Fumbling for the key in his pants pocket. Looking at him from an angle, she finds his face pleasing. Better from the side, she thinks. It's the moustache that does not quite suit him. Makes him look flighty. Maybe he is a weasel. David opens the door. The room is small with dark golds, greys, and off whites. Everything appears downplayed so that the fabrics, the walls, suggest nothing unusual in the room. Maybe that is what people want in a hotel room, Simone reflects. The room is designed so that you can only look at one another. David switches on a radio. The Cleveland Orchestra is playing a Bruch Violin Concerto.

Now an epiphany slams into her head. She wonders why it took so long to surface. He will want to make love to her. This in and of itself does not trouble her, even though she has never made love with anyone. Simone has had boyfriends in a mellow past, but none with whom she has felt a physical attraction. So, despite a kiss now and then, no man has ever gotten physically closer. When a boyfriend got too friendly, she tended to hold him at bay. Sex with any of them had no special aim. She never experienced lust. Men experience nothing but lust, she has heard. This, in of itself, does not concern her. She has also heard that sex the first time will be painful, perhaps even bloody, but a little pain, a little blood is undoubtedly a necessary ransom to pay in this situation. Cataloguing rapidly what little she knows or has read about sex.

Necessary for a spy to know how to seduce and be seduced. That would be part of the job, she judges. And in that vein, she is congruent with the world, for making love in this context. Offering herself to a stranger, is simply an aspect of the work she craves. David is opening a bottle of Scotch, pours two glasses.

"So, tell me about yourself," he says, sinking into a plush gray fauteuil, his face bland.

Perched on the edge of the bed. She sips the scotch and makes a sour face. She relates her pathetically trite childhood, the trifle of a story that passes for a life, the demise of her parents, the love she has for her sister.

"So, your parents deeded you your house," David says, sipping. His brown eyes now fix on to her face.

"The house we were raised in. Grace lived there with me for a while, then left."

"She is angry with you?"

Simone smiles. "Grace? Not at all. She is giving me space while trying on new spaces of her own."

"Interesting that you put it in those terms. Space, I mean. But let's get down to what brought you here. You want to become part of the movement that is sweeping the world, isn't that so?"

"Yes."

"Swell," he concludes adamantly. "Finish your drink," he says commandingly. Simone complies. He goes on, his tone harsher. Turns to her almost menacingly. "But why? I am told you tried to sign up with the enemy."

"The enemy?"

"Yes, the American government. You surely know by now that we will soon be at war with one another."

Pause. "I don't know that. Not for sure."

"Guaranteed," he laughs, revealing for the first time uneven, stained teeth. He offers her a Pall Mall. They are both smoking now. What caused you to change your mind?"

"I was angry they didn't take me," she begins, inhaling. She has rehearsed this answer several times previously and is confident it will be accepted. "And then I read Mein Kampf. True, it was only the abridged version, but I agree that power must be in the hands of the right people."

"Quite so," David agrees. "By the way, have you spotted Anderson's tell?"

"His tell?"

"I've known Anderson for several years. When he presses two fingers repeatedly against his mouth, he agrees with whatever is happening or said. Even if he tells you the opposite, don't believe him."

"Interesting," Simone avers. In fact, she has never thought about the human body providing clues as to what a person may be thinking. She finds this possibility fascinating. Lays the thought aside. She has heard that men like to talk about themselves and presses on. "Tell me about you," she continues.

His eyes shade. "There is little in my life which would interest you. I'd much rather know about you. To be with you." He gets up and sits by her on the bed. Touches her hair. "Women are able to do wonderful things with hair these days," he remarks clumsily.

Simone smiles. "Your hair flows," she remarks, touching his hair with her fingers. "The color is a mixture of blond and brown, and I bet you don't do anything to it."

"This is true," he acknowledges. Turns to her, pulls her in close, and kisses her fully on the lips. "You better put out your cigarette," she says. You might burn your finger."

Stamps out the butt. "I find you intriguing," he says. I'd like us to spend the night together."

Hmmm. She would prefer that he thought her so breathtakingly sexy that he couldn't contain himself from caressing every inch of her body. I better take what I can get, she thinks. She nods assent but does not look in his direction. His hands are now on her shoulders, lowering, probing, clumsy. He begins to undress her. She lets him do this, her breathing increasing in volume. After a moment, she is panting. He is pulling back the bed covers, and now slides naked between the sheets, a hand outstretched to her. She places a towel underneath the blanket just before sliding in. The sheets smell lemony as she pulls them up over her chest. She removes her bra, snuggles in beside him. I wish I knew what I am supposed to do, she is wondering. I'll just let go. Women report it is the man who always takes the initiative. She presses her lips against his. His mouth tastes acidic, a mixture of saliva and cigarettes. He touches her breasts, fondles them. She apologises because they aren't huge. Laughing, David kisses each one, teases a nipple. In a moment, he is thrusting inside her. Glandular scent. Musk. A sudden painful rip. Sure, she is bleeding. Cannot see it, cannot stop it. He is inside her. It hurts. She is undoing the tightness of her muscles before the onslaught of his thrusts. But he is at it only momentarily. His face contorts, and he exhales as he comes inside her. For an instant, she is alarmed by his guttural noise, his eyes closing shut, wondering whether he will pull through. Have I killed him?

She does not know whether he has put on protection or not. She is chiding herself for not exercising any control whatsoever. Suddenly the act is over. Ends before it has truly flowered, she thinks. Rush hour sex. She looks over and sees a hairy chest lifting up and down. The man's face is crimson. He falls backwards onto the bed breathing hard, but with a pleasant expression on his face. Rises on an elbow towards her.

"How did I do?" she asks, tentatively.

"For a first time, not bad," he responds gutturally, critically, "but you can't just lie there like a sack of potatoes." His voice edging fault-finding, almost mean." You do recall that you have hands and a mouth, yes?" Simone recoils as if she were slapped. A novice, she says to herself. Can't forget that I'm a novice at this. The thought little consoles her. In a few moments, David falls asleep and a few moments later, his throat erupts into a snore.

Simone arises carefully. Goes to the bathroom. Returns. David is manifestly out. His breathing laboured. Near the bed, by the sliver of light seeping into the room, she notices his pants askew on the floor. A wallet has fallen out of his pocket. A large brown, leather wallet. Simone looks up, eyes wide open. The man is asleep. She opens the wallet. Only now is she feeling the excitement she did not experience during sex. A small manila envelope inside. Undoes the flap. Opens it. A small round, black object. She has heard about such things. A microdot. The object may contain information. She takes it to the bathroom, holds it to the light, examines it, but the script is much too tiny to decipher.

Now what is she supposed to do? She can simply replace the object into the wallet, leaving everything as she has found it, including the pants on the floor. She could run to the church and hand it over to Anderson, or she can pocket the tiny envelope and deliver it to the German government in the morning. Isn't that what she is supposed to do in this situation? Could this be a test of how she must react as a spy? Unsure. The pants on the floor, the all too visible wallet falling out of it so conveniently creates doubt. Could be a plant. Probably a plant. Clearly, she needs to pocket the object and turn it over to the Germans. Deliver it via the priests, yes. For the moment, she sees no other avenue. Of course, if she is wrong, who knows what may happen to her. But she has made her judgment and trusts her intuition. As for David, she will simply leave him wrapped in bedsheets. Easy enough to dress quietly and find her way home. And that, finally, is what she decides.

Slips on her dress in the bathroom. Softly unlatches the front door to the room. She does not observe David's raised eye trailing her as she closes the door behind her with infinite caution. When she reaches fresh air, she realises she has stopped breathing. She lets out a cloud of air and tension. Better now.

On the next corner, a phone booth. She calls Father Michael's rectory. He answers.

"I have something for you," Simone says.

Father Michael answers fast. "Don't bring it here. You did hear me, did you not? Do not bring it here. Someone will be in touch with you before the end of the evening and you will deliver the item to that person."

Simone stops at a diner, orders a cup of coffee and a piece of apple pie. So, this is what spying is about. Have I played my cards well? Not for one moment does she consider that she has irretrievably lost her virginity to a man whom, several hours previously, she did not know. Sex feels irrelevant. She believes she has played the game correctly, but the proof of this assessment will lie in the next few hours. Chain smokes several cigarettes as she imbibes a second cup of coffee. Instead of taking the bus, she decides to walk. It will clear my head, and I can make it home within an hour.

Before she has reached the door of her house, she finds a man sitting on the stoop, snuffing out a butt on her stoop. He says his name is Erwand and that he works with the German Abwehr. She does not know what the Abwehr is. He snorts. He is a small, wiry man of fifty, she gauges, sporting a black suit with a blue tie. Shoes are polished to a gleam.

"And what is that?"

Erwand smiles. "Intelligence. German intelligence. But I don't wish to discuss the matter in the great outdoors. Let me come inside."

"It's late. The neighbours could be looking, judging," she observes.

Shrugs. "What could they possibly be thinking? Perhaps a new beau for the lovely Simone Valois."

Inside, she pours him a cup of tea. "I always preferred Earl Grey," he says approvingly. Erwand crinkles his cheek into a dimple when he speaks disparagingly. "Despite the fact that it is made by those silly, impotent citizens of Great Britain."

He sips at the tea, looks down, but intones forcefully. "You have taken something from your conquest last night. Where is it?"

"Show me some identification," she remarks quietly.

He produces a badge and an ID card. She scrutinises it without knowing whether it could be forged or not.

"It is genuine," he interrupts her glance. "Look, I know you stole a microdot from one of our men last night. The fact that you did not turn it over to the OSS is smashing. Had you done so, we would have put you on our enemy's list. Not a list to aspire to," he goes on, his dimple widening. "For when we end victorious, our enemies will be dealt with harshly. Or you could have left the item where you found it on the floor," he continues pensively. "Yet, you decided to take it. Why?"

"Because I wasn't entirely certain whether David was genuine," Simone responds.

"So, you brought it over to us, yes? Never doubted the wisdom of this action?"

"Yes, it was safer to turn it over to you. I have been in touch with Father Michael about it," she adds, and reaches into her purse for the envelope.

He scrutinises the dot slowly with almost endless curiosity, even though she is certain it cannot be read without a microscope. Now he lifts his head towards her.

"Good girl. This is exactly what we hoped you would do when we arranged for the wallet to fall onto the floor."

"You mean it was staged?" she asks with feigned surprise.

"Exactly to observe how you would treat the matter, especially after you had slept with the gentleman. Most women would have done nothing. Certainly not after having sex. By the way, how was that for you?" He asks looking at her directly for the first time.

"You mean having sex?"

"Yes," he says, "that is what I would like to know."

"Not glorious," she responds truthfully.

He is smacking his lips. "Did you initiate sex or did he?"

"He did, of course," she answers.

"He undressed you?"

"Excuse me," Simone responds sharply. "I don't think a description of what happened last night is appropriate."

Chagrined, the man lowers his head. "Of course," he responds. "Of course. It is just fun to hear and fantasise," he adds.

"But it is my body you are imagining," Simone says acidly.

"Forget what I said," the man says hastily. "You are quite a lovely woman," he adds. "You surely know that men lust after you."

"But I acted correctly. I'm referring to the microdot. Right? Isn't that the bottom line?"

"Yes," Erwand says, his tone less salacious. "Had you alerted him that his pants had disgorged his wallet, this would not have been a bad mark against you. Just a slovenly response. Sloppy under the circumstances. But you noted correctly that although he had agreed upon signals when you met, that he offered no additional identification. He could have been an enemy agent who had intercepted verbal cues. But had you done nothing, it might have indicated that you were not curious, inventive enough for spy work. So, you did just the right thing. We congratulate you on passing our little test. And as a result, we are provisionally inviting you into the Abwehr. Ours, as you know, is an international movement which will cleanse the entire world of troublemakers. Nonetheless, your appointment is provisional, I stress, but one which you may make permanent if you continue to do good work for us.

Each and every month, we shall pay you a small stipend as long as you are of service. When you travel or live outside of Atlanta, we will pay your expenses.

Speaking of which, next week we would like you to apply for a position in the Commerce Department as a clerk. I will provide you with the exact documentation. You will be offered the job, I promise you. So, you will need to move to DC in several months. We will pay your rent in addition to your stipend."

"And how could I be of service to you in this capacity? Simone asks. "This is not a small thing you are asking of me. Atlanta is my home, as you well know."

"We realise the inconvenience, of course. But it is a tiny favor to the Third Reich. Your work? We will let you know. In the interim, we also have an additional favor to ask. While you await the offer from Commerce, we want you to schedule surgery."

"Excuse me?"

Sipping his tea. Now lays it down, the cup rattling on the glass table.

"I will be blunt with you, Miss Valois. You are a fine-looking woman. Surely, you are aware of the potential of your body as a weapon. Your feminine attributes may be a great asset for us, especially in Washington. Yes, trim, an acceptable bosom, but your face, if you will accept the criticism, has a flaw. A small flaw, I grant you. You are no doubt aware of it."

She harbours no doubt about his aim. "My nose?"

"Yes, your nose," he responds carefully depositing the cup and saucer. "If your nose were shortened and angled just a bit, you would be especially ravishing. In fact, a little bundle of sexual dynamite, and few men could resist you. Your body could be of great use. To tell you the truth, my dear, we have few women in America working with us, and fewer still who have the wherewithal to seduce men. The bedding of key men is an important tool in our agency's bag of tricks. Men give up information more easily after their lust has been satisfied. Imagine yourself after a tryst with General This or That. He has had his orgasm. He's quite unwound, puffing a Lucky Strike next to you in bed, his free hand caressing your chest. First, he chatters pleasantries. Soon, he makes the leap, chatting about plans of the new tank his scientists are engineering. You see, Simone? It is important for us to optimise our product, if you understand that I speak of you in this manner. We have in our employ a plastic surgeon here in Atlanta who will do the work while you are awaiting your job acceptance. Are you willing to do this?"

Simone smiles. She has been carping about her nose all her life, and that someone else would pay to shorten and round it, is a dream come true.

"Of course," she gushes with a genuine smile. "Can I freshen your tea?"

3. Simone Undergoes Surgery

Dr. Ardi Mehta has taken ample measurements over more than an hour. In his windowless office, he touches, prods, and pulls at her nose as well as the flesh around it. He marks her face with a pen. Erases the marks, starts all over. Three separate appointments have led to refinements until Dr. Mehta is content. He is a man with a puffy hooked nose, a crusty black and white beard that swirls about his chin. A man who laughs easily but has eyes that seem blank. Impossible to know what he is thinking as he makes notations, returns to her face as if it were a blueprint on which his hands write. Finally, the verdict.

"Wednesday next at eight in the morning," he announces, pushing his stool back from the cot. You'll only be under for a couple of hours at most. There will be anesthesia, thus little or no pain. You will spend one night with us just as a precaution. There should be no bleeding. You won't have a fever unless I screw up the operation. Here he giggles. "I don't screw up surgeries," he confides quickly, his chest heaving from merriment. "When the surgery is complete, there will be a period in which there may be considerable swelling. Your face may look like a helium balloon for a while. We will need to attend to all of this, of course, but you will have little discomfort. You will take pain killers, aspirin frequently for a few days. But in a time, we will undo the bandages and I expect we shall reveal an extraordinarily beautiful woman. Not that you were not beautiful before," he hastens to add, "but I agree with you that your nose is presently an impediment to exquisite pulchritude. Movie star beauty, my dear, at its most exquisite."

Simone nods, at a loss for any response. There isn't much to say. Aware that her nose is a detraction from the beauty of her face, she welcomes the adjustment. But she is also concerned by what happens after surgery. In her past, there have been men who tried to get close to her, some who have come at her bristling. All her adult life she has parried assaults, some quiet and unassuming, some on the brink of violence. But now, she wonders whether suitors' assaults will be unbearable, constant, threatening her work, her every movement. Simone's truth is this: she is not in quest of romance through this transformation. For above all, Simone imagines herself a woman of intelligence, even of cunning. She categorises her body as an instrument, a tool for ferreting out secrets from the opposite sex. So, there may come some bad with the good. Still, she has agreed to this. And while she recovers, she is thinking through the options, determining how far she is willing to go for the Abwehr. If they have required this surgery as a test of her commitment, what else will they require of her?

The surgery lasts less than time than predicted. She awakens quietly in a recovery room and, as predicted, feels no pain. Nurses are hovering. One is pulling out an IV. Another one is dabbing her forehead. It is warm, she feels. There is a speck of blood. The nurse whisks it away. Doctor Mehta enters, smiles at her.

"Surgery went swimmingly," he says. "I did a heavenly job on you." Happy that he esteems himself, she tries to smile back at him but can hardly feel her lips moving. "No," he cautions her," nothing wrong. The rest of your face may feel a bit odd for a time. Don't concern your pretty little head about it. I have called your sister. She may now come and visit. Naughty girl! You didn't even tell your own flesh and blood about the surgery. How thoughtless of you, my dear," he adds, pretending to pout.

"My sister?"

"Yes, you left her phone number as next of kin."

Grace arrives in a huff. Sits beside Simone at the edge of the bed tapping her fingernails on the bedside table. She is dumbfounded.

"Someone else is paying for your nose surgery?" she asks. "Isn't that a form of prostitution?"

Simone grins, then grimaces at once. "Don't make me laugh," she says through her bandages. "I can't tell you who my benefactor is," she adds.

Her sister turns around to ascertain that nobody else is in the room. "Secret stuff," she says. "Must have to do with the OSS."

Simone sits up groggily. "Please don't speculate about all of this. I am sworn to secrecy."

Grace shrugs. "Your own sister left out in the cold. Well, if it has to be this way...I guess I won't tell you about my new beau, Faron Leifsen."

Perks up. "You have a new beau?"

"Yes, he's a Dane or a Norwegian, I forget which," Grace answers. We met at a fabric shop. Can you believe my luck? This man can tailor his own suits. He was buying fabric for a pair of pants and asked my opinion about the colour. I assured him that the shade he had chosen was excellent, that it matched his eyes. I then realised I had given away too much, but the next thing I knew we were together at Pandoria Pizza. I tried to eat in a civilized manner, but I fear I had pizza on the corner of my mouth for some time before he leaned over with a napkin and smoothed me clean. He seems to have a thing for neatness," she titters.

Hoot. Simone is laughing quietly despite the pain it causes.

"I'm painfully happy for you," She whispers.

"He has asked me out to the movies next week."

"Take this slowly," Simone warns with a frog in her throat. "You know how you like to fantasise about a new man in your life, and how you pay dearly later on."

Grace nods, lowers her head. "I intend not to mess this up."

Released the following morning, Simone takes a taxi home. She has asked Grace to buy groceries for her.

"I don't want to be seen at the store like this," she remarks to Grace, motioning to the bandages on her face. Lies down on the sofa staring at the woodwork around the ceiling.

Her front door opens with a bang. Grace!

"Sorry," she apologises about the thunder. "I have a bunch of food and I bought liquor," Grace tells her.

"You know I don't drink."

"You better start, I have never heard of a spy who didn't."

True, Simone thinks. Damn, very true! "Pour me a vodka. What do people put in it? "

Grace throws up her hands. "Not my drink. I suppose you can add any kind of juice or even soda."

Simone tries a glass neat. She squeals a bit reacting to the force of the liquid coursing downwards.

"Tastes awful," she avers. "Then she dilutes it with orange juice and finds this better. Takes a large swig. In a few moments, her head begins to spin. "Quite a lovely drink," Simone remarks to Grace, a drop of liquid spilling out of her mouth. "Oh, I've made a mess," she adds, giggling.

"You do realise you can just drink wine," Grace says to her sister. "Surely some spies are wine drinkers."

Simone spends most of the rest of the month at home venturing out in the evenings to stretch her legs, her raincoat high up against her cheeks. Towards the end of the month, she braves the grocery store and then the liquor store to buy a bottle of red wine. After a few evenings, she develops a taste for the wine, and decides that henceforth, that will be her drink of choice. It is better tasting than vodka or scotch, and the effect is milder. She enjoys the buzz of the drink but prefers a light high so that she does not feel out of control. As a spy, that would be the end of me, she judges.

The day of the great unveiling arrives. In the surgeon's office, Simone is placed in a chair. Told to raise her head and look directly in front of her. A nurse cuts free her bandages. She allows them to drop and accumulate on the floor. Dr. Mehta scans his work discerningly.

"Not a bad job," he declares. Holds up a mirror. "Have a look for yourself," he prompts.

"I'm afraid," Simone frowns, more excited than fearful.

"It's quite all right," he emphasises. "Even brilliant, if I may do my own trumpeting."

She takes the mirror in hand and lifts it to her face. "But I don't recognize this person," her trembling hand lowers the mirror as she faces her doctor.

Mehta laughs. "Quite. But do have a closer look. You may find that this unknown person staring back in the mirror is you. Not only you but an improved you. True or not true?"

Once again, she nears the mirror to her face. There is still a bit of swelling, a scab healing by her nose, but now she can gauge the effect of the surgery.

"I like it," she admits. "I will truly like it when I can apply make-up and see myself at my best."

"Soon," Mehta promises. "Very soon."

After several days, she decides to run errands. The grocery store where she has shopped for several years. The butcher hands her a slab of meat.

"You look different,' he says to her, his eyes shading.

"Different?"

"Yes," he says. "I think you've changed your hair."

At the cleaners, another guess. "You lost weight," the tailor says to her approvingly.

"That's not it," she answers provocatively.

"Hmm," he goes on, guessing. "You appear healthier. Eating better? True?"

"My face," she answers, pointing upwards. "Can you see no difference in my face?"

"Aah," he acknowledges, Looks at her piercingly. "Yes, there is a difference. I should have caught it earlier."

"Tell me," she prods.

"Different make-up. Around the eyes, of course."

Simone smiles and opens the door to leave.

"The earrings?" he calls out after her.

I need to go to church before leaving town, she thinks. Considers what else she may have to do besides packing. One day, while recuperating at home, she receives a letter in the mail. It contains neither forwarding address, nor the name of the sender. It contains a typed message:

> *2306 Filene Road, Apartment 2B in DC starting September 1. Apartment is furnished.*

Nothing else. Her assignment! But before packing and leaving for Washington, Simone has a plan.

4. Simone Makes her Plan Known

She dares not return to the Baptist Church. Not with the priests in constant attendance. How then can she contact Anderson? Simple: a phone call. Dials the OSS general number. Asks for Anderson. Told that no such person works for them. Stumped for an instant.

"Still there, miss?"

"Yes," Simone replies. "Tell the Anderson who does not work at the church where Simone has seen him work, that Simone has significant information for him and needs him to call her. Also persuade him not to come to my house.

"And why is that?"

"It is under surveillance," she intones crisply.

"I think you may have dialled the wrong number," the voice says.

"I have the only number I could find to connect me with Mr. Anderson. I assure you that he will want to speak to me. And here is my telephone number. Got it?"

Three hours pass. And then the phone rings.

"Simone?"

"Yes."

"Simone Valois?"

"Yes."

"Anderson here." Pause. "I thought we understood one another."

"We did. But since then things have changed. I would say dramatically."

"How so?"

"Too involved to describe over the phone," Simone retorts. "Can we meet?"

"Is that really necessary?" Anderson asks.

"Where?"

He answers immediately. "A new car wash called Macauley's Clean Car has opened on Peachtree and Tenth Street," he drawls. "It has quite a pleasant new car odor. Meet me there tomorrow at two. There's an office in the building."

"Can I show up without a car to wash?" Simone asks.

"Very funny. I hope you are not playing a joke at my expense and that my making this trip will be worthwhile."

"You can bet on it."

The following afternoon, Simone hops onto the streetcar to the intersection of Tenth Street at Peachtree. Indeed, there is a car wash advertising its grand opening with colored banners. Macauley's Clean Car. The car wash itself squats in an ugly low-slung gray concrete tube. To her nose, something smells offensively cheap as she wanders through the building, the odor is chemically induced and not fresh at all. Several men are hosing and soaping down a series of cars and then hand-drying each vehicle. The early afternoon has evolved hot and humid. Simone takes out a small fan from her purse with which she wands herself vigorously. Inside the building, next to the toilets, an office. She knocks on the door. A man in overalls answers, looks behind himself.

"She's here," he announces before leaving.

"Good afternoon, Miss Valois," Anderson intones, perched uncomfortably on a stool behind the metallic, clean desk. Clearly, he seems ill contented. "Wait a minute." Reaches into a cupboard and pulls out a fan, plugs it in before returning to his stool. Motions Simone to the other side of the desk where she sinks onto a wooden bench.

"You look different," he remarks, scanning her face.

"Yes," she replies.

"You wanted to show me how you've changed?" he remarks almost caustically. "Is that why I am here?"

"Not at all," she replies.

"But you have changed."

"For the better. I have had surgery. On my nose."

"Yes," he concedes. "You are different, altered, a sweller version than I remember. Looking swell." Clears his throat. "Go on."

"You rejected me, you remember," she begins.

Anderson shifts on his stool. "I have explained that to you."

"Yes, you have. But I didn't quite accept the verdict of the OSS."

"Get on with it."

"I went to what the German sympathisers in town call the Abwehr."

"Interesting." He sits up slightly although his face does not change expression.

"They gave me literature after they heard that you had rejected me."

"You told them, naturally, that you were incensed by me."

"Yes. And that their literature was intriguing."

Anderson sits up straighter, leans forward. He raises two fingers of his right hand and presses them against his lips.

"Plucky girl! Stupid girl. A dangerous game you play."

Simone now knows that Anderson is on board.

"I asked to join them. They gave me a test." Simone describes the meeting with David and the subsequent taking and delivering of the microdot.

"You didn't think to bring me the item?" Anderson asks sceptically.

"No," Simone replies, "Because it most assuredly had nothing of value on it. This was a test, after all. I was certain of it. The placement of the wallet was too obvious."

"Good catch," he responds approvingly. "Still, you were willing to hand over your virginity for this?"

"Not my favourite part of the evening," Simone replies. "I'm somewhat of a late bloomer in that category. Anyway, it hurt."

"Didn't the sex appeal to you?" Blushes. "Forget I asked. This is none of my business," Anderson interjects quickly.

"I considered the act puzzling," Simone replies. "It's discussed by an awful lot by people I know. I found it engrossing on the one hand; different of course, could be entertaining, but not delicious." She throws up her hands as if protesting that her comments aren't born of naiveté. "Some of my friends talk about sex as if they can't live without it." Now her eyes turn up chagrined. "I don't need to be telling you this."

Anderson shrugs. "Just part of what happened. And now? If you passed the test, surely they have plans for you."

"They want me to move to Washington and to work for the Commerce Department."

Taps the desk with fingernails. "Of course, you must do this," he says. They have an apartment for you and a monthly salary?"

"Yes."

"So, you are telling me this because…."

"Because I loathe what the Germans stand for."

Anderson exhales. Taps his lips

"Good. Clearly, we made a mistake turning you down. I thought so at the time. And you were gutsy, if foolish to join the Abwehr just to make the point that we had blundered. But you made it in spades," he adds. "I will need some time to confer with colleagues about this situation. Clearly there are uses for a gutsy girl with brains."

"So, you think I'll make the grade now? Simone asks with a wry smile.

"Bet your bottom dollar," Anderson booms. "We will be thrilled to have a female agent working for us in the midst of German intelligence. But I caution you. You are young, and as this action indicates, clearly impetuous. Be careful. These German sympathisers are tough. If they discover you are playing a double hand, they will dispose of you, probably as slowly and as painfully as they can. You do get that, eh?"

She shudders for an instant. "Clear as a bell."

Anderson writes on a pad, hands it to her. "My personal number. Call me day or night. Even if I am not there to pick up, someone is always near that phone and can get a message to me quickly. One tip: don't do anything rash. Don't try to outsmart the Abwehr. Just play their game and see what they are up to. Occasionally, when possible, report back. If you do that, you may even survive. Got it?"

"Trying to frighten me?" she asks with a coy smile.

"Just want you to be cautious. Look, my dear. They made you more beautiful because they intend to use your body to pry secrets from us. Any miscue on your part may be curtains. But you seem prepared to let them use you. May I ask why?"

"I hate what they do, what they represent. My body is as committed as my mind against them."

"I wish we had time to train you," Anderson sighs. "Maybe later! If you need me, call me. Otherwise, we will be in touch with you in Washington. And a vote of thanks for what you have already accomplished."

Simone arrives in Washington to a brown walk-up with a stoop, opens the stained-glass front door to find a delightful, if small apartment near Dupont Circle. Furnished nicely. A bed, dresser. Coffee table, loveseat. An empty bookcase. Probably needs to be filled with Nazi propaganda, she considers with a smile. She puts her copy of Mein Kampf into the top shelf. From the front bay window, she can observe much of the Circle. Traffic. People bustling. She watches them intently. Wonders where they are hustling in such a hurry. Sits in front of the window for more than an hour allowing her mind to wander. Grace has admonished her to reject this offer, even though Simone has not told her sister what the position involves.

"I'm being sisterly, concerned, and hate to lose you," Grace cries with a moan. Simone puts her arm around Grace and, just for an instant, feels sad, a sole tear edging down her cheek. Grace begins blubbering as Simone rushes to find tissues to dab at her eyes. In fact, she has told Grace that she has applied for and been accepted to a position as a clerk in the Commerce Department.

"I need to work," she confides in Grace. "I just can't sit around here and spend our parents' money until there is no more left." Of course, Grace understands. Nonetheless, she is concerned.

"Washington is an evil city, "she says overly seriously. "Politicians hang out there," she adds through cloudy eyes as if she were referencing the devil's accomplices. Simone laughs as if the idea of politicians living in DC might be novel. "So long as you are not working for the bloody Nazis," Grace insists.

Sitting by the window looking out over Dupont Circle, a parade of cars and busses shuffling, murmuring, spewing exhaust down the street. She remembers the last exchanges with Grace about her new beau. "Tell me about Faron."

Grace smiles. "We are connecting great guns," she says.

"You're not sleeping with him?"

Grace looks at her with surprise. "Hell no," she blubbers. "I don't give myself for free."

Her sister doesn't quite understand what Grace means. But for Grace, sex is useful to strengthen a bond with a man, but only at the right time. Used as an inducement, it has its role in a relationship. Also, true, Grace acknowledges, her eyes opening wider, she enjoys sex. Feels jolly good. A way to intersect deeply with a man. She has had one prior experience, the upshot of which was that her lover dispensed with her, she complains pointedly, after having absorbed her body deeply. Grace understood she had given herself too early and vowed not to repeat such folly.

But for Simone, sex is an instrument to probe a man, to gain his confidence and to exploit him. A woman's principle tool to cause a man to relax his inhibitions, and thus to speak freely, hopefully too freely to the flesh he has been fondling and is bent on continuing to fondle. For after all, according to Simone, the main difference between men and women is that the former cannot stop giving in to lust.

"I'll come visit you," Grace vows.

"I would like that. I don't know anyone in Washington."

Grace smiles. "You are a beautiful young woman. This will take no time at all. Still, you need to be judicious whom you allow to befriend you. I hear terrible things about people in DC, that they exploit one another to get ahead. There is an evil cabal of men there called lobbyists," she adds playfully.

Simone smiles, since these are exactly the people she believes she will encounter.

Yet she is unsure of herself, of her abilities in the world of touching, groping, sex. Not having had experiences other than the most recent one with David and recalling that David did not award her high marks for sexual aptitude, she realises she must learn better to perfect her skills in this area. For the moment, however, she has other concerns. She has arrived at the Commerce Department on her first day of work. First, she has to undergo several tests, fill out reams of paperwork, some of which are both repetitive and unnecessary, yet restraining her often acidic tongue, until finally, by mid-afternoon of the first day she is introduced to her boss, Alda Menotti.

Alda is a forty-ish giant of a woman with ham arms and a significant belly. In motion her legs strike the ground like massive bowling pins, and when she walks, an extraordinary girth separates them. Most noticeable about Alda, however, is that she has affixed on her lips a persistent smile. Never seen anything like this, Simone thinks. The woman seems to have the smile stapled onto her face. Instead of putting Simone at ease, it makes her tense.

"Your desk," Alda says, pointing to a chair and table. "You'll be sharing the room with another clerk."

"What will I be doing?" Simone asks.

Giant smile. "What I tell you to do, of course. Mainly filing, a bit of typing. You do know how to type, don't you?"

"Some." Simone replies.

"Lucky us," Alda says, her smiling broadening into what Simone believes is virtually a sneer.

"But I learn quickly."

"So," Alda says, holding up a sheaf of papers and thrusting them onto the desk. "These were typed up by staff. Retype them please after excising errors so that our bosses believe that we learned something in school after all."

For the remainder of the afternoon, Simone retypes these documents, editing them as she goes along. In fact, there are few errors to correct, yes, some typos, a few more grammatical errors. Always strong in this department, she captures the mistakes easily and fixes them at once.

By the end of the first afternoon she has completed two thirds of the documents and returns these to Alda.

Big smile! "Say. I think we have a winner," Alda chortles, examining the documents, and holding up a pudgy two fingers in victory.

Filing, making coffee, typing and re-typing. Chores for the first several weeks. During this time, nothing unusual has taken place. Nobody has approached her from the Abwehr. Dana, a little brunette from the steno pool with sparkling braces has asked her out to lunch. Thinking that this may be the contact she has been waiting for,

Simone accepts with anticipation. They walk to a Horn and Hardart cafeteria two blocks away, a place where with a handful of nickels she can purchase food from a glass vending machine. Find the food you want to buy, drop in the requisite nickels, and then take the food out and place it on your tray. But the girl has nothing to talk about except stenography, and her wastrel of a boyfriend. Disappointed, Simone nonetheless is pleased to make a workplace friend.

Three weeks elapse in this fashion when, suddenly, Dana indicates that she has something she wishes to communicate. Privately.

"I know a good café, the Dominex, on the Circle. In front of the café, there is a bench, almost always free. Meet me there after work."

The afternoon has grown heavy with humidity and lowering, unsettled clouds. A storm is brewing to the west, angry colored clouds bristling over the Capitol. Thunder in the distance. The wooden bench is empty. It squats next to a bus stop around which several people are waiting. Dana arrives.

She reaches over and kisses Simone on the cheek, surprising her. But once she has reached her ear, Dana stops for a moment.

"Our boss, Gus Eakin, has been charged with purchasing the elements of a new radar for the department of War. Pieces coming from Canada. Can you get to the right folder and take pictures?"

Looks at Dana with a mixture of interest and incredulity.

"What are you talking about?" she asks. Dana is fixing her long hair behind her into a ponytail.

"I'm your contact, silly."

"We had lunch a while back and, yet you said nothing," Simone protests.

"Had nothing to say. But now I've seen the folder. I just have no reason to go into the boss's office. You can pretend you are returning copied material."

"I have no camera," Simone protests again.

Dana opens the palm of her hand and slips a small, metallic object into Simone's pocket. "You do now. Don't you know we think of everything?"

"I don't know how to film."

"You open the lens and press the red button when you are ready. You can take up to seventeen pictures one after the other."

"Not sure I have the skill for this."

"Don't sell yourself short. Oh crap," Dana goes on, "Eddie has spotted us and is coming this way."

Eddie is one of the internal mail boys in the department. He has always had an eye for me, Simone thinks.

"Hey girls," Eddie says. "Have you already had lunch?"

"Not yet," Dana says.

"The cafeteria is right down the street," he says looking at Simone, his eyes dancing. "If you don't know how to use the vending machines, I can show you."

Later that afternoon, Simone takes a short walk down the corridor, turns left at the water fountain. Stops. Eyes Eakin's office. He's on the phone, leaning back with the receiver cradled by his neck, one foot on his desk. Folders, lots of them, crowd the desktop. Occasionally, a worker comes by. Simone lifts her face from the fountain, water dribbling down her cheek. Eakin hangs up and a worker comes in. He greets him. Eakin arises, reaches for his pipe, and they leave together, chatting. Simone thinks this may be her opportunity. She walks steadily towards his office with a sheaf of re-typed materials as a cover, and is about to enter the office when, from the corner of her eye, she perceives Alda waddling twards her. Damn! She retraces her steps to her office.

Two days pass in this fashion without solution. Finally, Dana enters her office one morning when she is alone to tell her that Eakin has an appointment that afternoon for approximately an hour. "Will he close his door? Lock it?"

Dana grins. "He has no idea that anyone would be interested in anything in his life in or out of his work."

At two, Eakin has already left. How correct Dana is, Simone thinks, looking at her watch. The fool leaves his office unlocked. Simone makes her way into it. Scanning the folders on the desk. Two minutes elapse. She is growing concerned about the time required to read the files. Turns as someone walks by. Stops and waits. Delves deeper into the pile. Notices that her left index finger is trembling. Tries to relax. Yes! At last, finds the folder. Turns her back to the door and begins to film as quickly as she can. Laughter in the hallway. She stands there fingering her sheaf of papers until the voices recede. Finishes the folder. All twelve pages. Camera in her pocket, sheaf of papers in hand, she turns and exits.

That evening, she has a phone call from a man named Redmond, Laurence Redmond.

"I believe you snapped some photos for us," he says after introducing himself. "Don't take the camera to a photo shop. Bring the camera with the film in it to Georgetown, to the Oak Hill Cemetery. Promise we won't bury it," he jokes. "Go there. I will meet you at the cemetery. I have red hair, so you can't miss me," he adds jovially.

"When."

"Yes, of course. That would be good to know. Saturday morning at Ten. In the morning, I mean. That would be the day after tomorrow," he adds quickly. "Does that work into your schedule?"

"I'll be there," Simone responds. "Should I dress in mourning?"

She rushes to the nearest post office to phone from one of the public instruments. Anderson answers. She can imagine him tapping two fingers to his lips. Murmurs:

"Good, good, very good. No, don't do anything but what you have agreed to do. Next time, however, when your contact gives you an assignment, let us know before you do it, not afterwards."

Chagrined, Simone sputters an answer over the phone, concerned that she wasn't exactly clear how to handle this.

"That's why training is so important," Anderson retorts. "Anyway, no harm has been done. The thing is not as important as it sounds. Hand over the camera as instructed. Try to find out the names, addresses, phone numbers, anything you can about the people you work with or those you meet like Dana and Redmond. Yes?"

"Yes," she replies. "You're not upset with me?"

"Hell no," he bellows. "Hell no."

Saturday morning, she locates the cemetery. Finds a very old, used oak bench with graffiti marked on it with a knife. She sits demurely, straightens her gray wool blend dress, fiddles with the heel of one shoe. A cloudy day, clouds skimming lower than usual, puffy, and turning black as they scamper above her. Ten minutes elapse.

People pass by. Some with flowers, often dragging children or parents along. Now a man settles in at the opposite end of the bench.

"Redmond?" she asks.

The man looks across at her and smiles. "I could be Redmond for you, pretty lady."

"Have you colored your hair?" she asks him, now scanning his face slowly. His hair is dark brown. The man wears a Van Dyke beard.

"I've come just for you," the man says seriously.

"Please. Tell me your name."

The man laughs. "As soon as you tell me yours."

"Simone," she replies.

"Redmond," he responds.

"What's your first name?"

Hesitates. "Joseph. Yes. Joseph."

Now she arises hurriedly and leaves. Turns after a few steps but the man is not following her.

After several paces, there is a hand on her shoulder. She looks up into the eyes of another man. "Sorry to be late," he sputters "Traffic." His hair is redish with a tinge of yellow in it.

"Excuse me," Simone says. "I need to know your name. Your entire name," she adds.

"Laurence Redmond," he says, guiding her to a bench in front of a mausoleum. "I could see that you were being engaged by that man, but I needed to know whether you could handle him."

"Thanks a bunch," she retorts sharply.

He ignores the tone. "You have the camera?"

She reaches into her pocket, looks in every direction before handing it to Redmond.

"Is this valuable information?" she asks.

"I can't say. Not because I don't want to respond but because I am no expert in the field. Our side, you know, has a pretty advanced radar capability. Better I'm sure than what the Americans have.

"Well then why was it important for me to take pictures of this?"

"We always want to see what the other side uses and what they are working on," Redmond grins. Slight pause. "I'd like to see you again," he adds in a more relaxed tone.

"You mean like a date?"

"Yes."

Redmond is quite a bit taller than she is, clean shaven, adequately built. Not the most interesting or expressive face Simone has ever seen, but there is something unhinged, possibly entertaining, about the man which she would not mind exploring. She finishes considering the offer.

"Yes, when?"

"How about dinner tonight? I have to leave town for several days tomorrow."

"All right. Take me to a good restaurant. I thrive on Italian," she adds.

"There is an Original Joe's in Georgetown. Spaghetti Bolognese to die for. I'll pick you up."

Starts to write down her address. He places his hand over her wrist. "No need. I know your address. Is seven OK?"

At the restaurant, they both order the spaghetti Bolognese.

"You were right," Simone says, a napkin wiping her mouth gingerly. "Quite a lovely sauce. It has fennel in it."

"Told you," Laurence gloats.

No shop talk. He clearly has something else on his mind. Probing that mind is more difficult that Simone surmises.

"You look deep in thought."

"Deep into you," he confesses. They hail a taxi to her apartment.

"Is Redmond your real name?" she inquires.

"No," he responds. "My name is Ernst Blacher."

"Your American English is spot on," she says admiringly. "How did you manage that?"

He smiles. "I was born and raised in Iowa. My parents took me back to Germany in the thirties. I'd like you to think that I have fantastic linguistic skills, but I'm afraid they are ordinary."

"Can you talk about your mission here?" she asks somewhat tentatively.

"Why not? You are, after all, one of us, and nothing I am going to tell you is unknown to the OSS. I am part of the mission known as Patrorious. We are a group of thirty or more saboteurs whose mission is mainly to destroy parts of American infrastructure...blowing up oil dumps, water facilities, that sort of thing. Give me a drink and I'll tell you more, he continues."

"I don't stock liquor in the apartment," she confesses, unlocking the apartment door. A frown.

"Pity, but not a big deal either," he responds, taking her hand. She is thinking. Thinking hard and fast. Wondering how to react to this man who is about to climb all over her. Finally, the wheels churn to a halt. I'll open up to him, she thinks, not because I'm randy. But because, Lord knows, after my first attempt which ended badly, I could use the practice.

"I'd like to make love to you," he says predictably, gazing into her eyes. Before she answers, he is already divesting himself of his double-breasted jacket. She peers into his eyes and sees something she has not yet encountered. In retrospect, she gleans that it is unadulterated lust.

"You are a beautiful woman," he remarks, unzipping her.

No reply. "You do know you are beautiful, don't you?"

"I leave that to others," she answers without a hint of coyness.

Runs a nail gently, slowly along the inside her arm. Tiny quiver. Now he descends the nail to the inside of her thigh. Another quiver. Kissing her. He tastes of red wine. Kisses him back. Something unusual in the touch of his lips. He does not force her backwards. Instead, his touch is firm but unforced. Soft but prominent. She rather likes it. Feels his tongue working her nipple. In a moment, she is naked sliding under the sheets, neither embarrassed by her nudity or by his ungainly advances as he approaches her on all fours. Simply looking at the man as his eyes narrow as if he were advancing onto her like honing onto a target. Learning.

"Relax," he whispers into her ear. "You'll enjoy this more."

She knows how to do this. Lets her muscles deflate. Reaches between his legs. A light snaps in her brain. She has never before touched a penis. An erect penis. Spreads wide, guides it into her. Hurts just a trifle. Wets her fingers and slides them into her. He is rougher now than she anticipated, but she hardly minds. Pulls him to her with both hands around his shoulders, her legs rising into the air. Cataloguing the sensations. He stays with her even after he has released.

"Can you?" he asks her.

"I have never," she replies. But she does not say this with sadness. Just a matter of fact.

"God, you are superb," he exclaims too loudly into her ear. "Superb!"

"Tell me the truth," she says quizzically. "How was I?"

He purses his lips, pauses momentarily. "Now you are asking for something unusual. The truth! You are ok in bed because you let me do everything. I think you enjoy it. Do you? Still, you never stop anything I start, but you would be sexier if you initiated."

"How? She asks.

"You need to ask that?" he wonders.

"Please tell me. I'm new."

"All right. You can start by rubbing my member," he begins. Then catalogues what else she may do with her hands and tongue.

Eyes glistening. Ashamedof her innocence, yet eager to digest this criticism. "Thank you," she acknowledges.

"And here I thought you might be angry if I criticized."

Sharing a cigarette, propped up on pillows side by side. She thinks she may have dozed off for a moment. When she opens her eyes, Laurence is on an elbow studying her.

"We have been discussing you," Laurence says finally, exhaling.

"We?"

"The Core. The group that makes judgments." She blinks. "We think you could prove to be a valuable ally.

Soon, within a few months, we gauge, this country will be fighting Germany. America will lose this struggle. Hitler has amassed an extraordinary fighting force. Obedient, trained fully, dedicated to the eradication of foreign elements in its society. Ready to spread his philosophy to the world. You have seen what he did in Poland and Czechoslovakia. France is falling on its ass. Yes," Laurence proceeds proudly, "France will fall, and Russia will surely be next."

She shifts uncomfortably. "You said you were talking about me?"

"Sorry," Laurence laughs. "I did say that, didn't I? A formidable female spy working for us can only be considered an important asset. Does the name Mata Hari mean anything to you?" he asks.

"No."

"She worked for Germany in the first world war, considered to have been among the greatest of all spies, although if you ask me to specify what she accomplished, I'm not sure I could tell you. Anyway, she is a legend. A Dutch beauty, a dancer. Her name in Javanese means 'Eye of the Dawn'. We have been thinking of an appropriate code name for you in our service. How about Dawn in honour of the greatest of female agents? Do you like it?

"Yes," Simone replies smiling. "I am one with Dawn."

"And the Third Reich approves completely," Laurence beams.

In the spring, just before Easter, Simone takes several days to return to Atlanta to spend time with her sister. Grace is now engaged to her man. Simone knows she has been sleeping with him.

"I hope you are being careful," she admonishes.

Grace giggles. "Most of the time. But once in a while, we are so starved to be with one another that we race to his apartment or mine, and literally tear into the other as if we were savages. We tend to neglect the niceties then."

"Risking pregnancy."

"I think I am going to marry this one," Grace replies.

"It is not considered kosher for an unmarried woman to bear a child."

"Stop it. Stop preaching to me," Grace responds angrily. "You have had adventures too, I know you have. And probably a hell of a lot riskier than me."

Simone pauses. "Yes," she responds. "You are right. I have had two adventures. One night in each case. The last one, Laurence, is after me to make it a steady relationship, but I don't see any need for that. He's small potatoes."

"You've always been so damned logical about love," Grace replies, shaking her head. "Love doesn't lend itself well to analysis," she adds.

A dinner with the tailor, Faron, and Grace. Does not stoop to judgment. Still, the man is swarthy, the comparison of his dark skin to her whiter than white complexion somehow doesn't seem to fit. As he speaks of his background, he describes early years working in the fields in California gathering lettuce. Simone observes Faron setting the table with amusement, moving each knife and fork as if they were elaborate chess pieces into their correct position. By the end of the dinner, Simone decides she could like this man. Unpretentious, but clearly smitten, his eyes rarely leave Grace's, his voice solid but hardly stentorian, not the voice of someone who needs total control over a woman. Simone has always worried about Grace's predilections for men who tend to be bossy. But Faron does not appear to be one of these.

"You have my approval, for what it's worth," she says to Grace in the ladies' room. "But you do realise you will never live luxuriously. If the two of you work hard and forever, you may have enough money at the end of each month to go out to dinner."

Grace cackles. "Not that dour."

"I just hope you know what you are letting yourself in for. Sure, you don't want to hold out for a professional man?"

Grace croons to her with doe eyes. "I love this man."

5. Training Dawn

Shortly after her return from Atlanta, Simone receives instructions which at first puzzle her:

'Go to the Atkins Gym in Alexandria this Saturday and every following Saturday at nine a.m. Ask for Hans. He is your trainer for the foreseeable future. You may need to work out one other time as well during the week.'

Simone arrives early. The gym is well stocked with implements of torture, Simone thinks, scanning the large room. Lots of heavy black and metallic things loosely hanging from the wall. Clearly instruments designed to hurt her. She shivers.

"We are going to build up your strength," Hans says. "Your body may be nice to look at, but it is weak, flabby. I wish to create a prime soldier out of you. And I don't have a great deal of time to do this."

Simone looks at Hans as if he were a little crazy.

"You need to get better clothing," he says to her, scrutinizing the woollen pants she is wearing. "Buy shorts. You can change here in the lockers. Wear tops which move with your body. Remember that you may even sweat from time to time," he adds with a chuckle.

"Sure," she says, somewhat amused by his gruffness as well as his impetus to meld her into a frightening person. "But you do see that I am a young woman, not a teenage boy."

"Madame," Hans retorts. "I know exactly who I am dealing with. But you are not to contravene my orders. Got this?"

She peers up into Hans' face. He has clear grey eyes, a shock of yellow hair that falls over one eye, lips that are too large for his face, full, almost swollen.

"Come," he says leading her to weights. "Pick up one of these."

She reaches down, tries to lift a weight, but cannot budge it.

"Start with the fifteen pounder," he says.

She lifts it. Puts it down.

"Lift it twenty times with each hand," he demands.

She screws up her face, suddenly grasping that this man is insane, but she tries to comply. She manages to lift the weight fifteen times with her left hand before dropping it. He notes this in a dossier.

"Pick it up with the other hand," he commands. Simone stoops, picks up the weight and manages a dozen with this hand before halting.

"Ach," he runs fingers along his scalp in consternation, says "I have my arms full with you."

At the end of an hour, Simone is afraid that she can no longer move either arm, and that her legs which are ablaze will be useless to her. Perhaps forever. She wonders whether Hans should call for an ambulance.

"Sit and take a coffee," he says un-gently. He pours a cup for her. "You will feel this for several days. Rest here a half hour before leaving. Come back Wednesday evening, and we start over. Yes?"

"Yes," she exclaims defiantly, fire in her eyes. "Yes."

Again Wednesday, the same routine. And also, the following Saturday. Weeks, then months of this. Just as Simone has become comfortable with the weights, two announcements.

"In three weeks, we begin a new phase. This is the physical phase to which now we will add movement, he continues, smacking full lips. "You shall learn unarmed defence. You will learn it exquisitely because to do so may one day save your life. Furthermore, in addition to the defensive side, I want to show you how you may easily slay an opponent. You do wish to learn to kill, no?" He looks at her with a hint of consternation in his eyes.

"I would be happy to learn how to kill," she responds, realising that any other answer would be tantamount to admitting defeat.

"Fucking good," he yells. "I am going to show you how to grab an oncoming fool with your bare hand, also with a knife. Then, on Sundays, we will drive to the firing range and I will show you how to shoot a pistol, a rifle and," he adds, wetting his lips, "A machine gun. Are you all right with acquiring such skills?"

"I've waited all my life to shoot a gun," she says facetiously, but Hans accepts her words as if they were serious. Just as well, she thinks.

Wednesday evening, she is standing on top of a mat in the middle of a mirrored room. Suddenly, Hans is rushing towards her while she cowers unsure how to protect herself. A burly man, Hans, well over 200 pounds moving at her with what she considers to be unusual speed, now strikes a glancing blow, and propels her off the mat into the air and against the mirror behind her with a thud. Slowly, he picks up this limp rag of a body which is both perspiring and breathing very hard. She opens her eyes slowly.

"You tried to kill me," she whispers, shaking her hair in disbelief. "Why did you do that?"

"I wanted to see how you would react," he responds nonchalantly.

"With panic," she huffs, still breathing hard. "How did I do?"

He snickers. "I could well have slaughtered you. You stood there like some cow waiting to be run over. I could have been a tank."

"What should I have done?"

"I will demonstrate."

"You mean there is a way to avoid being slammed?"

"Yes, of course. I don't do this only for chuckles, you know," he snickers, exasperated with her.

First, when the enemy runs at her, he teaches her to turn, to make less a target of her body, and then whenever possible, to yank the assailant past her. Once she has accomplished that feat, he suggests she could also stick out a leg using the enemy's momentum to trip him. In a few minutes, she has grasped the concept and has knocked Hans onto the floor.

"Not bad," he acknowledges, standing slowly. In the weeks to come, he teaches her how to deflect, then take away the oncoming enemy's blade, how to use the enemy's momentum to hoist him over her shoulder, how to aim her shoe, especially if she is wearing heels, to tread forcefully on his throat once she has floored him. Over fifty other techniques are ground into her. Finally, he points out to her the soft spot every male possesses just below the Adam's apple. "Stick your finger in there, especially with a sharp nail you ladies enjoy polishing, and your unlucky opponent will bleed to death swallowing and choking on his own blood," he chortles. "Quick and very useful. But should you miss the vital spot, kick this lucky man in his balls."

"I'd like to try that on you," she says feistily.

"I bet you would," he giggles uproariously. "But," he adds with less hilarity, "My balls are off limits."

Sundays, they meet at a firing range. Hans has brought with him a small collection of firearms in a large canvas bag.

"These will be useful to you," he begins. "Have you ever fired a gun before?"

"No."

"Start with the pistol. This one," he begins, handing it to her, "is a Beretta 1935 model, lighter than the previous year's version. Semi-automatic service pistol. It uses Browning cartridges. Holds eight rounds. Learn not only how to use it, but how to clean and maintain it. You can take this home with you. Caress it daily, like some kitten," he goes on. "Stroke it, let it meld into your hand from time to time until it begins to feel comfortable. Part of you. An appendage, if you wish. Bring it back each Sunday."

Now they proceed to the firing range. A handful of men shooting. A target is mounted against a backdrop some twenty-five feet away. She places earmuffs around her ears, aims, fires, and hits the edge of the target.

"Not bad," he acknowledges. He now shows her hold to hold the weapon with both hands to steady the aim. "I thought your first time you might miss the whole thing." But by the end of several rounds of firing, Simone is able to hit consistently somewhere within the target. "After a while, we move the target back," he says ominously.

"You mean there is another distance?" she asks with discouragement in her voice.

"Several," he responds almost gleefully.

Months pass in this fashion. Soon, much too soon for Simone, Hans announces that she will face an unarmed defence test.

"I doubt that I am ready," she says, dour and alarmed.

"I am the best judge of this," Hans retorts. "In two weeks, we fucking do it."

"And how do I prepare for it?"

"That is what we have been working at these past months."

Thank God, Simone thinks, for the exercise and the challenges at the firing range. Her work at the Commerce Department leaves her exasperated. No challenge. Typing, filing, carrying papers from one office to the other. Bored to shit. Her contact, Dana, has not given her another mission for some time. Hardly speaks to her. If this is spying, she thinks, there is more drudgery in it than activity. Thank God for Hans.

She knows she must be ready, as ready as possible. She is small, true, but lean, lithe, and now rather muscular. Her movements, even her reflexes, have quickened in the past months. She sees more, better, swears that sometimes she can peer around a corner before coming to it. This of course is nonsense, but the very notion speaks volumes with regards to her confidence. Hans has created a lot of this, making her work arduously, but never extending herself so far that she consistently fails.

So now the day is upon her. She stands in the middle of the room. At the farthest point of each quarter of the room, a man is standing. Each of them wearing shorts, bare from the waist up. Young, muscular men, lean and tall. But she is not quaking with fear, not yet, only mindful.

At a signal from Hans, the first man, perhaps the heaviest, moves towards her slowly. Stands in front of her. Breathing is shallow, gaze impenetrable, bares his teeth. Puts his two hands around her throat and begins to squeeze. His eyes are blank. Simone is beginning to gasp. With her two arms, Simone thrusts up both wrists forcefully disposing of the man's grip, now seizes him and twirls him over her knee to the floor. He dusts himself off, does not look at her, and gets up. No time to congratulate herself. The second man is at this moment running towards her, yelling in some foreign tongue. Steps aside, grabbing his arm, and trips him so that he falls heavily onto the floor. No time to turn. The third man, lithe, even wiry, is behind her pinning her arms. She moves a leg behind him and falls backwards so that the two of them recoil together. Turns in an instant. Now she straddles the man's throat with her legs. The man pounds the canvas indicating that he surrenders. As soon as she stands, a fourth man, virtually foaming at the mouth and screaming his head off, is rushing towards her with a knife. Turns to one side, allows the knife to pass her, grabs the wrist with both hands and bends it painfully so that the man has to drop the weapon, kicks him in the spine, raises her hand in a chop fashion to finish him off just as he drops to the ground. The man eyes her with fear.

"Stop! You won't need to dispose of him today," Hans chuckles, picking up the knife which is made of rubber.

"How did I do?" Simone asks breathlessly.

"Not over yet," Hans replies testily. "Get back to the middle of the room."

The four men have retaken their positions and now two of them are approaching Simone at the same time, one from the front the other from the rear. She seizes the arm of the man at her back and pulls him forward into the man in front. At once, the third and fourth men are running at her yelling at the top of their lungs. She bends down to let the momentum of the first man carry his body over her torso, reaches up to the second man, turns quickly, and propels him over her shoulder. Only now does Hans seem satisfied. Simone has sunk to the floor, her face on fire.

"You surely cannot be tired," he asks.

"Damn well near dead," she replies, her breathing laboured, her body quaking from the effort.

"You did fine," he responds. "However, the last duo would probably have stuck a knife in you and roasted you before you were able to disarm and knock them down. We'll be working on this. But I congratulate you. You passed the first test."

Blood streaming down her face. A bloody nose. She wipes it off with a sleeve.

"Nothing to it," she remarks. Turns towards the four men who are now together sitting on the floor observing her, smiling. "Nothing to it," she shouts at them. Now she gets up laboriously, and staggers to the bathroom where she sticks her head in a bowl and throws up.

6. Information for The Enemy

"Hello, Dawn," a voice intones.

"Redmond?"

"The one and only," he answers.

"You've never before called me."

"Intentionally. But today I need you for something."

"Go on," Simone says.

"Your boss has acquired some information which is important to us. Rather vital."

"Concerning?"

Pause. "The less you know, the better."

"Redmond, I can't do this unless I know what the job is."

"True enough," he chuckles, "He has rocket parts for Britain which America has been helping develop. He is shipping these parts to England, to Southampton, by freighter. Soon. That much we believe is true."

"Rocket parts? She says, her voice rising with incredulity, "I have no idea what you are talking about."

"Never mind. You just need to find out the sail date of the freighter and, preferably, its name, and whether the ship may be carrying anything else of significance."

"These are gigantic, these rockets?"

He laughs. "Actually, the technology the Brits are working on is just the contrary. They are developing three-inch rockets to be fired by a projector, but in volume. Over a hundred at a time, a little bit like shooting buckshot. But any one of these sting and could even bring down a fighter jet or bomber. They carry a sizeable explosive."

"When do you need this?"

Pause. "Hurry on this one. I don't want it to get away from us. Your boss is rather lackadaisical about his files, isn't he? It should give you a wonderful opportunity to locate the correct information. Keep Dana informed. She'll act as go-between."

Simone and Dana concoct a plan by which Dana will take her boss to lunch on the pretext of discussing some project with him. During this time, Simone will sneak into the office, lower the blinds, and rifle the files. On the appointed afternoon, Simone is busy scouring her boss's office, and checking through files for more than a half hour without success. Time is now of the essence. Either I find this in the next five minutes or I'll have to quit for this session, Simone thinks, looking frantically. She comes across several files with British sounding names. G. A Harbey of Greenwich. Opens this one skeptically. Still this could the one. Sketches. Engineering designs. Plans for rockets, yes! This is the one! But she feels she doesn't have time to take photos. They are spread out over seventeen pages. Instead, she looks for and finds a letter from Harbey to the Secretary of Commerce on which her boss has been copied. The letter indicates that the parts must be shipped by March 14 on the Marea Oro, a Portuguese freighter registered in Lisbon. It will take more than seven days to cross the Atlantic from New York, meaning that the goods should arrive in Southampton around March 21. There is a remote chance, the letter continues, that German U-boats which have been torpedoing freighters in the Atlantic may get wind of this. It's imperative that these goods get through since they contain ball bearings necessary for the project.

March 14! That would be in four days, Simone says, leaving the office. She stops. Returns to raise the blinds, closes the door behind her. She passes her boss in the hallway deep in conversation with Dana, winks at Dana who smacks her lips lightly in response.

Instead of taking lunch, Simone walks to a nearby park, searches for a battery of public phones, finds one which has an unused booth and calls Anderson.

Anderson mulls over the information. And then offers an extraordinary response to the problem.

"Tell your contact that the ship will leave March 21, not the 14th. Sadly, you were unable to locate the name of the ship. By March 21, the Marea Oro should have made its way to Southampton unharmed. You can't be blamed if the shippers changed the date of the shipment, right?"

Simone marvels. "Sounds like the perfect solution," she says. "I wonder whether I would have thought of that."

"Don't make me blush," Anderson scoffs over the phone. "You just have to learn to be as devious as the rest of us. And devious at a moment's notice! Good American spies learn how to lie quickly and well, and make it seem like a glorious moment of truth. Thank God for dissembling! But I better hurry now and make arrangements for another freighter to leave New York for Southampton on March 21. Of course, this freighter will be packing nothing of interest to the Axis," he chuckles. "Absolutely nothing."

That evening, Dana rings Simone. "By the look of you as we passed in the hallway, you must have unearthed the information."

"Well, some of it. I couldn't learn the name of the ship or anything else about it, but I do know that it is scheduled to sail about March 21."

"Brilliant," Dana says. "Knowing this will enable our submarines to intercept the freighter. You've done a great service," Dana continues.

***

Kapitan Wolfgang Neiderschnitz picked up the telephone. "You destroyed the freighter? You're certain of this? Yes. How did you do it?"

Kapitan Edmund Verein spoke quickly.

"We found the ship on its way down the Channel towards Southampton. We surfaced our U-boat and fired a shot over the bow signalling that they must indicate where they were sailing and what goods they were carrying. They refused, returning a rather obscene message. I did not stop for an instant. I gave the command and we fired two torpedoes. The first one struck the ship but, unfortunately, did not detonate. The second one, however, targeted midship just under the hull. When it exploded, the freighter virtually broke in half. It sank quickly in a total conflagration."

"So, you did not see any of the goods the ship carried?"

"No. This was impossible. It sank immediately."

Pause. "Before you fired on the freighter, did it cross your mind to stop the ship and board it?"

"No, Kapitan," Edmund Verein replied. "Our instructions were to sink the ship before it arrived in Britain. As I reported, we did ask them to signal us with information. We did so."

"And the name of the freighter?"

"Unknown."

Pause.

"Kapitan Verein, we are always happy when we sink a cargo ship heading for Britain. But the freighter you sank is not the one we specifically sent you to find and destroy."

"Really? And how do you know this, if I may ask?"

"Because that ship landed in Southampton, according to our spies, before you torpedoed your freighter."

"Mein Gott! Verein explodes. "Why was I not informed of this?"

"Because we only learned this information yesterday."

And the information is reliable?"

"Quite. As reliable it would seem, as the original information indicating that a freighter would leave New York for Southampton with the rocket pieces. Only the date was wrong. Presumably, that date was made available, deviously available, so that it could be changed later."

***

Unable to sleep for nearly two and a half weeks, Simone decides that she needs a soporific before bedtime. She chooses red wine, downs a glass and a half to sink her into unconsciousness. Nothing works. Most of the night, she tosses to and fro as thoughts and concerns impede drowsiness. If the submarines don't find a freighter bearing these rocket parts, will Redmond ever believe Simone again? Perhaps they will decipher the truth about whom she is working for. For the first time in her life, Simone is wracked with insomnia. She virtually stops eating, bites her nails to nubs and wonders what the fates have in store for her. She hears nothing for several weeks.

And then, finally one evening, Redmond calls in his usual laid-back style. He verifies that she is alone.

"About the shipment," he begins, "A rather important shipment..." he looks for words to describe what he knows and wants to convey.

"Get on with it," she says caustically, impatiently.

"Sorry," he replies with a lighter tone, "we could not locate the goods. Perhaps they were delayed...or, in fact, they may have been shipped earlier than you informed us."

Silence.

"And?" she asks at last, almost desperately.

"How could you know that the Americans intended to ship the goods differently? You did read the shipment date accurately, did you not?"

"Of course," she responds.

"Well, your information was spot on, Dawn," he continues. "We learned belatedly that the freighter docked in Southampton about a week earlier than you announced. The Americans may have decided to expedite the shipment then for a number of reasons, not the least of which may have been British pressure to send the goods over as quickly as possible. Not your fault, of course. As a result of your promising information, we are planning to send you overseas within the next six months. We consider you now a most valuable addition to our team."

Effusive with thanks, Simone downs two glasses of wine and collapses into her first genuine sleep of the past three weeks.

It is May of 1940. British troops are being evacuated from Dunkirk under heavy German bombardment. The war against Hitler, as predicted by German sympathisers, is not going well. Simone wishes she could advance the cause of defeating the Nazis. Their troops seem unstoppable. And as they ruthlessly gain ground, quickly the legend of the German superman begins to infiltrate the press. American troops are still not engaged.

The following month, a desperate phone call from Grace.

"You sound terrible," Simone says. "What's wrong, dear?"

"I discovered last week that what I hoped was impossible has happened," she says gloomily.

"Don't speak in riddles, girl."

"I'm pregnant."

"Ah!"

"Damn, I wish it were not so."

Simone thinks about how to approach this without undue criticism.

"You didn't use protection?"

"I thought we had, but you know, Faron reused his condoms."

"Oh, Lord," Simone sighs.

"Too expensive to buy," he used to tell me. "Ones he bought were made of cement dipped rubber with lubricants."

"So, he used one once too often."

"Apparently. But that's not the only sorrow," Grace continues. "When I was sure, I sat him down and told him what had happened. He jumped up, looked alarmed, sat back down, took a swig of his drink, and remained rigidly silent for almost ten minutes. Finally, I couldn't stand it and shouted at him. 'Say something, damn you, Faron,'

'All right,' he retorted, his face reddening. 'All right. This is what I have to say. The fact that you're a single woman and pregnant makes you no better than a harlot.

I'm not calling you a harlot, mind you. But others will.' Reached into his pocket for his Chesterfields. Pulled one out and lit it, sucking in smoke heavily.

I thought this was so disloyal and insensitive of him that my first reaction was to slap his face. Instead, I took a deep breath. 'But we can resolve this,' I responded quietly, sweetly. 'We love each other. Marry me.'"

Pause. 'We are too young to marry,' he stammered finally. He spoke, never looking directly at me, looked out of the corner of his eye suspiciously. Suddenly I saw that his paranoia was based on a simple idea that my pregnancy was a means to force him into marriage. As if I ever had such power.

'Too young? You are twenty-seven years old,' I blustered.

'I think I am too young,' he persisted, tugging at his little scruffy beard.

I decided to plunge right in. 'Maybe what you are truly saying is that you don't love me enough to marry me.'

He hid his face in his hands and lowered his face. For an instant, he remained still. Motionless. I thought he might cry. Instead, he jumped up. 'I have to go now,' he said without further response to my statement.

'Go. Leave? That's no way to resolve our dilemma.'

'Our dilemma?' he cried out his voice rising. 'This is not our dilemma. I don't have a dilemma in my stomach. It is only in yours.'

'But, my dear,' I responded flushing, stifling my rage, 'I could not have had the dilemma without your help.'

'And,' he continued grimly, 'I will do everything to assist you to resolve the problem. But marriage is out of the question.'

'You're proposing to get rid of our child?' I asked alarmed.

'There is no other way.'

'But this is life within me. I don't want to terminate this life.'

'I think you have no choice,' he responded sullenly.

'And how do you suggest we do this?'

He threw up his hands. 'Women have had abortions from forever,' he boomed. Pause. Then, calmer. 'I've heard that if you sit over steaming water and let the steam penetrate your private parts, you shall miscarry. That doesn't sound so horrible, does it? Isn't it worth a try? No doctors, no instruments, just a bit of vapour'

'Just a little vapour up my canal. That's your solution? Maybe you should inject a little vapour up your ass,' I shouted. I despised him, this insensitive, craven fool. And what a liar! He had sworn his love and his allegiance to me a hundred times. Facing our first real problem he attempted to resolve the problem in some spineless manner.'

'Then go to a hospital to have the procedure performed,' he added harshly.

'Get the hell out of my sight,' I thundered. When he left with a sullen look on his face, I crashed onto my bed and emptied my eyes out for three hours straight."

Simone is incensed. "Grace, you do need to abort at the hospital. You can't find a coat hanger to do it in some shabby tenement. He is right about that."

"I know he is, even though I hate the idea. I realise I cannot keep the baby with all of society judging me every day. Every walk with my son or daughter would be subject to scrutiny and gossip. Society ladies whispering to one another about my lack of respectability. I couldn't stand that."

"I know this is so," Simone says. "Poor dear. Poor careless dear. I wish I could take the pain away from you. Do you need me to come down to Atlanta?"

"No," Grace says. "I'll calm down in a day or so and then I will make a decision about it. In the interim, I have to make up my mind whether I love Faron more or hate Faron more."

That evening, alone in her thoughts, Simone is strolling in Georgetown. It is late for her. Almost 11, but she is not tired. Fired up by her success with the freighter, and troubled about her sister. She stands in front of the cathedral. She believes the door is open, but she decides not to enter. As she turns, she notices a man leaning backwards on a railing smoking a pipe. A man with a moustache, a blond moustache but with somewhat darker hair. I've seen this man before, she says to herself, but cannot dredge up the exact memory. Now, the man turns, and descends the stairs into the street.

A half hour later, as Simone is about to enter her side street, she has an intuition. Turns quickly. A shadow behind her is fading behind a building. But she can tell that it is a man. And furthermore, she is certain that it is the man with the pipe. She hurries back to the spot, but the shadow has vanished.

7. The Eye of the Dawn

Another month whisks by. Grace undergoes an abortion. Physically uneventful, but mentally, it casts a devastating cloud and impels her into melancholy.

"I really wanted that baby," she confesses to her sister. Her man has apparently disappeared into the ether. He does not visit or call. At Christmas, she receives a card from him asking whether he is indeed a daddy. A card she tears up without answering.

Simone has not been commissioned to do anything further but continue her work in Commerce. Any day, she hopes, she may be asked to pilfer information, but weeks pass without instructions. She continues with unarmed defence and marksmanship. She has now graduated to a Sten gun, and learns to fire it at will with scattergun accuracy, to take the weapon apart, clean it and re-assemble it. She can manage this in relative short order.

"Make sure," Hans insists as he examines her work with precision, "to look for carbon build-up on this weapon." He is timing her assembly. When she has completed it, holding the machine gun in a firing position, crouching on one knee, he nods. "Better. Not perfect, but better."

She works on her stamina, running around a track. First one mile, then two. Finally, a half dozen. As she starts training, Simone cannot believe she will ever complete a mile, but having accomplished that feat in a rag-tag fashion, is dubious about the next mile. After three months, she is running six miles at a pace of ten minutes each. Hans wants her to lower it to nine-minute miles.

Impossible," she cries. "I can barely manage ten. Nine is completely impossible."

"Only for those who decide it is," he catcalls.

She knows this to be true. Isolates one mile and lowers her speed to 9:15. A second mile in 9:20. Then a third in 9:30. A month later she is running three miles in twenty-seven minutes. Now she works on the next three. Three more weeks pass.

"Good," Hans praises her. "You are damn close."

One day, short of her mark, breathless after a run of six miles, having given everything and still short of her goal, Simone slips down a gymnasium wall onto her butt, her chest heaving, her cotton shirt sweat laden.

"Why are we doing this?" she demands. "Surely, it can't matter whether I can run two miles, six miles or ten-minute miles."

"Few things matter more," Hans suggests, giving her his hand and pulling her upright. "It matters because it is a goal, an achievable goal. Just as you will be asked to finish a job and the job may be out of reach, or so it appears, still you will remember how you covered six miles in fifty-four minutes and you will say to yourself that you can, of course you can, manage this job, any job. And one day, your ability to prevail may even save your skin."

Two weeks later, having lost four pounds, Simone runs six miles in fifty-four minutes.

December 7, the Japanese bomb Pearl Harbor. A few days later, FDR declares war on Japan and Germany. The country is in shock. Despite the fearful apprehension that America must enter the war, nobody is entirely prepared. Aware that thousands, perhaps hundreds of thousands of lives will be lost. American lives. While learning to take the belt in a notch. There will be shortages of food, of other goods used in the war effort. Already there is talk of a rationing system as the military ramps up. Droves of men, both young and old, enlist. Women as well. Many women co-opted to build the machinery that makes modern warfare possible. Simone's inclination is to join some branch of the Armed Forces, but she realises that her present position may be significantly more valuable. Several nail-biting months pass as the early engagements favour the Germans.

Then a visit from Richmond. Dapper as always, a beautiful black and stripped double breasted suit with a yellow foursquare in his vest pocket to lend colour. His face is clean shaven; hair slicked back, cheeks radiantly pink as if he had been tweaking them before knocking on her door.

"What are you doing here? She demands.

"That's a hell of a welcome. Let me in," he scoffs at her tone.

He edges into the house, she shutting the door with a slam.

"Everybody is listening to the radio these days," he explains, "not watching you, my dear. Hope that's not too much of a disappointment. I have some news for you and I wanted to bring it myself."

"But if you are seen…."

"Nobody knows who I am," he answers. "Just another beau for the beauteous Simone Valois. Anyone seeing me enter your house will think that we are having a cup of tea together…or perhaps brewing up a cup of passion."

Snorts. "You are naïve."

But he is laughing. Stuffs his pipe with tobacco, lights it with a match he scrapes against a fireplace brick.

"I don't enjoy the smell," Simone complains.

"Don't be so damned fussy," he snaps.

"I assume this isn't a social visit," she begins. "You have news? A development?" she prompts, sitting primly in front of him.

"Yes. You are to leave for France."

"France? But France is already occupied."

"True," Redmond agrees, "but there is a serious resistance brewing and we would like to nip it in the bud. The fighters call themselves Maquis."

"Go on." Now interested, she leans back into her chair, fingering the cotton fabric.

He stands. "You'll use your real name. Your code name, Dawn, will be reserved for special contacts. We'll transport you to Paris. The occupation is in full swing. Hitler rode down the Champs Elysees and people applauded him. Can you believe it? The French applauding the Fuehrer? But as you can imagine, not all Frenchmen are supporters. The Maquis is already turning fierce, dangerous."

"What will you need to know?"

"Who the resistance leaders are, their names, addresses, their cohorts, the size of their following, their meeting places, and any other information which may be of use to us. You speak French perfectly. You will fit in. We will establish a cover story for you, and a place where you can stay. Listen, fraulein, Paris is spectacular. I envy you living there. The food is elegant, the streets extraordinary, the museums to die for. And I believe there is even a casino there, so that if you get bored, you can drop a franc or two."

"I don't play," Simone retorts.

"Pity," Redmond acknowledges. "No play, no fun. No fun, no personality."

"You didn't complain about my personality the night we made love," she retorts.

"But yes, my dear, I wondered where was the real girl underneath the bountiful flesh she exposed?"

"Never enough for men," she sneers.

"Look Simone, I am not here to joust with you, only to prepare you for your trip. First by plane, then by train to your destination. In the meanwhile, you will learn all the information you need to memorise with regards to your name, your past, and so on. Yes?

"Yes."

"Good! Now," Redmond continues. "Give me a kiss before I leave."

He leans towards her, but she ushers him away.

"No, no," he retorts. "You misunderstand. I want people to see lipstick on my cheek, just in case anyone is nosey enough to monitor your house."

She kisses him forcefully on the cheek.

"Ouch," he says. "Pretty potent lips. How do you say ouch anyway in French?"

"Aieee," she shouts. "Now get out of here so I can scrub my lips. And when you deliver my new identity, how about a pair or two of silk stockings to make it more believable?"

"You drive a hard bargain," Richmond allows, bowing with a flourish and cackling before reaching the door. "We'll have to see whether the Abwehr can afford it."

"And some Eve Arden hand crème," she adds. "I have rough hands from the all strenuous exercise you put me through."

"No Rolls Royce?"

"Don't tempt me."

"Mademoiselle is learning, I see," he remarks snidely, closing the door behind him.

Ten days later, a package arrives by mail: A French passport with her name and other pertinent information. An expert forgery.

"I was born in Roscoff in Brittany," she reads, "in 1918. According to the passport, I have travelled little, rarely out of France."

Other papers accompany the document. Birth certificate. Parents, Lalo and Marie-Claude Valois, boulanger and patissier as professions. Birth information about them as well with locations. Jean Valois was a well-known cyclist, having participated in several races at the Paris velodrome. Marie-Claude had only one child, Simone. Pity! Simone jokes to herself. She could have had so many other siblings. There is a French ID card, two other passports, one American, one German, a driver's license (I probably should learn to drive a car before I leave town!), the address in Paris of an apartment near the Marais as well as but detailed instruction to reach it. Third floor walk-up. One bedroom. Can't be very fancy, Simone thinks. But they have also supplied her with funds in Portuguese, Spanish and French monies. One other name. Odette Reamur. Landlady? Contact? Unknown.

As Simone awaits further instructions, she has given her notice at the Commerce Department. When co-workers or her boss ask her why she is leaving, she says she wants to support the war effort. Praising her, everyone thinks her motivation stellar, but when they ask her how she expects to contribute, she says only that she is studying several possibilities.

Walking in the evenings after dinner, a long-time habit now of many years, she is convinced that someone is following her. Is it a protective tail? Someone certain to step in between her and any assailant that approaches? Or is it someone from the OSS? Occasionally stopping, checking out the streets that adjoin her house, looking under her skirt, she observes a shadow sliding along a wall, disappearing behind it. Could be a cat. Or a rat! One evening, she doubles back towards the phantom, but when she reaches the wall she figures had engulfed her tail, nobody is there. She must acknowledge that whoever is shadowing her is quite professional about it. Anyway, she wonders what she would say had she trapped the person.

"Good day, sir or madam. How can I be of service to you?" Awfully polite. Instead, how about: "I don't care to be followed. Do it again, and I'll unleash the dogs on you."

Yes, that's better. That could mean anything! How menacing. Good. Tough. Just the way Simone must learn to be, she thinks biting her lips.

"I have to go away for a while," connecting to Grace over the phone.

"Away?"

"Wish I could tell you exactly where, but that is supposed to remain a secret."

"I'll miss you."

"And I you. Tell me how you are."

A pause. Simone can hear Grace rising up in her seat.

"Well enough."

"You're getting over…"

"Don't mention that ugly, woebegotten name," Grace replies. She smacks her lips together. "If truth be told, I think of him every day, but with less and less longing. I truly hate this coward."

"As you should."

"Be safe, Simone, wherever you must travel. You're the only sister I have."

"No blubbering," Simone replies. "I'll be in touch when I can. But it may not be for some weeks."

The day before departure, she rides the train to New York, and takes a room in the Henry Hudson Hotel on the west end of town near the port. A small, somewhat dingy room. Clean, but dark. A clock and a radio for company. She listens to Walter Winchell and his entertaining gossip. Later, there is a series on the Lone Ranger and subsequently, the Shadow. With nothing else to do, she listens to both of these, allowing her imagination to illuminate the dialogue, until fatigue sets in and sleep dominates awareness.

In the morning, she hails a cab to the port. The freighter, Excambion, takes passengers as well.

"How do I know this freighter won't be torpedoed?" she asks Redmond.

He chuckles. "We would be wasting a promising asset," he replies. "Don't concern yourself. I am certain that you will have safe passage until Lisbon."

With that, he slips her a file. Things to study, to memorise, the name and rank of a German officer to see in Paris, and how to make contact, how to travel from Lisbon to Madrid and, from there, on to Paris.

"You won't be resting once you disembark in Lisbon. You will make your way to the main train station. Take a taxi," Redmond counsels. "You will have less than two hours to board the express train to Madrid. Don't miss it. The next one only runs the following morning."

She mulls all of this over in the cab to the port, excited, even a bit nervous as she is about to enter the realm of the unknown. She does not speak Portuguese or

Spanish. She has never in fact been to Europe. She wonders how well she will handle new challenges. On the other hand, a deep-seated wellspring of confidence with which she is in touch. So far, after all, she has handled life quite easily and even with aplomb. The thought bucks her up.

Up the gangplank, then down into the bowels of the ship. Not terribly elegant, she thinks, looking around. Walls are scarred, gouged. Oak flooring cracked in places. Crew members are running in every direction while shouting to one another in Portuguese. One she corrals directs her towards her cabin. She has forgotten to ask which number is hers. She returns to the top deck and is brought back down by a young, pimply faced sailor. He leads her to her cabin. They pass several boisterous men milling around.

"There are no keys," the boy remarks.

Swell, she sighs, opening the door. She sees a small room with a cot, a dresser and a musty smell. She looks out onto the Hudson from her porthole, calm for the moment. She has never been on a large ship before. The idea of a world existing on and with water for days on end seems improbable. Simone does recall being a passenger on a sailboat once as a child.

"What do I do if I have mal de mer?" she had asked Redmond.

"Stick your finger down your throat and get rid of anything in your stomach," he told her gleefully.

"Crappy advice," Grace had said. "Tell him what he can do with his own finger. Lie down and try to relax as you get accustomed to the rhythm of the ship's bobbing. I also hear that if you look out and fix on the horizon, you'll be all right."

"The bathroom is down the hall," the pimply face boy interrupts her memory.

Simone treads the threadbare carpet to the end of the hall. There are two stalls for women. Italian graffitti. A single shower.

"How many women on board?" she asks the boy.

"You're the only one, I think. Most of the time, we don't see women sailing to Europe. But on the return passage, we're crammed with immigrants. Last voyage, we had a young boy of only four sail alone to New York. Must have strange parents! He was deposited on the ship by his nanny. His mom and dad awaited him in the States at the foot of the gangplank, but when he saw them he ran the other way. We also had Mme Curie sail with us. There was a lot of commotion with her on board. Apparently, she invented something important."

The boy tells Simone about the dining room.

"Only one serving period," he announces. "Seven in the evening for about an hour, and then mornings, between eight and nine. Lunch is brought out around noon. If you're late, you rely on the kindness of the chefs to feed you leftovers. But, knowing them," he continues, "You can trust in nice folk."

The Excambion's heavy ropes are jettisoned. The ship backs out, its tower belching black smoke, and sets sail. Simone stands on the upper deck leaning on a railing, watching the Statue of Liberty pass. For some reason, the sight of the gigantic statue thrills her. Unused to such emotion, she has to check herself for a moment. She caves into the thrill so that the feeling passes quickly. Now, the ship edges out into the sea. Soon, there is nothing but water in every direction, its gentle rolling motion rocking back and forth. A smokestack above shoots out clouds of carbon. Several men are on the deck next to her agitatedly observing landmasses fade into the distance. Shrieking seagulls hover round the rear of the ship awaiting garbage. Simone wraps her sweater about her neck and stretches out on a lounge chair. A boy serves her tea and cookies.

Days pass slowly if effortlessly. She thumbs through a cooking book she has purchased in New York, although she rarely cooks. But she is not into novels. The fantastic does not appeal to her. Reality must be observed, focused on, studied, analyzed, and dealt with. She finds a history book on Germany in the limited ship's library but feels uneasy whenever she opens it. Probably because her mother was Jewish, she thinks. Noontime, she joins the men at lunch. Mainly soup and sandwiches. Ham seems quite popular. Swiss Cheese less popular, but equally filling. The cook, a Malaysian lad, makes apple tarts that are quite tasty. She has one every day for dessert.

For the most part, she does not mingle with the passengers. At lunch, they try to speak to her but often in a language she does not understand. She is told they are Norwegian. A few convey in broken English. She asks them why they are returning to their country in wartime. They answer vaguely, defensively, and this makes her believe that they are returning to wage war against the invaders. Dinners, she tends to sit at a designated table. No one offers to have her join them. They respect her privacy.

Once, a hubbub arises. In the distance, a ship.

"A military ship!" the pimply faced boy shouts at her. He thinks it may be German. They have already practiced war stations, jumping into lifeboats their first day at sea. A siren rings out prompting them to repair quickly to their station with life vests fastened. In a few moments, the alarm is lifted. It proves to be a British destroyer.

British sailors stand at the railing looking at the little freighter as their powerful vessel steams by. Some wave, some salute. One waves a flag with the British emblem. Simone waves back. The others do not return the salute, but they are buzzing with excitement.

Most days are calm, days in which to reflect on the vastness of the sea, the enormous panoply of stars at night. One morning, a driving rainstorm. Violent swells roiling the ship, the world gyrating. The pimply faced sailor suggests she eat something to settle herself, but the thought of food knots her stomach. She declines and chooses to ride it out.

On the ninth day, as the sun hoists upwards towards noon, land is sighted. Portugal. Lisbon. The ship approaches port slowly, almost discretely. Sailors are at the ready with the heavy ropes to stabilise the docking ship. Everyone runs up on deck to scan the port. It is as if they are expecting armed men to patrol the harbour, but there is only a single policeman strolling with an unlit cigarette in his mouth.

Debarked, immigration and customs dealt with, Simone hails a taxi to the Lisbon train station. The taxi driver loads her luggage, says to her in stilted English:

"Too bad you are not come sooner. Our World's Fair is finish, digested. Maybe you see the replica of the 17th century galleon in harbour?" She has not. "Pity," he says with a sigh. "It's awfully remarkable." In a few minutes: "Here we are, the Rossio train station. If you stare upwards," he continues proudly, "you shall witness the statue of King Sebastian."

The train station is a brooding nineteenth century stone edifice. She enters through the main gate, locates an information counter. A woman with a bright green sash directs her to quai two.

"You must change in Madrid," she says to Simone in a British accent. "The connecting train arrives in another hour. But also, if you do not care to dine in the food wagon, you may purchase sandwiches in the café within the station."

One seat remains in her compartment. As she enters, five passengers crane their necks to look at her, examine her. Once she has settled, a man on the opposite bench reaches into his pocket and produces the carving of a church. Holds it up and thrusts it into Simone's hand.

"I take this to the capitol to sell." The workmanship is not fine, but at least Simone identifies the object as a church. She nods and returns it to the man. A woman with a Pekinese on a leash crosses her legs. Simone reaches over to pet the dog's head. The Pekinese emits a shrill howl, retreats onto its hind legs, and bares its teeth.

"This dog is a trifle shy," the woman holding it announces in French.

Just before Madrid, several Guardia Civil officers enter her wagon and examine her passport. The Spanish civil war has ended, but there are still occasional incidents. The police take few chances. Two of the men in the compartment appear to be shrinking in their seats. The police verify everyone's credentials and tickets. They peruse Simone's passport perfunctorily, then start to walk away without another word. They stop at the door to allow a passenger to pass through the corridor. Simone reaches for a Lucky Strike. The second policeman turns, holds up a finger, then produces a lighter. He doffs his casque when he lights her smoke.

At the French frontier, the Paris train grinds to a stop. German soldiers board each wagon. The shrinking men are now puffing themselves up and out. They speak German fluently. The woman with the shy dog is gripping her dog's neck tightly. The dog is wiggling, trying to free itself. For a moment, Simone notices something she has rarely encountered. Her wrist is quietly shaking. Tremors, she thinks. Others might term it fear, certainly agitation. She herself cannot dredge up a word for the sensation. Blood is pounding. Thigh muscles bristling. Breathing shallow and quick, yet in a moment, recalling her relaxation technique, she is able to quiet her tightness, to diminish her unsettled breathing. She regains her steady state momentum, and she is calmer. Her wrist is now silent. Whole. Assuming control.

This time, she produces the German passport.

"Your destination?" one soldier asks her. She notices another soldier just outside her compartment with a submachine gun at the ready. Its barrel is pointed at her, but the soldier isn't looking in her direction.

"I am going to Paris," she replies in perfect German. "I have an appointment with a German officer."

"Your German, Fraulein," the soldier says approvingly eyeing her documents, "is quite fluent."

"Vielen dank," she says, thanking the soldier for his compliment, tells him that she learned well in school. He bows, and slowly backs out with a smile on his face.

Simone leans back into the cushion of the headrest. Notices she is breathing a bit more quickly. But she has passed this first test with aplomb. Now she unwinds and soon begins to doze. The train plods through the countryside, the steam engine bursting forth with occasional whistles and spewing ash into the air. She leaves her compartment only to stop at the bathroom and to dine in the food wagon. The train is a bit unbalanced, lurching on the rails whenever it rolls around curves. She has ordered an escalope de veau with potatoes and green beans. Plates slide along the table from time to time. The butter plate sails off the table and onto the carpet. The food is generally good when she can catch it. She downs a glass of red wine. A soldier saunters into the dining car and stops by her table. He asks whether she would enjoy his company. She replies that she is tired and is about to retire for the evening. The solider shrugs and moves on.

Simone dozes in her compartment. From time to time, the train halts. It belches black clouds of coal dust, so much so that she urges her fellow passengers to shut the window. They do so, but they seem irritated. It is close in the compartment now with the window shut. At dawn, the train limps into the Austerlitz station. The station is noisy with the shriek of trains arriving and departing, passengers calling out to one another as they board. When Simone disembarks, a porter totting her suitcase, she is halted at the entrance gate. French policeman, Vichy style. Sporting a wide moustache, his uniform grease spotted and torn at one wrist he asks:

"You are here for business?"

"I am here to visit a German officer," Simone replies.

"You don't possess the accent of Paris," he says. Now checking her rayon dress with its flower motif, the daisies that dot the sides of the garment. "And the name and rank of this officer?"

She produces the information.

"A male friend? Perhaps a lover?"

Demurs, eyelids shutting down.

"We have business. A Captain," she adds. "Do you know Paris?" he asks her with what passes for an agreeable smile.

"No," she replies.

"I would be pleased to squire you to the important, cultural sites," the policeman offers.

She thanks him politely, but remarks that the German officer has already proposed to do so. The man grimaces, urges her with a dismissive wave of his hand to pass the barrier. Simone, however, is pleased that she has lied so easily and effectively. Wouldn't Anderson be proud!

At the sidewalk, a French taxi from the queue. The driver sits in the open part of the car, while she enters the enclosed rear. He is driving her slowly over cobbled streets to the Marais.

"It is not so far," he shouts back at her.

"And how is Paris these days?" she shouts back.

"With the Boches here?" he complains crudely, referring to the Nazis, his hands leaving the steering wheel.

"Better not to speak this way about the occupiers," she chides him.

"Ah, you are one of those," he concludes darkly.

"Not at all," she sniffs. "I am concerned about your welfare."

"So, I shall take the direct path," he shouts pleasantly, then explains. "The indirect path costs passengers a trifle more."

Before long Simone is ringing the outer door bell. She rings it again. Then for a third time. Finally, someone answers. A nose appears first, quickly followed by a wrung face. A small woman with a red shawl about her neck, her hair in a bun, and spectacles drooping about her nose, opens the door.

"I'm hard of hearing," she offers apologetically. "Here," she continues, "let me take your valise. I suppose you are the one I have been waiting for."

She picks it up with some difficulty, but shrugs off Simone's entreaty. "I can do this. I promise you. Follow me. Your apartment is on the third floor."

The concierge presses the commutateur, an electric device that produces a light for thirty seconds. "Ha!" she cries gleefully. "I thought it was no longer functioning."
They begin the steep climb holding on to an old wooden banister scarred from unusually difficult contact with people, suitcases, and furniture, bruised and groaning as they occasionally slide against it.

They are both out of breath on the third floor.

"I hope I remembered the key," the concierge says. "My name is Odette."

"Simone," she answers, holding out her hand.

The concierge takes her hand, then fishes into her pocket for a master key. She opens the door. There is one light, a bulb against the ceiling. She pulls the string and the bulb produces a pale sliver of light.

"The bathroom is down the hallway," Jacqueline says. "You might buy your own toilet paper. I tend to forget to do so."

"And where would I buy toilet paper?" Simone asks.

The concierge shrugs. "It's almost impossible to obtain these days. The soldiers need to wipe their asses more than civilians. I do understand this, of course. It's in the national interest. But the local newspaper is not bad also. I prefer Le Figaro. Seems a shade softer than Le Monde. The cleaning woman comes once a week. Stay out of her way. She is not to be crossed when she starts to sweep."

The room is a rectangle. A single unbalanced chair stands against the window, next to it, a dresser. Outside, Simone glimpses an alleyway with garbage cans and an acrobatic cat. A small elm tree striving to grow despite the lack of sunlight. Against the wall, a cot. Spongy mattress. Coiled springs underneath groan when the mattress bears weight. There is a pillow. Sheets and pillow cases which have been washed so often that the fabric is skimpy.

"I'll have to buy a lamp," Simone says to the concierge.

"If you do so, I must charge you ten percent. Electricity is frightfully dear these days."

"But I cannot live without a lamp. There is not enough light in this room to read by."

"True, but there is ample light during the day." Odette leaves the key and descends the stairs.

Simone trudges down the hallway to the toilets. A shower with a hand wand, a bar of skinned hand soap. The toilets are unisex. She begins to blush even before she enters. Silly me, she chides herself. Yet, the toilets are relatively clean with an acrid odour of cleaning fluid.

She wonders why the Nazis have given her such an inexpensive, no, cheap, apartment. They must not value my work, she considers. Later she appreciates that they want her to appear inconspicuous, just one of the labourers.

In a flea market in the Marais, she unearths a lamp, but it is broken, and she has no means to repair it. She decides not to buy it. At any rate, there are no bulbs.

"Bulbs are rare these days," the salesman says. He is not upset, only stating the fact of the matter. "Wartime, you know. Stroll down the rue de Rivoli. Sometimes you may stumble on a place that has a fresh shipment."

She studies the walls of her room. Someone has marked one in pencil. She tries to read it. It appears to be a poem of some length, but she cannot decipher it. I'm painting this room, she says to herself. But first things first. Simone prepares for an appointment the following morning at the Hotel Meurice. She declines into sleep early, interrupted only once by the boisterous sounds of several men calling to each other.

8.   A Meeting at the Hotel Meurice

She makes her way through the throngs down the rue de Rivoli on a misty late morning. The street, a major thoroughfare through the heart of the city, is invariably crowded with shoppers and passers-by. The elegant hotel, the Meurice, has been in existence since the early nineteenth century, and has recently been commandeered as a governing headquarters of the city by the German general, Von Choltitz.

Blocked at the door by a heavily armed, helmeted soldier, she produces papers. The guard looks her up and down, studies her passport picture.

"Kapitan Anselm Baer is waiting for you in the parlour. You're early." Then he smiles. "Naturlich, he is always earlier." He points the way, then adds that he will accompany her.

Simone is dressed in a black cotton dress with a white pearl necklace. Applied red lipstick and powder, a bit of eyeliner, hair curled. The concierge has produced white paste which she uses in place of silk stockings on her legs. A bit of rubbing and the legs appear as if they are the essence of silk.

The captain, wearing the green gray tunic and breeches of the Wehrmacht, rises quickly as she approaches. Fiftyish, tall, greying at the temples, a pleasant face save for a slight harelip. His narrow mouth remains closed as if it were a vice. Anselm seems clearly aware of the deformity to his face, masking his lips often. On a side table, a phonograph is playing a Brandenburg Concerto. He quickly turns it off. Clicks his heels. He clearly appreciates the vision before him.

"Fraulein Valois," he says, "an honour to make your acquaintance."

"The honour is mine," she responds, offering her hand to the captain.

"You are a splendid young woman," he remarks, kissing her hand even as his eyes meet hers. "The Abwehr did not do justice to your loveliness," he continues. He offers her a seat on a plush red sofa. Simone sits, settles her purse next to her, looks about. Perennial gold trim over crème stucco walls, carpets dating from either the seventeenth or eighteenth centuries depicting war scenes in red and gold, lush red and white sofas, rich covered scarlet armchairs. Eighteenth century oil paintings in the style of Watteau adorn the walls. An enormous chandelier with Irish crystal hanging in the centre of the room catches her eye. A Steinway piano sat in a corner. A soldier closes the phonograph, and now lifts open the piano case. Begins to play softly, but is shooed away by the captain.

"Bring us tea," he remarks off-handedly to the soldier. Then to Simone: "I used to play the violin in my town orchestra. I miss it." he grimaces slightly. "Perhaps music later. English breakfast tea," he points. "You enjoy this tea?"

Simone nods her approval.

"Your first time to Paris?"

"Yes, it is."

"So, tell me how you find it," he inquires.

She tells him how she made her way from Portugal to the Gare Austerlitz, describes her apartment in the Marais.

"I would kill for a lamp," she scowls, "but it has not been possible for to find one."

The captain laughs. "I will have someone bring you a lamp this evening. Tell me what else you need."

"A bulb to read by."

"Naturlich," he grins, nodding assent. "Your needs are not impossible, at least not so far."

"I went to a nearby restaurant last night, "Simone goes on. "I found it strangely empty. I had an entire table to myself. I scanned the menu and found a steak, a fauxfilet with potatoes and green beans, and ordered it. The waiter politely informed me that the restaurant was out of this item. So, I ordered the hamburger tartare. But I was informed that they had no hamburger. Finally, I asked them whether he had either the chicken or the sole. The waiter sadly shook his head. "Well then, what do you have? 'We have a can of peas,' he intoned solemnly. 'And perhaps I can also find cauliflower in a tin.' So that is what I had for dinner," she concludes with a quick smile.

The captain returns her smile.

"This is quite common in Paris these days. But you don't need to starve while in town, my dear. I am going to provide you with a list of several restaurants around Paris. When you enter, you will show them the ID I provide for you, and I think you will find that they can offer you more substantial meals."

"I cannot thank you enough," Simone says, her lips softening.

"I don't want you to starve while you are in my town. Henceforth," the captain goes on switching languages, leaning towards Simone, I shall call you by your new name, Dawn. Quite a charming name, I think. It suits you well."

"So, you know English."

"I did study it in school," the captain admits. "It comes in useful to interrogate British prisoners. Americans, we haven't seen yet, but I expect to interrogate a slew in the near future," he adds confidently.

"So, tell me what you require of me."

"I do have a quarry for you to hunt," the captain reveals, accepting the tray of tea and pouring a cup for Simone. "Your German is excellent, and I am told that your French is every bit as good. My plan is this: I want you to infiltrate the French resistance, tell me who the ringleaders are, their names, where they live, gain their confidence so that you can bring me their plans as well as any other pertinent information."

Simone leans forward, sips her tea. "You must have a place for me to start, perhaps a street or a name."

"Indeed," the captain answers.

"Tell me about the resistance. We have not heard much about them in the States."

"They are only now beginning to form in groups," the Captain begins. "Very pesky mosquitoes," he adds stoically.

"Who are they?"

"Since our soldiers are fighting on multiple fronts," the captain says, toying with a pair of gray leather gloves in his hands, "we need Frenchmen, particularly young ones, to labour for us. Making ammunition, construction of weapons, building airplanes, tanks, other machinery, even clothing. We can use millions of workers to this end. So, we require that all young Frenchmen spend time in this endeavour. Many have agreed to do so, but there are hundreds, perhaps thousands, who have decided they prefer to fight us rather than work. These are the groups we want to apprehend and eliminate before they attract too many other adherents. My man who brings the lamp and bulb tonight, will also furnish the name and address of someone whom you will want to meet at once. When you have information, do not return here. Every Wednesday night at seven, go to the Jardin du Luxembourg. There is a fountain there with a bench facing the fountain. Sit there. Someone will contact you and you can pass along information."

"A soldier?"

"Someone in civilian clothing," the captain smiles. "Perhaps even a woman. Which do you prefer?"

Simone looks up surprised at the question. "Either one," she answers simply.

"My question was somewhat indiscrete," the captain admits, his lips parting slowly. "A half-hearted attempt at flirting," he adds. "Sometimes it is tiresome to be away from home for so long. I have a family in Dusseldorf, a wife and three children. I see them rarely."

"Send for them to come to Paris," Simone suggests.

The captain's face grows sombre. "I would fear for them," he admits. "Once identified, they would be subject to harm. No," he continues vigorously, "I cannot bring them to the city, although I know my wife would love to visit this beautiful town. We control Paris," he adds, "but there are forces smouldering, forces building strength which will eventually cause us strife. These are the units we need you to identify for us. Their ringleader is a young man."

"Why haven't you already arrested this man?" she asks the captain.

"He is much more valuable to us as a key to others. Once we have this information we will imprison all of them. We have a particular interest in Jews, homosexuals, and gypsies, of course. These are the lesser beings in the food chain but surely there will be others who struggle against us."

Stupidly, she cannot refrain from asking the captain why the Germans have chosen specifically these groups to assail.

He looks at her with virtual disdain. "You must know, my dear, that we Germans are a race apart. Surely that is what attracted you to our cause, nichtwahr? How did we achieve our grandeur? By remaining as pure as our Aryan blood would allow. Certainly, there have been poisons that emptied into our bloodstream, and these we need to ferret out, suck out, if you will, and destroy. Of course, all men make these distinctions. You are either one of us or you are not. Do you think the English, the Germans or the French are any different from us? Perhaps they pretend a veneer of civilization which glosses over their ardour to remain unadulterated. The difference for us is that we have the desire, the order, and the power to make us unique among men. Unlike others, we will destroy those who don't match the purity of our bloodlines. Our race is superior because we strive to make it so. Look at yourself, my dear. Do you associate with loose women?"

"Of course not," Simone cries out.

"But why not? They're women. There are American prostitutes who may be as pretty, as intelligent and as devious as you."

"I find them repugnant," Simone says.

Encouraged by this response, the Captain continues. "It is because they are unlike you. Take your negro. Coloured men in America were slaves because as white masters you could make them slaves. You won't marry a black man, will you?"

"No."

"It is because you are different from the black race. Not even a matter of colour. They are simply an underclass. And you, as an educated, attractive white woman are clearly superior to them in so many respects. As a result, we use them. We use the weak, the Jewish profiteers, and so many others. Why? Because, my dear, we can. Once Germany has ruled the world, we will institute policies which will shield you further from the encroachment of blacks, Indians, Asians, and others who may strive to adulterate your race."

Within herself, Simone feels a giddiness. On the one hand, she finds it difficult to believe that this intelligent, sophisticated man is spewing such garbage, while on the other; she wonders what he might be saying to her if he knew that she was half Jewish. Clearly, if he only knew, their conversation would come to a speedy end. And her end would be even speedier!

"The wheelwrights of the world, the valets, they too have a place in our story, but their place will always be subservient to their masters," he concludes.

She won't argue with him. That would be stupid, revealing too much of her. Instead, she sits before this man, legs crossed, pretending to drink in each and every syllable, nodding here and then to acknowledge what a wise man the Captain is, and how fortunate she has become to find a mentor in such a man. Another hour passes in this fashion. At a certain moment, he pulls out a disc of Rhapsody in Blue and plays it for her on his phonograph. Half way through, he has to stop because the needle, now worn, defaces the sound. He replaces it quickly, apologizing. But then, with a beatific smile, he leans back to hear the entire piece played. At its conclusion, he turns to Simone:

"A lovely piece, don't you agree? True it was composed by an American Jew. Had a Hugenot, a Lutheran, or an atheist composed it, the sound would be even sweeter."

9. The Maquis

Undecided as to whether her assault should be more frontal or perhaps more restrained, Simone finally decides to open herself completely to the man she is to meet. His name is Clovis Rastine. Mornings, he reads and studies in the Bibliotheque Municipale under a green, shaded light in the main reading room. She pulls out his photo from her purse and studies it as she enters the large, quaint chamber.

And there is where Simone locates her target. For a moment, she simply walks by him, turns discretely, and checks him out from the corner of her eye. She expects to see someone strong, even burly; someone, if called upon, capable of acts of brutality. Instead, she is peering into the face of a young man with a tranquil, bemused face, a slender man with curly hair, hair which wafts about his forehead in the manner that some young women wear it. His frame is rather slight. Tall, lanky, clearly studious. He wears glasses. Focuses completely on the book he is reading. At first, she does not understand that he is speaking to her. He is mouthing words while reading. But suddenly, clearly, she realises that he is addressing her.

"It's a work by Martin Heidegger," he says without looking up.

So, he has noticed me, she thinks, despite his attention to his book. Maybe there is more to this young man than I thought.

"I am fascinated by man's relationship to time," he goes on.

"Simone Valois," she says, and holds out her hand. He does not take it. Instead, he lays down the book carefully, placing a marker into a page, and lifts his eyes. "I have heard about you, but I don't know what to think," he says evenly. "I don't like spies. Or trust double agents. They tend to make for double trouble. You don't ever know which side they are truly playing."

"I only play one side," Simone affirms somewhat testily.

He bids her sit.

"Don't speak loudly," he whispers to her. "They don't permit it here."

"Only one side," she whispers back.

"Yes, but which one?" he asks suspiciously. "That is yet to be determined."

"You have heard of me...I must have been referred to you..."

"For sure," he says. He gets up briefly to stretch. Tall, thin, long arms, wearing gray pants, a blue shirt and tie; he is clearly not given to promoting himself. Nor is his face special. It is that of a young Frenchman without special attractive features. And yet, there is something fetching about this young person. He traps her glance without demanding it of her. He holds me, she thinks. How does he do this? He has some kind of aura, but she cannot identify it. She has no answer.

"So," he goes on, "we have now made contact. Sit here opposite me and pretend that we are discussing Heidegger. I'm somewhat surprised to meet you so quickly. I understood that you had arrived only the day before yesterday. You must have something you wish to convey."

She relates her conversation with the captain in the hotel Meurice. Clovis appears deep in thought, his eyes lowered. He does not respond to her immediately once she has finished.

"I know he can arrest me at any moment," he muses. "I do know that."

"He seems to be in no hurry."

"He wants information about my cohort," Clovis says, now rising. "Let's get out of here. There is a café around the corner where we can chat more freely."

He takes her arm to cover the hundred yards to the café. They sit outside beneath electric heaters, and order two cafes. There is no coffee. The waiter brings them two cups of hot chicory.

"I do plan to provide you information about them," he says at last. Her head shoots up. "You look surprised. Don't be. I will write down the names of many who are either captured or serving in labour camps. I will also provide the names of wanted men who have perished or disappeared. But I will not give him the names of any person still active within the group."

"Perhaps that will be enough for him," Simone speculates. "At least, it will buy time," she adds. "He knows that I am new to all of this in France. My information cannot be totally correct, can it?"

Clovis shrugs. "You do understand that eventually you will be upended. Undoubtedly. Once captured, you will be tortured to spill everything you know. Hardly anyone can withstand ongoing torture. You will confide everything you know and even what you do not know, anything to stop the cutting, probing, the hitting and perhaps in your case, the raping."

Chills. She tries to recover her aplomb.

"I understand this." Simone's face settles into classic restraint.

"And you are still willing to proceed?"

"Yes," Simone says. "Yes. I won't let them win."

"Right," he scowls. "It is their incredibly selfish and stupid ideas. How magnificent they are and how lowly and dirty and poor the rest of the world! We're going to put an end to those theories. Once and for all."

They sip chicory in silence for a moment. He grimaces at the sourness of it, searches for sugar.

"I will also want something from you. To prove yourself, my friend, I have some work for you tomorrow night."

"Work?"

"I won't tell you what the job is. Not yet. But be prepared to spend the night. Come dressed as if you were on a cleaning crew. Do you know how to use weapons?"

"Yes."

"A Sten gun?"

"Yes. I learned from a Nazi sympathiser."

"Good," he remarks, pleased. For the first time, a sliver of a smile tugs his tight lips. "Meet me at the rear of the Madeleine tomorrow night after dinner. Nine o'clock. Don't be late." Pause. "If you betray us, Simone, I will personally kill you. Slowly! I have no compunctions about murdering a female if she is treacherous." There is steel in the voice.

She recoils. She has not heard this tone before. "Please don't say things like that. I am working with you, not against you."

"On verra," he concludes. "We'll see."

Simone is both shaken and calmed by her first meeting with Clovis; reassured by his authority, disturbed by the brutality lurking underneath his mild manner. And yet, she understands clearly that without such ability to murder, to fight back, there would be no resistance.

That evening after dinner, Simone makes her way tentatively to the Madeleine. She walks around to the back. The evening is calm. Stars abound. The moon is shining clearly, big and low in the sky.

At the rear of the church, there are large steps. She rests on one of them. In a few moments, men are arriving, two by two, slowly making their way towards her. One of them, accompanied by a woman, is Clovis. He says nothing to Simone as he passes. Nor does he look at her. The young girl also stares straight ahead. In another moment, a truck arrives, slowing by the steps. It is a vintage truck, constructed in the thirties. Its clutch makes a grinding racket as the driver downshifts. There are two men sitting in the front seats. The driver wearing a cap firmly planted on his head, the passenger beside him with a grim expression on his lips. The back of the truck is covered with a tarp. The men now pile into the truck under the tarp one after the other, Clovis as well as the young girl.

"Come on," he waves to Simone. "Get in."

She complies. Side panels on either side to sit on. The truck starts up slowly. Passing couples on the street. German soldiers in pairs, occasional a lone soldier walking. One Nazi soldier is strolling with a woman. They are laughing together, his arm around her waist. Clovis glances at her with disdain. The soldier gives the woman his hand to cross a street. The truck continues onto the Latin Quarter, past the Sorbonne. Simone is asking questions, but for the moment, nobody is responding. Instead, everyone is concentrating on another large structure looming ahead, the Lycee Louis-le-Grand.

"What are we doing here? "She asks when she reads the sign. "It's too late in the evening to take a class." The joke is lame.

"Quiet," Clovis frowns, his finger reaching over to her lips. "Quiet. This is now a Nazi barracks."

The truck stops. The men get out slowly, effortlessly, virtually without sound. Three of them carry large canvas cases. One reaches into his case and pulls out a box of hand grenades. He hands several to each person. Now, another distributes Sten guns and MP 40 submachine guns. A third, Welrod pistols. Simone takes a Sten-gun and sticks a Welrod in her waistband.

"Remember," Clovis whispers, "If anyone is caught, you know nothing. If you can just resist for a little while, this will give us time to move to a safe place. All right now, let's go. Time is of the essence."

Simone cocks her Sten gun, lodges the pistol into her waist belt tightly. Two by two, the men are moving across the yards that separate the truck from the school. At the entrance to the main courtyard, soldiers are standing guard at attention.

Clovis and one other man hide their weapons. They signal to one guard. The pair approaches the guardhouse from two sides.

Simone can hear a request for identification. Clovis is reaching into his pocket. She is watching his hands for the slightest quiver. There is none. On his face, a studious pose. He produces a piece of paper. The guard props up his rifle on the guardhouse behind him and is reading it. Suddenly, Clovis grabs his shoulder, turns the man deftly and, in the same motion, slits his throat from behind. The second guard is felled by a blow from a pistol butt. Clovis signals the others with a wave. They rush towards the guardhouse brandishing their weapons. Entering the courtyard. In the middle, there is an ample flower garden with blooming red and white roses. The group is moving on either side of it through the darkness, lit only by the aura of the crescent moon. Now a cloud obscures the moon, and, for an instant, they halt awaiting its passing.

"Stay with me," Clovis says to Simone. "Follow my lead." He sucks in a large gasp of air.

Simone is astonished. Clovis has changed from the mild mannered intellectual in the library, whose mornings are consumed devouring Heidegger, into a panther who hunts effortlessly, in total command of both his emotions and his men. She swallows hard and follows.

Suddenly a side door opens to the left, and two German soldiers exit strolling together, joking, lit cigarettes in their mouths. Clovis and Simone are crouching behind a rose bush.

"Simone," Clovis whispers, "Shoot the one on the left."

Simone looks up at him, her mouth ajar. For a moment, her mouth is too dry to answer.

"Now!" he commands. The voice is stern, but not acidic. "Kill the one on the left."

Simone raises her Sten gun. She stops for a moment to undo the fog from her eyes. Lifts up her body. Shoots two crisp rounds. The soldier on the left drops to the ground. In the same moment, Clovis raises his gun and shoots the other soldier who descends onto his knees before collapsing.

"Good," Clovis says quietly. "Swell. But now all hell is going to break loose."

As if responding to this thought, doors crash open everywhere in the main courtyard and soldiers spill out in various stages of undress. Clovis elevates three fingers to prompt his group to launch grenades one after the other at the opening doors. Fire, noise and convulsions reign. Soldiers are catapulting into the air, many decimated by shrapnel and explosions. A soldier raises his rifle when suddenly his arm shatters into thin air. Blood is raining everywhere. The crying, the shouting...it is as if a human earthquake had erupted into the night air, turning the unhurried peace of the night into total chaos of endless airborne cartilage. The smell of gunpowder infiltrates the nostrils. Shouts of confusion and rage mix with gunfire. Streams of blood are draining towards the sewers. Soldiers are firing unrestrained in every direction, running through the flower beds.

"Use your gun," Clovis commands her.

She looks up, sees a group of advancing soldiers, one now kneeling. She fires, dropping two of them. Three others are shooting at her as they advance. The noise of the whistling bullets passing by her head startles her. Clovis throws a grenade and the soldiers carrousel in a cloud of yellow fire.

Now he revolves, and, with another wave of his fingers, his entire group begins to edge backwards, heaving grenades and firing as they retreat. One man, the driver of the truck, has left hurriedly, running low virtually on all fours. Simone can hear the engine revving behind her, the clutch now engaging, screaming through the caustic night air, as bullets target them, cracking concrete slabs at their feet, whistling by them. The truck pulls alongside the curb. They scamper into the truck's abdomen still firing at the vestiges of troops shucking and diving in their direction.

"Quickly now," Clovis cries, out of breath. "There will be armoured personnel following. We have to make for the side streets and our garage." The truck veers onto a pedestrian walkway, yanks off it and careens down a street paralleling the Seine. Behind them in the blackness of night, a tumult is swelling. Simone can see an upraised hand of a German soldier trying to signal just as shots ring out, his hand detaching from the remainder of his shoulder. Machines are moving in their direction, men shouting, some crying, others whining. More sounds of mechanization. Tanks? Armored vehicles? Jeeps? They cannot tell at this distance. Floodlights search through the brilliant night sky. The driver picks up speed, the truck lurching from side to side on cobblestone streets, its clutch groaning. Eyes open wide, Simone is expecting to hear the terrible mechanical fury of vehicles behind her. She is sure that they will catch up. Her breathing has tripled in volume. Sweat clouding her eyes. In the distance, the tumult of a thousand sirens, lights exploding throughout the evening, the moon obscured.

On the Ile Saint-Louis, the truck enters an open space, an alleyway. Clovis signals the driver to halt, leans out of the passenger window and examines the street. It is empty. The truck moves another hundred feet. Stops. The moon suddenly disengages from a cloud appearing like a searchlight, its cloud dissipating into the stars. Clovis jumps out, pulls down a garage door. The truck enters the garage. At once, the group empties out of the rear of the truck, the men piling boxes one on top of the other to shield the truck should the door be raised. Sirens are filling the night air as vehicles swarm in their general direction.

They're hunched down behind the truck. Waiting. Waiting for the hubbub to pass, to ease, to silence. Clovis quiets a cramp in his right leg. He pulls a piece of paper out of his pocket and begins to shred it.

"What's that?" she asks watching him decimate the paper bit by bit.

He smiles an ineffable smile.

"It's a list of false Nazi sympathisers. All of us, except for you, had a copy of it so that if any of us was captured or killed, the Nazis would find what they consider to be a treasure trove of information."

After an hour, Clovis reaches into his pocket and hands Simone a candy bar.

"Eat it," he urges her. "Good job tonight," he praises her. "But you used up a lot of energy."

Simone, however, is virtually frozen in a foetal position. Her mind is fixed, picturing the eyes of the first soldier she has slain, eyes that opened wide in denial as her bullets penetrated his flesh. His mouth had quivered as if he wished to issue a final word, yet without sound. She saw him drop to the ground in a heap; blank eyes remaining wide open, inexorably trained on her.

She turns slightly. She has not noticed that one of their men has been shot, and the others are attending to him. He is just a boy, perhaps seventeen. A flesh wound in the arm. They have arrested the bleeding.

"We'll need to pull out that bullet before the night is over," someone remarks. The boy grunts. He is in pain, but he is not crying. His pride is stronger than his pain, the bravery of fighting for his country while so many others have abandoned themselves sheepishly to the Nazis. It dominates his anguish. The arm will heal, he knows.

"Anything I can do?" Simone asks, shaking herself out of her lethargy.

The other woman is attentive to the boy and says she is managing. Clovis knows the mention of the shooting of the Germans is taboo to Simone in this moment. Too fresh a wound to cope with. Yet, he persists, because he strives to snap her into reality.

"This was the first man you killed, right?"

"Yes."

"And then there were others you shot." His eyes are sombre. "This takes time to digest."

"Yes," is all she can reply.

"But you are a patriot," he adds, in a hopeful tone. "You are one of us. You did what any soldier does in wartime."

"I am no soldier," she demurs.

"Never say that," he answers adamantly.

That evening, after she has ridden the metro, she is disgorged into the fresh night. Simone finds an empty bench at the Place des Vosges, the full moon overhead now illuminating the square, utterly drained. A quivering right hand undoes itself. She sits quietly. Sirens are receding. Armoured vehicles are slowing in the Marais. Her watch has been shattered, but she doesn't give a damn about the oncoming curfew. Before finding her apartment, she will remain in the chill of the night air until it is the right moment to get up; to head home. Her hand stops its tremor. She observes a pair of lovers kissing on a bench across from her, and uncharacteristically, as emotion attains the depth of her being, she begins to well up.

That night, sleep is out of the question. Whenever she lays her head on her pillow, the eyes of the man she killed floods her brain. After a time, unable to dispose of the dreadful scene, to abandon herself to unconsciousness, she decides to engage once more the scenes she has witnessed, even lived.

The killing, Simone tells herself, is unlike anything I imagined. I thought it would be easy, because the man I murdered is an enemy and deserved to die. And yet, the act itself, while so unbelievably easy because it took only squeezing a trigger, was the hardest thing I have ever done. It was not I who squeezed that trigger. It must have been somebody else, some other volition. I never thought I would ever wrest life from anyone. To the contrary, as part of the OSS, I expected to save lives. I could break codes. I could even obtain information by theft, or by offering my body in an exchange, but never for a moment did I imagine causing such harm. Confusion sets in.

True, I was trained to do this. But the idea of murder and the act of murder are not identical. In the idea, I can shoot a gun, and nothing happens save in my visualization. But this night, I actually took the life of someone I did not know. Perhaps he had a family, children, and a wife. He had a childhood and lived his adulthood and would have expected to reach old age. But no, I stole that from him. I don't know whether I killed the others I shot, perhaps not. But this man, I locked eyes with him and I am certain he died. Life emptied from his pupils. How could I do this? This is not me. I was brought up to think, to read, and to enjoy life. Not to murder. And yet, when I remember the event truthfully, it was frightfully easy to do. So damned easy. One finger does the trick. One finger alone!

The night with its host of self-recriminations wages on hour after hour. In the morning there is a rap on her door. Simone slides on a bathrobe.

"You!" she exclaims. "What are you doing here? This could be dangerous."

"I was concerned for you," Clovis answers. "I brought croissants and a can of juice."

"It's dangerous for you to come here. I've had the impression from time to time that I am being followed," Simone remarks.

He laughs, sits. "If they wanted to arrest me, they know where to find me. No, they are patiently waiting until they have all of us in hand."

"You are kind to visit me," Simone says, once she calms down. "And the croissant is tasty."

Combing back the curls before his eyes, leaning back into the velvet of the sofa, he remarks, "I used to be a student at that Lycee."

She looks at him uncomprehendingly. "How could you have returned to your former school in that way? I can't believe you planned it."

He shrugs. "I made myself forget that it was my school," he answers. "I only thought of it as barracks for the occupiers."

"But what did you hope to do there?" she asks. "Yes, we injured many, killed some, but was that worth the risk?"

He smiles crisply. "It was a message, not only to the Nazis, but to the rest of France that the resistance is alive and well, that at any moment, we can return fire."

"You could have been killed."

He looks up and smiles again, "I am aware of that. Let me explain. I am a young man with a hopeful future. Once we eject the occupiers I intend to work with the underprivileged, with the homeless, veterans without arms and without legs, and I shall do my part in guiding them.

Having said this, I concede that I shall probably not attain that life before the day comes when the Nazis are vanquished, I will have been captured, imprisoned, tortured, and perhaps killed."

Simone is amazed "How easily you say such a thing."

"I have thought a lot about my passing," he answers. At this moment, he looks younger than he is, his thoughts weighing on his lips, turning them downwards. "You can't forget the truth. We all die. Only the time and place of our death matters. Had I been born at a different moment, I would wrap my life up considerably tighter than I have done so. But today, given the circumstances, I choose to offer it to France."

"Because you are religious, I suppose," Simone suggests, "and expect to find a new life after death."

"Not at all," he responds. "I have no illusions about life everlasting. I don't expect to lounge about heaven all day. What an extraordinary notion," he snorts. "When my life departs, so does my consciousness, and that is the end of everything. I don't want bullshit about this life on earth. Either it is useful, or it is not. Either it has purpose, or it means nothing. I can trivialise my life by giving in, by sitting in cafes, drinking beer, and ogling pretty girls that walk by. Or I can make it mean something. Not to anyone else, because I do not believe that, but it must mean something to me. Do you get this?"

"No," she responds shaking her head, drawing the string of her bathrobe tighter. "No."

"I may be giving up years of living to my ideals," he ventures on, attempting to make Simone understand, "but without ideals what do I really have?"

"You could have love, work, a family, a future."

"It has to mean something," he insists, breaking a piece of his croissant. "I don't give a damn whether it has significance for anyone else, for you, for my parents, or even for Charles DeGaulle. But it must represent something for me."

"You are very secure in your beliefs," she says, wondering about such confidence in this young man. She goes to the window and opens it to let in the morning air. He leans back and smiles. A charming smile, she thinks, almost as if what he has said is communicated for effect. But as soon as the thought arises, she eliminates it. The man is transparent, she says to herself. It is her scepticism about men that she must overcome.

That evening, a piece of mail arrives from Grace. She opens it with anticipation. She has heard nothing from her sister in almost two months.

Simone,

I hope this letter gets to you. I am mailing it with my fingers crossed. We are hearing all sorts of rumours about ships sunk in the Atlantic. Supposing this letter finds its way onto one of those ships. Then all will be lost, and you will wonder what happened to me, whether I am alive or dead. Very much alive, sis. I miss you. That is one of the ways I know that I am alive. Your absence burns a hole these nights.

I have other news. Faron and I are back together. I'm not even sure how this has happened. Not that I cared for it to happen. But one day he came over and we sat together, and he apologised for his bad behaviour, and he looked so crestfallen, that I planted a kiss on his mouth and one thing led to the other. And so, we have been seeing one another virtually every day. I don't love him, I think, because the anguish he caused me during my pregnancy can't be effaced so quickly. But I enjoy his company. I like sex. You know that, of course. So, we are having sex quite a bit. *I look forward to it. I look forward to him holding me in his arms. After sex, he is like a kitten, very quiet and whispers to me as we cuddle. He talks about doing the dishes or making the bed. Silly me, I like this very much. I know you won't approve, but I won't change anything.*

So, write me of your news. It must be terrible for you in Paris. The Germans are in town, right? And we are told that you have shortages. Even of electricity. So, it can't be too pleasant for you. I know you can't write me exactly what you are doing, so write me inexactly what you are doing, and I'll have my imagination fill in the rest.

Love you,
Grace,

Simone folds the letter and puts it into a pocket pensively. How uncanny. For some reason she expected that Grace and Faron were not through, but hoped that her intuition was wrong. She fears for Grace overall. The kitten could be a masked predator and rip her to shreds when things go wrong.

But Simone intends to write her, to tell her that all is well, that she, her sister is managing famously, perhaps to add a small lie to assuage her sister's fear, that the shortages have not stood in the way of her enjoying this incredible city.

10. A Train from the East

Wednesday. A day Simone dreads, but one in which she has a duty to perform. It's seven in the evening. She has not dined; her mouth is dry. She is sitting up straight on a bench in the Jardin du Luxembourg facing a statue. The statue depicts a boy whose pouting mouth is a fountain raining water into a pool below. Small goldfish are leisurely meandering through murky waters. A gray and chilly day, the moist air wrapped around Simone as she huddles on the bench with her raincoat pulled tight about her neck. She has not seen him arrive, this man edging next to her, now assuming a seat. It is Anselm, the captain, but in civilian clothing. The trench coat he is wearing is not the one she has seen countless times worn by German officers throughout town. His is lighter with a bluish tint.

"Good afternoon," he says casually. "You're prompt. A fine trait," he adds, fingers surrounding his mouth.

Small talk continues for a few moments as squirrels chase one another up the statue and into a nearby tree.

"I have something for you," she says, reaching into her pocket for an envelope.

"Good. I hoped so."

She hands him the envelope and he pockets it without opening it.

"I'll peruse this with great interest," he says with a slight grin, his thin lips rising slightly. "But there is something else I need to know from you."

"I am listening," she responds looking straight ahead at the pouty mouth.

"A few evenings ago, there was a raid on German barracks in town. Several men were killed, many more injured. The people who did it got away. In a truck," he adds. "Of course, we shall have reprisals. For every man killed, we shall kill three of theirs." He is no longer smiling. "You must know something about it," he pushes on.

"I heard about the raid," she answers evenly, 'but no one has confided any details to me."

"So, it was one of Clovis' group, yes?"

"Yes," she replies, not knowing exactly why she agrees, but fearing for a moment that she would be uncovered were she to hide the truth. In the depth of her being, she thinks Anselm already knows who did it and is testing her. "Yes, Clovis himself told me."

"He led the attack?"

"No," she answers. "Someone else. He was not present."

"Interesting," Anselm cackles, crossing his legs. "He sends others now for his dirty work. Perhaps a bit of a coward in a rather insignificant person."

"He is a rather frail, skinny person," she admits.

"True," Anselm says, processing the remark. "Very true. So, who led the attack?"

"That I don't know."

"Damn. That would be important to learn!"

"Of course," she answers. "I will know more as they gain confidence in me."

"Naturlich," Anselm says, somewhat agitated. "I simply hoped that you had made more progress with Clovis."

He pauses to brush a speck of dirt from one of his boots.

"I do have news," she interrupts. "There are more Maquis coming into Paris in the next few weeks. They are arriving to join his cohort."

"Really! Where are they coming from?"

"I don't know."

"And how many?"

"Dozens I heard."

Angry now, he shifts in his seat. "You have to be more precise than this, my dear. Obtain an exact number. And once they are all here, we will corner and round up all of them including our young leader, Clovis. That should make good reading for the Fuhrer, and perhaps a bump in rank for me." Now he emits a rather dour sigh.

"You seem out of sorts," she says to him softly. "Something wrong?"

His lips cross together.

"Why yes. In fact, I am not pleased. We need reinforcements here in Paris as opposition grows. So, I asked Albert Speer, the armaments minister, for one thousand men. Instead, I was told this morning they are sending six hundred. They always know better, damn beurocrats," he curses angrily. "Always. And yet they're not here on the ground where the need is real. They always believe that whatever we ask for is unnecessary, hyperbolic."

"Still," she says, "six hundred men will help, won't it?"

He smiles at what he perceives to be her naiveté.

"Of course, Simone. Of course."

"I hope they arrive quickly," she goes on, "so that you aren't in such a raw mood."

"They will be here next Tuesday afternoon," he answers. "Not soon enough for my taste. By the way, my dear, are you a fan of American film?"

Simone looks at him with caution. "Why, yes. I like movies."

"I so appreciate American film," he goes on in English with a hard German accent. "I like Mr. Bogart. He enjoys bumping people off, no?"

"Certainly," she hastens to respond.

"To make lettuce," Captain Anselm continues chuckling. "Very hard boiled, private dick. Is this correct?"

"Oh yes," she chuckles. "A private dick."

"I also like Mr. Duryea. Dan Duryea. He has a splendid German face."

"And how about Greta Garbo?"

"Very swanky," Anselm continues in English. "The cat's meow. I talk good American slang, nichtwahr?"

Later that evening, despite the sensation that someone is tailing her, she ventures out to the club where she understands Clovis sometimes takes an evening drink with friends, but she cannot locate him. The library is closed at this hour. Nor does she know where he lives. She has important information for him. Upset that she cannot deliver it. The evening drags on in a kind of clumsy slow motion, apparently without end. Finally, with the rising of the sun, the dawn arrives, and she quickly showers, dresses, and imbibes a cup of chicory. A croissant will come later. Hunger she can forestall. The library does not open for another hour. So instead of taking the bus, she walks the distance. About three miles. The morning is agreeable. Men and woman hurry on their way to work. But as she crosses the rue Chauchat, in a thicket, she sees two soldiers with raised arms. Drawing near, she witnesses them beating an older man and woman with clubs. As the old woman drops to the floor, her face scarred and bloody, Simone can discern the Star of David patch, stained ruby with her blood. Simone pushes on angrily, feeling impotent that she does not have the right to intervene.

She sits in front of the library steps waiting for it to open. When it does, Clovis has not yet appeared, Rain descends in a kind of dewy mist causing her to pull her raincoat tight about her. Mini rainbows flash through the rain, colours vibrant as the probing sun fights to drive the rain out. And then she spots him at a distance. Brown corduroy pants, a plaid shirt, glasses hanging from a shirt pocket, his curls dancing about his head as he walks. He moves with intent and the gait of an athletic young man. When he sees her, his mouth evolves into a slight grin.

"What are you doing here?" he asks her.

She conveys Anselm's story about the six hundred soldiers scheduled to arrive Tuesday afternoon.

This brings a scowl. "Not much time to set this up," he says. "Wish I had another several days."

"What are you planning?"

"We are going to intercept that train," he glowers, his brow furrowing. Eyes spread open as if he were visualizing the total destruction of the wagons in a fiery explosion. "I need some time to plan this through," he says. "I'll come visit you tonight and we can take dinner together at the student cafeteria of the Sorbonne."

That night, at the Sorbonne, they are sitting in the cafeteria munching stale bread and cheese. It is late, and most students have left.

"Can you come with me Tuesday morning?"

"Where are we going?"

"Tell you in a bit." He looks at his watch and gets up. "I need to make a quick phone call," he says hastily. "Come with me." In a nearby post office building, they reach a bank of phones. He takes out a slug and drops it into the phone. The phone calls eats up five minutes.

"The train will be coming in from the east," he confides to Simone. "It's the only path that makes sense," he adds. "I am aware that there is a freight train that comes through at about one thirty in the afternoon. That is the only one scheduled…at least that is what is on the train list for the Gare de l'Est. So, any train directly after that is the one we are targeting. This means that we will have a short period of time somewhere east of Paris to tie a bomb to the tracks. When the train strikes the trigger, the charge will explode. We are aiming for the engine because if it ignites, then the whole train could derail."

In the truck, late Tuesday morning a half dozen of them are riding east of Paris towards the town of Bar-le-Duc. Near there, they stop at a café. Omelettes and salads for lunch with a baguette, washed down with red wine. Clovis examines the time and waves to the others to hurry eating.

"I see no Boches," Clovis remarks quietly to the bartender, paying the bill.

"They come later," the bartender replies.

"And how long do they stay?"

"Quite a long time…normally, at least two hours. They enjoy the saucisson and the red wine for a snack. They have nothing else to do in town but eat, smoke and pick up French women."

"Don't mention that you have seen us," Clovis replies.

"Such a pity that we had no business at lunch," the bartender complains, wiping the bar clean.

The truck edges out of town to a secluded spot along the railroad tracks. Within twenty minutes, a freight train roars by. Clovis's men are walking up and down the tracks checking the perimeters. They wave to one another to indicate that the tracks are clean.

From the truck, Clovis throws down a bag. He holds in his hand a demolition charge.

"We call the detonator the Clam," he remarks to Simone. "It emits a warning signal to the engineer to slow the train down. After he does, the explosion follows. Just enough," he says to Simone, "to derail the train. For the rest, nature will take its course."

He sets it carefully inside a rail, packs it in tightly. In front of it, he carefully lays down two small Clams. He signals for the others to retreat to the truck.

"We are not waiting for the derailment? Simone inquires.

He shrugs. "Too risky. We will hear about the explosion later on tonight." With this, they spring back into the truck and return to Paris.

But in fact, there is no news of an explosion. They scour the afternoon Figaro, Le Monde. No radio gossip.

"Find out from your admiring Captain Anselm what happened," Clovis tells her.

The following evening, she is sitting nervously in front of the fountain in the Jardin. Promptly at seven, Captain Anselm, this time in military garb, wearing his peaked cap, seats himself next to her.

"How are you, my dear Dawn?" he asks. His tone is overly agreeable. Simone is taken aback by it. If the explosion derailed the troop train, she would certainly have become a prime suspect.

"I'm feeling quite wonderful," she responds. "The weather this time of year is so temperate."

"I have something to confess to you," Anselm remarks, now turning to her. "After I asked you for the names of the Maquis, and you gave me a list which turned up nobody we could arrest, I confess I was suspicious about your information, that is to say, your allegiances. And that is why at our last meeting, I let slip the news about the troop train coming into the Gare de l'Est. Had this train been attacked, you and only you could have provided that information to the Maquis."

A vice closed about Simone's throat. She coughs, turns away from Anselm, pulls out a handkerchief and blows her nose.

"After the afternoon freight train passed, we sent a lone engine from Nancy through Bar le Duc into Paris. But this engine passed without incident. I have to apologise to you for even considering that you were a possible double agent."

Her head turns to look into his smiling face. Now he reaches over to plant a fatherly kiss on her cheek. "Forgive me for doubting you."

She shrugs, her nerves steeling. "It's only natural. I would have done the same had the situation been reversed. So, there were no new troops?"

"An unabashed lie," Anselm laughs. "I should be ashamed, but we cannot be too careful in wartime. We have all the troops we need at present." With this, he arises. "You will have more information for me next week, nichtwahr?"

As soon as he leaves, Simone releases her breath. She has stopped expelling air for the past several moments. I was an inch away from being arrested, she thinks. How enormously lucky that the explosive we set did not ignite.

When she relates this meeting to Clovis, he scowls, but says he has an idea.

"I am going to build a new list for your captain," he starts. "You will tell him that these are the most secretive members of the Maquis, but in fact, they are all Nazi sympathisers, especially the ones who have called out their Jewish neighbours. I will give you a list of about fifteen. The same list we always have on our bodies during raids. These people will be detained, certainly interrogated. They will cry out their admiration for the Third Reich, but Anselm and the Gestapo will not believe them. To the contrary, they will see through their so-called admiration. They may be tortured. Some may even by shot. But most will be sent to camps in Poland and elsewhere. A rather fitting end to traitors of France, don't you think?"

142

11. A Voyage to the Mountains

Simone has never before seen Clovis in distress. As he trudges wearily towards her, he appears distracted, even depressed.

"Something has happened?" she asks.

"Come with me," he responds, taking her arm. They walk in silence along the cinder path into the Tuileries, to a concrete bench overlooking the Place de la Concorde.

"Things are changing quickly," Clovis says to her. The fire in his eyes has dimmed, she thinks. "The Nazis have started to round up Jews in Paris. They are corralling as many as they can find, stuffing them in cattle cars, and sending them on to Poland. To work, they say. But they have a million Frenchmen working for them already. It is not credible. They have more sinister plans."

She looks into his eyes, his crestfallen expression. "They intend extermination," he claims. "There had already been reports of mass killings, but these were hard to confirm, and I was never sure whether to believe them. But now…"

For a moment, he remains silent. Then he turns to her once more. "My parents live here in Paris," he begins. "My mother is Jewish." Then as an afterthought: "Of course, this means that I am as well whether I want to be or not. I have to get them out of town."

"Of course," Simone says. "How can I help?"

"Come with us," Clovis urges.

"Anything," she says. "But what about Captain Anselm?"

"You will meet with him as scheduled Wednesday evening as you always do, and you will tell him that I know a dozen or so Spanish Maquisards who fought against General Franco in Spain and who are now ready to come to Paris to fight against the Nazis."

"Is this true?"

"Entirely," he says. "I have thought this through over a period of a day and a half. It is probably no secret that some Spaniards are ready to fight against Hitler. But leave that aside for the moment. I have the sketch of a plan. First, all of us we will go to the Pyrenees to meet the Spaniards. My parents will come along. Simply not enough time to take them to Nice where they can hide. We can initiate these Spanish fighters into what needs to be done. I can assist them on the path to Paris and whom to contact there. As for you, Simone, you will establish a list of Spaniards and present the captain with it. Of course, the list will be bogus. This will be your last contact with the Captain. As he is awaiting the arrival of the Spaniards, we will be making our way south. Once we have settled the new members of the resistance, then I will go on, take my parents to Nice. First of all, Nice is not occupied by Germans, only Italians. No problems with them. We have a cousin there. Her name is Kitty. My folks can stay with her. She runs a tourist bus line. Food is much more plentiful because Italy is nearby, and she has access to the Italian markets in Ventimiglia. So, what do you say?"

"First, I need to contact the OSS…" she responds.

"Of course. We have a wireless connection with England. We will send a coded message to the OSS on your behalf and the Brits will transmit it to the States."

Simone smiles, "I'm in this all the way then." In fact, she is happy that she and Clovis will not be separated.

"Come meet my parents this evening. They are expecting both of us," he adds. "I hoped you would agree."

"So, you think you know me that well?" she asks, but her eyes are dancing. "Pretty presumptuous!"

"I hoped…"

Suddenly, her lips are grazing his cheek. She has no sense as to how this happened. She did not do it willingly, she believes. It erupted out of her as if it had been an involuntary gasp. Embarrassed, she recoils. But Clovis is now drawing her towards him. He stops, Looks around. Alone. They are alone in that area of the park. He pulls her to him and kisses her on the lips. Simone is returning his lips. She finds his pliable, soft, but eager.

"Not such a good idea for us to get involved with each other," she remarks quietly, opening her eyes.

"A terrible idea," he agrees before pulling her face to his once more.

"We won't let anything get in the way of our work," he assures her, lounging in her arms, smoke circling above her head from a Gauloise.

"I wouldn't allow it," she agrees. In her embryonic heart, a place she once thought vacant, something is stirring, a feeling, a longing. This person, this studious hero, the bookworm become warrior has found his way into her emotional garden. Never felt anything like it, she thinks with a slight quiver.

"Better split up now," he says. "The longer we sit here intertwined, the more likely something will go wrong." He writes down his parent's address on rue Monsieur le Prince. "Second floor. First door to the right. Come around eight," he adds. Before leaving with a lighter step, he kisses her gently on the lips.

Her body feels heavier as she arises, watching Clovis disappear into the bustling street near the rue de Rivoli. What have I done? She asks herself. It's so unlike her to give in to an unknown feeling. She checks her legs. They feel burdened. Stupid girl, she chides herself. But she does so with a wispy little smile around her lips. There's something magnetic about this boy-man, she says to herself. Surprised by her uncharacteristic action, she realises it is rare for her to give into him, to anyone. She turns, quickly aware that someone may be observing her. But there is nobody. Body lapses into a relaxed mode. Now she descends the stairs, strolling by the nearby bus stop, sits for a moment on the covered bench with two other people reading newspapers, waiting silently. When the snub-nosed bus arrives, she follows them onto it without knowing where this bus is heading. She sits in the rear, onto a raised bench. Looks straight ahead. The bus weaves its way to the Gare de Lyon and pulls in. Everyone descends. She does as well engrossed in thought, sensitive to the parts of skin which Clovis has skimmed, those parts tingling, alive, aware of her hand which grazed and held his arm, her mind hazy.

Simone muddles into the Gare beyond the two French police guards with machine guns. They are not interested in her. One is smoking. The other one is leaning against a front wall; one leg perched on the wall behind him. She stops at a newsstand and buys the afternoon paper without any intention of reading it.

Just then, to her left, a commotion. She hears it before seeing it. A woman has fallen onto the concrete floor of the station. Simone approaches. She is wearing a Star of David: A little heavy, around fifty years old with round, rosy cheeks. Comes closer. An older man wearing a beret basque is down on one knee by her side.

"I was a medic in the first war. She is having a heart attack," he says to no one in particular. "We must get her to a hospital." Just then, one of the French guards arrives on the scene.

"There are taxis outside," Simone says to him. "Call one, please." The guard looks down at her indifferently, finally speaks:

"This woman cannot be taken to any hospital in Paris. Jews are not accepted there."

"How will she get treated?" Simone asks the guard trying to check her rage. He shrugs.

"Don't ask me."

The woman is breathing heavily. "Her blood pressure must be flying," the man on the floor says.

"Where can we take her?" Simone asks.

"A clinic outside of Paris....if you can find a taxi driver who will drive a Jew there."

"Can you walk?" Simone asks the woman.

"Yes," the woman responds shakily but with resolve. "With help"

They lift her, the woman resting on the shoulder of the man on one side and Simone on the other. Slowly, they near the front of the Gare.

"Stay here," the man says. "I will find a taxi."

They see him running to the head of the taxi station. There are perhaps a dozen cabs in the queue. The first driver clearly is interested, but in a moment, Simone can see him waving the man away. A second driver does the same. Finally, a third agrees. The man returns, and they walk the woman into the cab and gently stretch her out in the back.

"Thank you," the woman says, her face pale, her lips barely moving. She raises a pudgy hand to Simone. "It is not easy being a Jew in this town these days."

"I'll go with her to the clinic," the man says. "If you can spare a few francs, that will help," he adds with an embarrassed tone.

"Of course," Simone responds and pulls out two bills to hand to the man. "Good luck," she shouts to the woman as the taxi pulls away.

That evening, she arrives at the apartment just before eight o'clock. Trudges up the flights of stairs. Turns to the door. Knocks.

Clovis answers, "Come in quickly," he says to her. He kisses her on both cheeks. Behind him are an older man and woman. The gentleman is tall, slender, with a silver beard framing his cheeks. A pleasant face, one she responds to. If I were on the metro and this man turned and smiled, I would smile back. The woman is tiny, hair greying, graying over ten years. She has veiled deep-set eyes, a perpetual frown on her forehead seemingly permanently etched. Her hands are rarely still, illustrating points she makes while speaking. But even silent, hands intertwine, loop around snakelike. Once a pretty woman, Simone imagines. But her beauty has been stripped away not only by time, but by circumstance.

"My parents," Clovis says. "Jean-Luc Rastine: former professor at the University in Astronomy. My mother, Odile. Mother is a poet, a published poet." Simone shakes hands warmly with them.

"Our son has spoken highly of you," Jean-Luc beams. "He claims you are a warrior even though you are a woman…and a small woman at that."

"Your son exaggerates," Simone replies. Compliments have a way of disturbing rather than gratifying her. She blushes, embarrassed.

Somehow, Jean-Luc has been able to lay his hand on a rabbit, and his wife has concocted a stew.

"Very tasty," Simone says with satisfaction. In fact, it is her first meal of the day.

This apartment has average sized two bedrooms, a bath with a tiny shower with a hand-held wand, a small dining room and a medium sized living room. The furniture dates for the most part to the early nineteen hundreds, to the Belle Epoque period.

"Some of the furniture came from my mother," Odile remarks. "As did the paintings." She is referring to a dozen oil paintings which cover the living room wall, paintings by Dutch and French painters of the seventeenth and eighteenth centuries.

"Beautiful," Simone says, breathing in the power of the works in front of her.

"So," Clovis begins, once they have settled themselves in armchairs in the living room, "so we have agreed to leave Paris next Thursday. That will give you time to visit with your friend, the Captain, for a final time. You can hand him the list of traitors and explain that you are leaving for the south of France to welcome the Spanish Maquis who intend to make their way to Paris. That should intrigue him, don't you think?"

"He will be frothing at the mouth," she replies.

"I'm not clear," Jean-Luc says, how we intend to make it to the Pyrenees. "You never know any more when the trains will be running. Often, they are commandeered at the last minute by the Germans. How can we plan an orderly voyage without knowing what trains will be available?"

"We can't," Clovis remarks. "We will try to board the morning train Thursday from the Gare d'Austerlitz, and if it is running and available to passengers, to take it as far south as it will go.

"I believe I can handle a rough journey," Jean-Luc says. "But what about mother?"

Odile waves him away with a smile. "You won't hear any complaints from me," she says.

"Once we have made it to the Pyrenees, that is only a portion of the journey. Afterwards, we will continue to Nice where you can stay hidden of course, at our cousin's," Clovis says.

When Simone makes her way home, another missive from Grace is awaiting her. Her writing style is so personal, so detailed. It is as if each word is a piece of calligraphy:

Dear, lovely, Simone,
The big news is that your priests have been arrested and charged with treason. They're facing lots of years in the hoosegow if convicted. Everyone is amazed. The FBI did it. They are cooking with gas. If you were here, you would be flipping your wig over the news. The men claim they are innocent. How can it be that men of God are working for the Nazis? Incomprehensible!

Anyway, that's the local news. Elsewhere, we seem to be losing the war against the Germans. But it is early yet, right? I know that you are involved somehow. Don't tell me. Better that I don't know in case I am captured and tortured, ha ha. Food is abundant, but never the food I want. We are rationing everything now as the war intensifies.

As for my personal life, Faron and I are on an even keel. He seems to have settled down. He has rented a new, swanky apartment, but I don't see where he gets the money. I stay there several nights of the week. I wake up in his arms; my eyes open out through a great plate glass window towards the centre of town, the grand hotels. A brilliant sight. Near Piedmont Park.

I know you want to know how we are doing together. Don't disapprove. We are steady now. I have made it clear that he needs to treat me like a real woman, not some broad he met at a dance hall. He agrees. I think he is genuine. I trust him. Sort of. Stay safe, little one.

Write me if you can. Love, Grace.

Wednesday evening finds Simone preparing to leave Paris, perhaps for good. She keeps her appointment with Anselm. It's a chilly evening, with a cold fog that slips around the monuments and buildings into her body. She pulls up the folds of her coat around her ears, wound tight like an eighteenth-century clock. She sits watching the squirrels scampering up and down trees. The sound of a mini-carrousel at the far end of the park startles her, its lights twinkling in the dark as the wheel turns with laughing, wiggling children. Behind them, a puppet show: le Grand Guignol. To the right a chestnut vendor. The scent is appealing, warm and nourishing. She walks over quickly and buys a cornet.

The Captain arrives in a great coat, his peaked hat pulled low over his eyes. Suddenly, she spies a great dog next to him. A German shepherd. A dog with dangerous black eyes, a soft trickle of drool, and its ears raised to attention.

"This is Wotan," Anselm says, caressing the nape of his neck. "We walked from the hotel this evening," he says. "Don't feed him," he adds.

Simone spies Wotan, but does not extend a hand to pet him. "You mustn't be afraid, Dawn," Anselm says. "Wotan is gentle as long as I am not threatened."

"And if you are in danger?"

"He attacks faster than any of my troops,' Anselm smiles. "Not only that, he does so by stripping bodies of their parts quickly and efficiently. I have often told my troops that were they all as quick and resourceful as Wotan, the war would be over much quicker."

"I don't get along with dogs," Simone says. "They don't act reasonably."

Anselm chuckles. "Silly, we don't expect reason from canines," he responds. "Friendship? Loyalty? Yes, always. From time to time a fierce set of teeth and claws can be unleashed. He's always ready to defend me," Anselm continues in English.

Simone reaches into her purse, pulls out a Gauloise. The Captain lights it. She hands a list to Anselm.

"These are the names of Spanish Maquis we believe are crossing the border into France. Not the entire list by any means. And it is possible that the list is not precise," she adds.

Anselm studies it for a moment before pocketing it, waits another moment before speaking pensively.

"You know, Dawn, you should really go to the border to greet these men. In this way, you could get close to them, and you would be capable of a correct count with exact names. Yes, that would be the preferred thing to do. And when you have met them, you can guide them to Paris, nichtwahr? And deliver them like lambs into my manger."

"I have also thought this would be a good plan," she confesses.

"Better to imprison them before they create trouble," Anselm adds. "I will miss you, little one. I should tell you that your prior list has produced a number of interesting developments. Everyone on your list claim to be Nazi sympathisers, but under torture many admitted that they were not what they appeared. We have sent the lot to concentration camps. This is exactly what we hoped you would do for us, Dawn. Provide us with the names of the enemy. And once you have brought the Spanish terrorists to Paris, we will then arrest them as well as your friend, Clovis."

"Perfect," Simone agrees. "Perfect."

"I have told Goebbels about you, and he hopes soon to dispatch someone to interview you, anonymously, of course; an article for propaganda purposes, without identifying you by name. Would you like that?"

"Anything I can do to help," Simone replies.

"You are so modest," the Captain says, clucking his tongue against his cheek. "You need to do more to promote yourself, my dear."

That evening, after dinner, Simone hopes to fall asleep early and sleep long. It is clear to her that the voyage as far as the Pyrenees, especially with two seniors, cannot be easily managed. True, she has obtained from Anselm a laisser passer. Curiously, he has specified that two individuals may use it without specifying who they are. He has had it delivered to her within the hour after their meeting. Will this pass be invalid for Clovis's folks? If her math is exact, two is not four. Still, she is confident in her ability to make four out of two. Sleep is fitful. She awakens several times, once to walk down the dimly lit corridor to the bathroom. This little stroll invigorates her somewhat, rendering her mind clear. When she lays her head on her pillow, she is unable to find the solace of abandonment. Finally, she dozes into a carrousel dream, children and dogs whirling about her and a man, clearly Captain Anselm.

At six, she awakens with a start, descends the staircase to the shower. Finds it occupied by a gentleman from the fourth floor, scrubbing his back. He hears her and opens the door gently. He invites her in jovially. She declines. Waits. When he departs, a towel surrounding a pudgy, rose coloured belly, she enters. Simone suppresses an initial shudder, for she hates to use bathrooms where others are bathing on a daily basis. They don't smell or feel clean. Her hair is greasy. She shampoos it with soap. Time elapses, and she must now rush. Upstairs, she packs a small suitcase and trundles it down the stairs. She remembers to say goodbye to the concierge who has been welcoming to her. The concierge kisses her on both cheeks and wishes her Godspeed.

Now Simone hails an early morning black taxi to the Gare d'Austerlitz to board the train to Bordeaux. She has learned to expect everything and nothing. The immensity of the project she is about to undertake is seeping through into awareness. Still optimistic, she is open to the day's offerings. The morning is clear, orange slips of clouds skimming the horizon as the sun struggles to rise. Roads are empty at this hour. But as the taxi approaches the station, a world of traffic congregates clogging each avenue. Taxis, buses, automobiles and trucks are all intent on driving to the station, all at the same time. My God, she thinks. Total congestion! Do they all expect to board my train?

She looks at her watch. "Anyway, you can get around the traffic?"

"Malheuresement, non," the driver retorts with a Gallic frown. "Everyone tries to leave Paris this morning. It is the end of the month. The whole of Paris goes south for holidays," he adds. "Or maybe they leave and don't intend to return," he giggles.

She and Clovis had not counted on such a mob, nor had they taken into account that so many Parisians might flee southward at the end of July. The driver is clearly irritated by the turn of events, and suddenly pulls out into another lane. As he does so, his cab is impacted by another car. Immediately, Simone's driver stops his engine, leaps out, skims the damage and engages the driver of the offending vehicle in a shouting match. Other drivers storm out of their vehicles to join the hubbub. Nothing is moving. After two minutes of shouted barbs, Simone snatches her valise, exits the cab, and runs the several hundred yards to the train station.

Stopped at the entrance by a uniformed guard, Simone has her papers examined.

"You better hurry," he says to her. "The train waits for no man...or woman."

She locates the quai number on the central board and runs to it. There she finds Clovis and his parents nervously awaiting her. On the quai itself, there are hundreds, perhaps thousands of people attempting to board the train. Clovis has a grim look about him.

"We must go now. Quickly."

"You have tickets?"

"Yes," he says, "and reserved seats, but I don't know whether in this hellhole they will count."

"Which wagon?"

"In second class, number eighteen," he replies. He is lifting three heavy leather suitcases and begins to carry them while running as best he can, passengers crossing in front of him, crisscrossing, screaming at one another as families lose touch with other family members. He looks back at her. "Stay with my parents. Get them on the train."

She links arms with the two of them and moves forward. The train is already belching smoke emitting a fog onto the quai. They are moving as swiftly as Odile's legs will transport her. At one moment, Odile stops, winded.

"I don't think I can go on. Go without me."

"Impossible," Jean-Luc shouts at her. "We must go forward together. Try. Try. Please try."

Again, Odile moves forward, her legs buckling, but suddenly she catches a second wind and is moving with them at a fairly good rate of speed. Simone checks her watch. They have about two minutes to board the train and wagon eighteen is not yet in sight."

"Look," she says to them. Get on the train on any wagon and simply move through it until you come to the right one."

She watches Jean-Luc and Odile mount the steps into the train. A male passenger is yanking them upwards onboard. And then Simone takes off running down the quai through the teeming, bewildered, sweltering mob searching for Clovis as well as their wagon. She finds neither. Instead, she encounters someone who was standing next to Clovis at the head of the station and she asks whether that person has seen him. There is no answer, no physical response. She yells the same question into the person's ear. The face simply turns away as if her ears were impervious to sound. She continues running. Now the train is beginning to jerk forward when, suddenly, she glimpses Clovis boarding a wagon, pushing a heavy woman forward and hoisting himself into the train.

Simone will not be able to make it to that wagon, she knows, so she boards the one behind it. Just as she enters the train, she looks down onto the quai as the train slowly picks up steam. She sees Clovis on the platform. Why has he jumped off the train? She is screaming at him to board, holding the door open despite the quickening movement of the wheels. He turns to her, his hands high above his head.

"I left the luggage down the tracks," he cries.

"Forget the goddamn luggage!" she screams. "Jump onto the train." And suddenly, she is grasping his hand as he leaps onto the metal steps and winches himself up into her body. "My God," she says, shivering, holding Clovis tight. He is exhaling reams of air, his body heaving. "You almost didn't make it."

"My parents?" he asks, shaken, with a pathetic, accusatory tone. "I asked you to be with them."

"They are somewhere on the train."

"Yes," he says, now the beginnings of a smile crossing his face, one hand wiping the sweat from his brow. "Good. I'll go back and look for them."

"And the luggage?"

"To hell with the luggage," he replies. "I'll find someone in town to pick them up and bring them to us as soon as he can."

Four people are sitting on a bench in the compartment which Clovis has rented. Interlopers. Simone moves them out of the carriage and into the corridor. She hates to do this because she realises that the train ride will be arduous over many hours, and to stand the entire duration, especially for older people will be virtually impossible. They will have to sit on the floor, she reasons. In a few moments, Clovis enters the compartment with his parents. His mother's face is pale, her breathing shallow, hands intertwined, fidgeting together as if they were conducting a tune.

Jean-Luc looks drained. "I'm no longer a young man," he exclaims, sitting heavily onto the bench. He is looking across into the wan, exhausted faces of men and women, too weary to speak.

Chugging on, the train rattles into Tours after several hours. And then crawls to a grinding stop. Outside, on the platform, a platoon of German soldiers are brandishing weapons. There's commotion in the wagon, a soldier coming through.

"Get out," he shouts into one compartment after the other.

"But we are on our way to Bordeaux," someone says.

"This train stops here. It does not go beyond this point. It has been commandeered by the German army."

"But how do we proceed to Bordeaux?"

"Not my problem," the soldier exclaims. Before moving on to the next wagon, he adds. "There will be no further trains travelling south. They have all been co-opted for use at the front." Passengers are scrambling off the train and onto the platform with bewildered looks. Children are howling in distress. A poodle is barking as it escapes down the platform, a teenager in hot pursuit. Several benches outside are quickly occupied by older travellers. Some distraught passengers are sobbing, some with heads in their hands. Luggage is everywhere without a single cart to transport it.

Jean-Luc helps his wife descend laboriously as Simone and Clovis follow.

"I suppose we are lucky," Jean-Luc smiles wryly on the platform. "We don't have to carry our luggage."

"Splendid at finding the bright side of every dilemma," his wife remarks, but she is not smiling. "What do we do?" she asks.

"Walk!" Clovis responds. "We may be able to hitch a ride now and then."

"But the trip to Bordeaux will be hundreds of miles. Even then, we are still not in the Pyrenees."

"Do you see an alternative?" Clovis asks, but his question is posed softly. Simone can hear in the question sympathy for his mother's plight.

No response, but Clovis knows what mother is considering. A walk of several hundred miles will be impossible for her to complete.

"Cheer up, mom," Clovis says. "We will find a way."

They begin to walk. They are not alone. Many travellers accompany them, carrying valises, pets, even mattresses. Some are pushing carts laden with goods. Both men and women struggle with carts meant for horses to pull. The day has worn warm, the sun engulfing man and animal. Sweat is profuse on brows. Many are walking in the middle of the road, for there are virtually no vehicles.

"They would have trouble finding gas," Clovis remarks about the dearth of cars. "No point starting out without being able to finish the ride."

An hour later, Odile can no longer go on. She sits down heavily by the side of the road.

"We can't just stop here," Jean-Luc observes in a low voice mainly to himself. "Wait," he says. Pushes on in one direction, returns, tries another before he spots a farmhouse a few hundred yards away. "I'll go down there and see what I am able to find." They watch his lean figure amble down the road. Clovis is trailing him by about a hundred yards. He sees the farmhouse door open and an old man ushering Jean-Luc in. After a few moments, Jean-Luc appears, waving for them to come to the farmhouse. An older man in overalls follows him out.

"I think we may have found a solution," Jean-Luc begins, as they near. "This gentleman here is Jerome, the owner of the farm. He says he can give us a bit of food and water and an opportunity to rest."

"But what about continuing the voyage?" Simone asks.

Jean-Luc smiles. "I have a solution also. Jerome has a wheelbarrow which belongs to a friend a few miles down the road. We can wheel my wife in it. Furthermore, Jeannot, the friend, has a larger farmhouse and may be able to put us up for the evening. I have directions."

Jerome has a steaming bowl of broth for everyone along with some bread and cheese.

"I'm afraid we don't have special food every day," he complains. German soldiers found my cache of potatoes and stole everything, along with tomatoes and other vegetables. From now on, I'm going to bury anything I grow."

Two hours later, fed, and rested, the group starts out. Jerome provides a tarp which when folded functions like a mini mattress. Jean-Luc and Clovis lift Odile into the tarp. They alternate sessions in which each pushes the wheelbarrow.

"I rather enjoy the transportation, "Odile remarks smiling. "It's not quite a limo, but in a pinch…."

An hour passes. They arrive exhausted at the farmhouse indicated by Jerome, owned by his friend, Jeannot. He himself is rushing to the edge of the property to slide open the gate.

"So," he says laughing, "You are returning my wheelbarrow. And returning it with something extra."

"But you can't keep what's in it," Jean-Luc declares.

"Thank you, I really don't need another woman," Jerome laughs. "I have one of my very own."

This farmhouse is more modern, even a bit luxurious. There is an upright piano in a corner with music on the adjacent stand, plush sofas and antique side tables. A large plate glass window looked out into the woods.

"You haven't been looted by the Nazis?"

"I'm on a side path in these woods," Jeannot remarks. "They haven't located me yet. I do expect one of these days they will track me down, but I have taken pains to hide my valuables. By which I mean mainly flour. I am the baker for the entire area." Pauses. "I am furious with what has happened to my country." He pours himself a gin and breathes deeply. "I have two extra bedrooms upstairs which I offer you for the night. Without compensation, he continues, waving away Jean-Luc's wallet. You will be my guests tonight for dinner and for breakfast in the morning. And then, I may have one more agreeable surprise for you."

Nothing would coax Jeannot to tell the group what he has in mind. His wife, Flore, puts together a dinner of sole, potatoes and green beans, with plenty of bread and even pastries at the end of the meal.

"This is extraordinary," Clovis remarks. "It's absolutely astonishing to find this in France."

Jeannot laughs. "Have a good evening. I have to turn in early because baking begins about three in the morning, I shall try to be quiet as a church mouse, but if you hear anything it is only me working the oven. It's a bit rusty from decades of use."

After his parents settle in for the night upstairs, Clovis offers Simone a drink of Ricard.

"I would like that," she says. "But not more than one. It will certainly knock me out after the day we have had."

Clovis pours two glasses, adds a shot of water, watches the liquid turn into a green yellow mixture. They clink glasses together, their wish that the morrow may be easier than this day. Afterwards, they climb old wooden stairs to their assigned bedroom: a small room with a fairly narrow bed. Its mattress may date from the nineteenth century, Clovis thinks. An open window allows cool air to enter as the night has fully descended. It has a small bedside light and under the bed, a chamber pot.

"We won't have to search for the bathroom," Clovis chuckles.

"Lucky us," Simone agrees, tongue in cheek.

Too fatigued to make love, they entwine in one another's arms, and in this fashion, fall asleep quickly and profoundly.

In the morning, Jeannot fashions a breakfast of toasted bread with jam and croissants. His wife is pouring cups of real coffee.

"We won't forget you," Jean-Luc says. "I don't know what we would have done without your kind assistance. My wife was simply unable to do more yesterday. How can one repay such a debt?"

Jeannot smiles, "I think I may be able to help just a bit more. I own a truck. I also have stocked extra gasoline, enough to make a trip to Bordeaux and back. I need to drive the truck there periodically to buy flour if and when it is available. I am told I have an opportunity this weekend, so I am leaving this morning. If you don't mind a couple of you riding in the back of the truck which will not be comfortable but surely better than walking, then we can leave within the hour."

And so, an hour later, astonished by their good fortune, Odile and Jean-Luc take their seat next to Jeannot in the front of the truck while Clovis and Simone spread blankets underneath them in the back of the truck.

Jeannot's truck is painted a deep red. It starts up noisily, but then glides easily with each shift. Miles pass without incident.

"Will we be stopped by the Germans on the road?"

"Probably," Jeannot says. "But they are only interested in weapons and Jews, it seems."

"No problem," Jean-Luc lies.

From time to time, the road is blocked by travellers with horses, goats, and pets, many travelling on foot. Once cleared, the road opens up for several miles. At one point, a blockade looms ahead. Several German soldiers check identity papers. There is a small Peugeot in front of them. One of the soldiers orders both the driver and his wife out of the car. The young man offers the soldier a set of documents. The solider examines them, and then searches both the young man and his wife.

"What do you have in back of the car?" he asks.

"Nothing," the young man says at first, then corrects himself. "Only our baby in a bassinette."

"Stand back," the soldier says. He affixes a bayonet to his rifle, opens the rear door and looks down upon a baby sleeping soundly in a basket. The soldier lowers his bayonet towards the baby."

"Heah! What do you think you are doing?" the young man cries out.

"Checking to see whether you have hidden grenades or other weapons under the child." He probes his bayonet under the blanket covering the child. The man's wife is holding on to her husband with total anxiety affixed to her face, but in an instant, the man breaks free and attacks the soldier with the bayonet. Another soldier opens fire, hits the young man in the arm with such force that he careens into the vehicle before slumping onto the ground.

"So, satisfied now? What weapon did you find? The wife asks shrilly. "Perhaps a diaper bomb?" The soldier with the bayonet shrugs and waves them on. The young man slumps into the car, his wife sliding in to the driver's seat. Their vehicle pulls away slowly. Now the soldier with the bayonet comes to Simone and Clovis.

"Stupid bastards," he curses the couple who have just left. "Show me documents and also some respect," he says to Clovis. As soon as Simone shows him the document signed by Captain Anselm, they salute.

"I've never seen them cowtow to anyone so quickly," Jeannot laughs. "You must be an important person."

Simone returns his laugh. "Very important indeed," she says.

Up ahead the Peugeot has pulled off. The young man has exited the car, and is kneeling by the woods, throwing up, his wife holding his head in her hands. His wound is bristling blood.

"We have to tie that off," Jean-Luc says to the woman. The young woman produces a clean towel which Jean-Luc wraps above the wound. "You need to get him to a doctor to have the bullet removed," Jean-Luc insists. The young woman takes his hand and kisses it.

That evening, they arrive in Bordeaux. Jeannot leaves them at a fork in the road, indicating the direction to Pau.

"If you follow this road a mile or so, you will come to an inn. Tell them you are friends of Jeannot, the baker. Tell them also that I will be bringing them pastries and other baked goods next week. The owners will find a place for you, I promise."

They watch his red truck pull away. "What a good man, "Odile says. "We have been very lucky so far."

In fifteen minutes, they arrive at the inn crowded with travellers. The owner says she has room for all four people in one remaining bedroom. She has an extra cot she can put in that room. She also has beer, but only a few sausages to go with it.

And so that evening, the four enter a rather large bedroom with one good-sized sleigh bed in the middle of the room, and a cot on the floor.

"You take it," Clovis says to Simone.

"We'll trade off during the night," she says. "I suspect the floor is rather hard."

"True, but we have an extra blanket to put underneath one of us."

In the morning, the inn owner tells them that this far south, trains are actually running into Pau and even beyond.

"Too far for the Boches to use for their war work in the east. The train station is down the road another twenty minutes or so on foot. You may have to wait for a train however. Schedules are meaningless these days."

That morning, after a meagre breakfast of chicory and apples, the four walk some twenty minutes to the train station. Jean-Luc buys four tickets for Pau.

"The train should leave in about two hours," the train master says. He is a young man with perfectly coiffed hair covered by a brindled cap, and gray pants. "In the interim, there is a waiting room you can sit in."

"Is there any food around?"

"To buy? Possibly, but probably not on the train itself, despite claims to the contrary. Your best bet is within the station. Watch as the café opens if any large packages are delivered."

"We'll wait in the café," Odile says.

The café opens some fifteen minutes later. "We have nothing to offer," the sole waiter tells them with a sad expression around his lips. "But we are expecting a shipment this morning. Sit in one of the booths. I'll bring you water."

About an hour later, the back door of the café opens, and a man pushes in a shipment on a trolley.

"We have jam, a baguette for the four of you to share and some tea. Chamomile, I believe," the waiter says.

"That will be perfect," Clovis remarks.

Three more hours pass before the train to Pau is announced. The foursome head to the quai and watch a very old, rusty and graffiti laden train shuffle in with wisps of dirty clouds emitting from its smokestacks.

Forty-five minutes later, the train chugs out with an immense roar from its engines. Within a few moments, it reaches a speed of some thirty miles per hour which it manages to maintain. Late that evening, the train chugs into the train station of Pau. The train master has no recommendations for them.

"There are thousands of refugees on the road who have arrived before you. None of the inns have room. There is some food in the café of the station. And it never closes. You can get a bite to eat there and, if I were you, I would remain in the café all night. You can sleep on benches there. Not terribly soft, but better than nothing."

And this is how the foursome spends the night.

"Not quite what you bargained for." Clovis whispers to Simone.

"But I also didn't bargain for you, my sweet," she replies, "and see how lucky I have become." He kisses her gently on the mouth. Sleep that night is fitful at best. And yet, Simone is thinking that she would not prefer to be elsewhere. For the first time in her young life, she is beginning to experience and understand loving someone. I have a feeling for this boy-man, she says to herself, a feeling I have never before felt with anyone, I look at him and my body becomes warm no matter the temperature. My mind at times grows dizzy with the wonder of him in my life. If this is not love, then I don't know what to call it.

In the morning, they are offered cups of chicory and, by some miracle, a half dozen croissants. Now fortified, they are ready to proceed into the mountains. In town, they learn about a bus which will ferry them part of the distance to Oloron Sainte-Marie. As they're let off, in the Radigou Café, they partake of a meal of roast chicken leftovers and beets. Their first bottle of red wine.

"How can we go up the mountain to Arette?" Clovis asks the proprietor.

He is an older gentleman wearing an apron and a beret. "There is no transportation these days in that direction. You will have to walk."

"No cars for hire?"

He nods. "Nothing that I know of. But you can make it to Arette by nightfall if you walk quickly. It's a bit under thirteen miles, all uphill."

"Not possible," Jean-Luc says. "My wife will not be able to travel so quickly."

"And what do you hope to find in Arette?" the proprietor asks.

"My sister owns a house there," Jean-Luc replies. "We intend to stay with her."

"Escaping the Boches?" the proprietor asks as if asking the time of day.

"Not really," Clovis answers easily. "Just visiting relatives."

12. Arette and the Pierre Saint-Martin

After lunch, they start out. It becomes clear within a half hour that Odile will not be able to walk with them at their speed.

"Leave me here," she huffs, exhausted after two miles. "Have your sister send her car for me."

They look at one another speechless. Yes, it makes sense for them to push on, if risky, leaving Odile alone at her age. Behind them, there is a small hill with an opening, a mini cave in which she can possibly find shelter as well as rest

"I just don't know whether Marguerite's car is even working," Jean-Luc says to her.

Odile shakes her head. "I can't climb up this mountain. Somehow, you will find a way to collect me either tonight or tomorrow morning. I have faith," she adds, taking her husband's hand. He squeezes hers and then lets it go.

"There isn't even any water here," Jean-Luc says concerned, "in case you get parched."

Odile smiles. "I'll have lots to drink in Arette."

Now the three begin the ascent up the mountain. As promised, the road veers, zigzagging uphill with elevations of ten percent or more in places. Jean-Luc is becoming weary, and periodically they need to halt. Simone and Clovis, admittedly worn, are nonetheless committed to the final assault up to Arette, and they now lead the way. When they enter the village of Aramits, they know there are but a few kilometres remaining. Simone turns around. The road in front as well as in back is empty.

Not a single car has come by in the hours they have been marching.

Dusk descends. Thirsty, now hungry, they plod on into the oncoming night. Finally, they pass the Arette town marker. And just then, they hear a motorcycle throttling behind them up the mountain, a headlight bearing down on them. They signal the driver to stop.

"I know Marguerite very well," the driver smiles in the accent of the Bearnais, removing his helmet. "In fact, we are cousins. Everyone in town is a cousin of everyone else," he continues with a short laugh. He diagrams the location of Marguerite's house. "Less than a kilometer from here," he adds. Then as an afterthought: "I can take one person behind me up the hill. Jean-Luc decides he will ride with the motorcyclist.

"In this way," he remarks, "I can prepare Marguerite for the rest of us."

It is past ten o'clock when Jean-Luc raps on the door of his sister's house. There's commotion inside. A light illuminates. An indistinguishable voice emanates from inside. Then Marguerite appears. She is an elderly woman in a bathrobe, somewhat stout, with a pleasant, ruddy face marked by a series of dimples, and very sharp blue eyes.

"Jean-Luc," she cries, her eyes alarmed. "I didn't expect you."

He takes his sister in his arms. When her head moves back from his chest, he sees tears. "I wondered whether I would ever see you again," she sobs whimsically. "Married to a Jewess, you are fair game for the Boches. Are you alone?"

Jean-Luc explains the situation to Marguerite. "You must be starved," she says to him. He smiles. This is the first thing that every person in the village says when someone comes to their door. "You look famished."

"The others will be here shortly," he remarks. "I'll hold off. Then we will all eat together."

"I can prepare a vegetable soup," Marguerite says, drawing her bathrobe tightly around herself. With this, she pours the elements of the soup into a cauldron in the chimney, starts a fire with twigs adding larger wood fragments, until the fire is flaming, and the cauldron begins to simmer.

"Odile has had great difficulty making this trip. She will need to rest for several days."

"But what are you doing here? I always thought that if you escaped from Paris you would go south to Kitty's in Nice. It has so much more to offer than our poor village."

Jean-Luc shrugs. "Our Clovis is meeting some people up the mountain," he says.

"People you say?" She gives him a quizzical glance.

"Spanish partisans," he admits.

"You know my heart is with you," Marguerite says with concern, "but you may bring down the first Nazis into our village if you create too much of a stir."

"A chance we must take," he replies. "We have to risk in order to gain."

She nods sympathetically, a large draught of air emitting from her in a sigh. A few moments later, Clovis and Simone have made it to her house. They too are terribly fatigued.

"We have to fetch Odile down the mountain," Jean-Luc says.

"I will send Pierrot for her on his motorcycle," Marguerite exclaims. "This will be much faster." She picks up the phone and calls Pierrot on the other side of the village. "He lives close by with my cousin, Jeanne. "He knows every inch of the mountain," Marguerite says. "Tell him where you left her."

Within the half hour, Odile has arrived at the door, her arm wrapped for support about the solid torso of Pierrot.

"I think I need to eat and drink something," she says, her lips parched.

Marguerite has a miche of bread which she cuts with a great knife. From a large pot, she pours glasses of spring water. And now she brings out the simmering soup, the odours of which have been teasing them for over a half hour.

"I also have some cheese, goat cheese," she adds, "from the flock in the mountain." She turns to Clovis. "You, young man, I have not seen you since you were a teen-ager. Give your aunt a hug." In their embrace, she breaks free to ask about Simone.

"My friend," Clovis says simply. She is travelling with us."

Marguerite embraces her, Simone profuse with thanks for her gracious welcome.

"But, my dear, we have a problem," Marguerite continues with a frown. "I only have two bedrooms available: one for Jean-Luc and Odile, and the other for Clovis."

"Simone will stay with me," Clovis offers.

Marguerite shakes her head. "I'm afraid that won't work. I am Catholic, you know, and this is a Catholic village. No, I could not permit a young unmarried woman to share a bed with my nephew." She shakes her tousled hair. "I will find a room for you nearby. There may be one available across the street."

Clovis looks helplessly at his father. "No use crossing swords with your aunt," Jean-Luc says. "Her morality is legendary for a reason."

Marguerite is a spinster. She has lived her entire life in this town and, for the past forty years, in this very house. The house was built by her father before he died, large by village standards, a two-story stucco building with an attic and a small storage space in a basement which the old man used to store wine. Weekdays, Marguerite works as a bookkeeper for a sandal factory three minutes away on foot down a leaf lined path, by a tennis court. She picked up her skill without formal education. For the rest, she tends to a fruit orchard on one side of the house, and a vegetable garden on the other. A tireless worker, each row of carrots or leeks is impeccably straight, weed-free, and groomed. She says she lives on the vegetables she grows here all year round as well as the fruit from the orchard, much of which she cans. In the little basement of the house, once reserved for wine, she maintains her canned goods. For the rest, after intense inspection, she buys a slaughtered pig each year, quarters it on her own, and lives on the meat year-round. A large slab of porc has been hoisted to the ceiling in the dining room. As she needs a slab, she lowers it, washes off the salt preserves, and cuts the pieces she requires. In virtually every respect, the woman is self-sufficient. She has heard of fairs in Pau and Oloron but has never attended. There are restaurants which abound in the large city down the mountain, but she has rarely ventured that far. Yet she does not feel constrained. Always occupied, her life is in her house, the food she must maintain each and every year through the orchard and garden. For special occasions, her sister Jeanne fetches her over to her side of the village for a feast and celebration. It is enough to fill this woman's soul. As a child, Clovis could not pronounce the name of his aunt Instead; he referred to her as Rite. Tatie Rite, and the name stuck into adulthood.

"Adalia and her daughter, Abella, have a small property directly across the street." Marguerite muses. "Occasionally, they rent out a room to earn extra money." She picks up the phone and calls. Nods. "Yes, they will have a room for you. An inexpensive one," she adds.

So, Simone prepares regretfully to leave for the night. "They will feed you an Algerian breakfast as well," Marguerite adds as a further incentive. But Simone is ignoring Tatie Rite's inducement and is looking into Clovis' eyes. She has his hand in hers. "The boy is pretty tired and can't go to bed unless you let go of his hand," Marguerite insists with a soft smile.

Adalia meets Simone at the door and shows her to her room. She is a middle-aged woman with raven hair, in a gray dress, a shawl about her head, lacking make-up. Simone gazed at a quaint, small bedroom with a mattress on the floor, a chair and a table facing the window. The shutters have now been closed so that she cannot look out onto the street or at Marguerite's house.

"Next to this room is your bathroom," Adalia tells her. "You may wish to take a bath there. We have no shower," she adds. "I am going to bed, but my daughter Abella is awake for an hour or more. So, if you need anything, please ask her."

The bathtub looks inviting after a day of hard hiking. The room itself is rather large, quite a bit grander than the bedroom she has been offered. Discrete cloudy windows block views to the outside. On the wall, a gas heater. The tub itself is large, white, curved at the back to allow one to settle in comfortably. She undresses as the hot water is running into the tub. Once the water has risen a couple of feet, she tests it with a finger, then realises she has to practically vault into the tub due to the height of the sides. She climbs in carefully, settles down and leans back, a bar of orange soap in one hand. Enjoying the comforting heat of the water, watching little clouds rising from the waters, Simone mentally retraces the day's hike.

After a time, she is feeling sleepy. The water is cooling. So, she decides to get out of the tub, and begins to lift her frame upwards. To her dismay and progressive horror, she realises she cannot do this. Her muscles are failing her. They seem to have collapsed. She simply does not have the strength to raise herself out of this tub. For an instant she is both flustered and upset about this peculiar circumstance. Something isn't right. I'm probably just tired after such an exhausting day, she says to herself. But after a while, she realises that something is terribly wrong. Now panic begins to mount within her. She stills it, turns her head to the heater on the wall. She cannot quite see it for the clouds obscuring it. Something about the heater she now understands is wrong, and she must make a special effort to propel herself out of this tub. With a force only available to her from her strict training regime, she lifts a leg over the side of the tub and pushing as hard as she can, manages to careen and fall out of the tub onto the solid porcelain floor.

The thud causes her mind to race. She is being poisoned. Sure of it now. She is, in fact, dying. She looks at the door: closed, shut tight. She tries to scream, but her throat emits only a croak. I have to make it to the door; she says to herself and strives to move her limbs. Slowly, painfully, she grunts along the floor, crawling an inch or two with each exertion. So sleepy. All she really wants to do is submit into blessed sleep. Yet she knows that if she allows herself this blessing, she will never again awaken. Her love is waiting for her asleep across the street. This thought prompts her to move some more. Now Simone reaches the door. But she cannot attain the handle from the floor. Somehow, she has to reach that handle. She looks at it. It appears so close and yet impossibly far. She manages to stagger onto a knee. Lifts up. Still short. I have to stand, she says to herself, fighting with every ounce of power within herself to achieve this. Shakily rises to the handle, grabs it, holds it for an instant out of breath, turns it until the door opens, and when it does and the air from the corridor rushes in, she collapses unconscious with a thud onto the floor.

Abella finds her ten minutes later stretched out naked, half in the bathroom, half out. The girl can smell the gas now. Realising the heater is leaking she covers her nose, rushes to the heater and shuts it off.

Simone opens her eyes on the floor of the bedroom. A blanket covers her. She shudders. I could have been killed, she thinks. Maybe I have been mortally damaged anyway! Abella is sitting on the bed holding her hand, looking abject. The girl's mother has crossed the street to inform Marguerite of the accident. Marguerite, dressed in her bathrobe, pads across the street in her sandals, ashen-faced. She has not awakened the others.

"My God," she says, finding Simone on the floor, pale, still unable to verbalise what has happened. "I'm so truly sorry, my child," she says.

There is no doctor in the village. The closest one is in Oloron.

"Should I have someone call the doctor?" Abella asks.

Marguerite is looking at the inert figure of Simone.

"I think I'll be all right," Simone responds lifting her head slightly, the words issued more as a gurgle than as actual speech.

"So, let's not do anything for a while, Marguerite speaks to Abella and her mother. "It would take the doctor more than an hour to get here."

"I cannot tell you how sorry I am," Adalia speaks to no one in particular.

"It was an accident," Marguerite replies.

"I told you many times we need to check that heater," Abella says, now in tears.

A half hour later, with assistance, Simone has crossed the street into Marguerite's house.

"I've made a blunder," Marguerite says ruefully to her. "Believe me! I would rather have you and Clovis together than have you dead."

A bit later, Simone, under her own power, and covered entirely by a large blanket, mounts the stairs to Clovis's room and slips under the covers. The young man does not awaken.

***

Gruppenfuehrer Hausser removes his gloves and sits primly. His face is tightly serious, the demeanour of someone who brooks no nonsense. Still, the tone in his question slips out inoffensively.

"Nothing yet from your Dawn? You know you have Ribbentrop's interest in the girl."

Captain Anselm stands up from behind his desk.

"Nothing yet. But it has only been a few days. I thought she might need a few weeks, perhaps a month before she could relay information back to us.

"You're certain that she is not playing both black as well as white in her chess match?"

Anselm laughs. "A double agent? Quaint idea. The girl seems fearless, but terribly innocent. Too innocent in my estimation to act on both sides of any issue. She has already given us some preliminary information which has proven itself valuable. But the pay-off as I indicated to you last week is to stop the Spaniard resistance from forming in France while we undermine the French Maquis at the same time. And this young, pretty girl has all the attributes to produce this for the Reich."

"Then we will by all means wait," Hausser responds. "But not forever."

13. A Time for Peace

In the morning, Simone finds the other side of the bed empty. Clovis is downstairs in the dining room, reading. He has brought with him two books on existentialism. Now he peers up beyond his glasses.

"I just wonder at the meaning of it all," he says to Simone. "No, I'm not talking about existentialism. This stupid, stupid war. It's as if some orchestra leader decided to let loose all the evil players at the same time. The cacophony of death stinks to high heaven."

"Good morning to you too," Simone laughs.

'I'm not kidding, "Clovis responds. "What's the purpose of all this misery? Religious people believe it all has meaning, purpose. I see nothing but the misery itself."

"But you are still young," Marguerite says, opening the door. "Besides, the world will look different after breakfast. Slices of fresh bread, jam, and a bit of butter that Jeanne and I scraped up last time we were down the mountain. Good food, some tea, and you will look at the world with brighter eyes," she admonishes. "Come and eat now."

"There is more to life than a tasty breakfast," Clovis responds, but he is smiling at his aunt who smacks his bottom as he walks by.

Later, he takes Simone on a walk through the village. A late September morning, warm, but the air is dry. The air on the mountain is pure, unfiltered. Nothing up there corrodes it. It has the effect of opening the lungs. She sucks it in contentedly.

"What does one do in this village?" she asks Clovis.

He smiles. "We do pay a lot of attention to eating, and eating well, even as the war is waged around us. Look at the mountain. It's full of surprises; lots of animals, even food that can be garnered from under trees. Way up in the mountain, there is a shepherd with a flock of goats. Later, we will bring him provisions."

"Have you forgotten completely about the Spaniards?" she asks.

"Not at all. I am expecting word any week now."

"Not a very satisfactory timetable to wage war against an enemy," she claims.

"True," he acknowledges, "but the best we can do."

Marguerite has started out for the sandal factory. She leaves behind a note that there are tennis rackets in the closet if anyone cares to play on the factory court. Simone takes them out of the closet and shakes the dust free. They are vintage rackets from the twenties, intact, but heavy, old, the stringing not quite taut. There is a pack of balls alongside. So, they walk to the courts. The concrete flooring is jagged in spots. Chestnuts have fallen on much of the court. They sweep them to one side. Try to raise the sagging net and hit for a while. Neither of them has much ability in the sport. Balls fly outside of the court.

Afterwards, they are striding up the mountain to a spring to fetch water in a bucket.

"Put your mouth there," Clovis says pointing to a natural stone spout between rocks. "You can drink directly from the spring. It is water coming down the mountain, fresh, clean."

"And it tastes good too," Simone marvels.

"Not only that. It has a way of flushing out your insides. There'll be a lot of peeing after intake from this spring."

In this manner, days pass quickly, languorously. Afternoon naps are plentiful. Odile likes to putter around the garden, while her husband enjoys hiking up the mountain or down to Aramits for an occasional beer at a local café.

One morning, Clovis has another idea.

"We are going crayfish hunting this morning," he says to Simone.

"And how do we do that?"

"Tatie Rite has fishing nets. We need to bait those for the little buggers. There should be bait coming by shortly," he laughs. A half hour later, a meat truck rumbles up the street stopping every tenth of a mile, the driver calling out his wares. He opens the back of the truck to show the rabbits, squirrels, beef, lamb, and pork he has available for sale. Women empty out their houses and apartments to check out the offerings.

"I'm looking for old meat," Clovis says to the driver.

"How old?"

"Rotten preferably," Clovis responds.

"I have just the thing you need," the driver responds, rummaging in the back of his truck. Now he pulls out the remains of some liver which has seen fresher days.

"This has a superb, stinky odour," the driver continues. "And you can have it cheap."

Clovis cuts up the rotten meat, ties it to the bottom of the nets. From inside the house, he finds a bottle of Anis del Mono, and sprinkles a few drops on top of the meat. He leads Simone up the mountains and into the woods where there is a stream.

"Hold the nets," he says as he peruses the waters. In a shallow spot, he takes a net and drops it carefully next to a pile of shallow rocks. He repeats this step some ten yards farther down.

Now he returns to Simone and suggests they find a soft spot under a tree to stretch out.

"This is fishing?" she asks sceptically.

"Absolutely," he grins. "We wait until the crayfish come forth. Slow movers they are, but the Anis is irresistible. Nor will they be able to resist the clarion call of rotten meat."

About an hour later, Clovis wakes Simone up from a doze.

"Time to collect our winnings," he announces. She gets up, smoothes out her dress, follows him uncomprehendingly back to the stream. He holds out a large canvas bag,

"Open this wide," he says. Enters the stream quietly, reaches for the net, and yanks it out of the water. There are dozens of crayfish in its centre scrambling one on top of the other. Clovis deposits these into the canvas bag. Repeats the same steps with the second net.

"Dinner is served," he says, as he looks at the contents of the bag. At the house, Odile has pulled some leaks and is cooking them into a soup. She prepares the cauldron for the crayfish.

A week elapses without words from the Spaniards.

"Maybe they have no intention of coming to France." Simone says.

"Patience," Clovis responds. "Remember they're leaving a war site of their own. Everything takes time these days."

And so, they wait. More weeks elapse. They are spending afternoons in the woods hunting mushrooms of the season, 'cepe' and 'girolle'. The cepe are plentiful this late summer but must be pursued. Found usually snuggling in groups near a tree. Occasionally, up to a half hour goes by before they find a plot. Pushing on into the forest, mushrooms abound. Just have to locate the buggers, he says to Simone. The mushrooms range from the small, perhaps the size of a half dollar, to the gigantic, larger than a head. Clovis shows Simone which mushrooms to eschew, for some are poisonous. But the girolles are fine and easy to locate thanks to their yellow colour. Their medium size tends to be rather uniform.

As the sun reaches its zenith, they halt underneath an elm tree, lay out a baguette with cheese. Clovis has brought a flask of red wine. A simple, but filling meal. Afterwards, as is their wont, they stretch out underneath a tree. Clovis is fond of mint, holds a sprig of it to his nose and breathes in deeply. Sometimes, it causes him to sneeze, and he always seems surprised by this. Then, he undoes Simone's sandals, and massages each of her feet, always beginning with the left one. This is relaxing, intimate, and afterwards, Simone reclines immobile. Up the mountain, in the distance, a flock of sheep is grazing on the hillside. An eagle parades in ever loftier circles above them. Simone and Clovis stretch out under the tree and nap. Sometimes, sleep eludes them. Instead, they reach for one another. The air is dry, balmy. The mountain is quiet.

"I have a surprise for you," Clovis beams.

"Tell me."

"I can do better than that," he says, searching in his pocket. He brings forth a little bottle and hands it to Simone.

"Where did you get this? Simone asks holding the bottle of nail polish high in the air. It's a miracle."

"A present from Tatie Jeanne: she got it from Pierrot, but the boy won't tell her where he found it."

She opens the bottle carefully. The colour is a deep red. She begins to apply it with the applicator onto each of her nails. She holds her fingers in the air, waving them back and forth to dry the lotion.

Then she slips off her sandals. "My feet are quite warm and relaxed," she says.

Clovis takes the bottle from her and colours each of her toes.

"Very sexy," she says to him.

"Quiet," he admonishes her. "I'm painting."

Silence as Simone lays back and closes her eyes. They hear nothing save for the beating of their hearts as they touch. Joining together, wordless, they feel as if they are slipping into one another's auras. They make love unhurriedly, passion subdued by the need to please the other. The other feels a projection of themselves. They sense that they are slipping into one another's orbit, touching gently. Fulfilled, hearts racing, they now find release in the embrace of the other.

Occasionally, they venture up the mountain to the shepherd, Dany, who is tending a flock of sheep. They bring him provisions to last for the remainder of the warm season. Dany is a young man with a beard…too difficult to manicure every day to cut, he insists…but not much interest in conversing. He has little to say about his time on the mountain. He does not mention the spectacular sunsets, the cold, dry evening air that requires him to slip on a coat even when the day waxes warm, the evening fires against which he dozes. Nor does he speak about the animals he tends. Perhaps there are unspoken bonds between him and the nature he inhabits. It's impossible to know. Dany scarcely grasps that a war is waging below him on his continent, that his own country has been invaded, and that his own people surrendered easily, much too easily. When Clovis speaks about the ongoing conflict, Dany's eyes turn glassy and he looks upwards as if to say he has no interest in this alien experience, whatever it may be. He has one weakness: chocolate, but these days little chocolate is available.

And then, in the course of a morning, everything changes. A messenger comes into the village. A man named Caleb Bracado. He is here to connect with Clovis. The two of them walk to the fronton, leaning against the pink wall.

"I expected you weeks ago, Clovis says, accepting a Spanish cigarette, tapping it against the fronton.

Caleb doffs his beret under the hot sun. He spits onto the ground.

"We do what we can, Clovis. Some of the group is only now released from jails. Others have been working to keep their families in food. Of course, they want to join the resistance. They hate what Franco represented in Spain, and Hitler in the rest of Europe is but a mirror image. The Fascists must be defeated."

"So, when will they come up the mountain?"

"Hard to say, we are aiming for a specific day, the treaty day. After that, winter sets in and it is much harder to climb easily."

"I agree. It must be done quickly."

"And then? Caleb asks. "What will you do with them?"

"We will go to Paris and join the Maquis there. Much to be done there. Many targets, but difficult as well because for every Nazi life we take, the Germans exact three times the price. Yet, we cannot stop. We cannot give in."

"Expect from thirteen to eighteen men."

"Good," Clovis concludes. "Join us for dinner tonight."

"I would like that, Caleb replies. My feet are weary, and I have acquired one or two blisters."

"How did you come up?"

"Climbed from the Spanish side to the Pierre Saint Martin before I descended to the village."

"And this is the way the others will come as well?"

"Yes. You know that there is a feast day on the mountain in about three weeks. A Saturday. By the treaty signed in the middle ages, the Spanish must bring up a slaughtered cow and pastries, while the French bring wine, bread, and condiments. If we can accomplish it, we will try to have the Spanish Maquis come up on that weekend."

"Genius," Clovis remarks. "The celebration will give them cover. I had forgotten about the treaty."

"Perhaps you would also have a room for me in the village to stay the night? When I came through town, I saw a sign for Abella's place. Apparently, she has a room to rent."

Clovis smirks. "True, you can rent the room, but you may never leave it," he laughs and tells Caleb the story of Simone's arrival in town.

"I prefer to leave Arette on my own two feet," Caleb concurs with a soft grin.

***

Gruppenfuehrer Hausser is polishing his braids with the tip of his fingers.

"How long has it been now?" he demands.

"Too long," Captain Anselm responds. "Something clearly has occurred. Perhaps our Dawn has been discovered or killed."

"Or," Hauser adds cynically, "Perhaps she never worked for us in the first place and is conspiring with Clovis."

Anselm chuckles. "I doubt that. Her information while in Paris was generally reliable."

"Not entirely as you yourself informed me."

"All right," Anselm concedes, somewhat irritated. Wotan lifts off the ground next to him to stand. Anselm pets the dog. "What do you propose we do about it?"

"You did receive one note from her, correct?"

"Yes," Anselm says, "From the Pyrenees asking me to be patient."

"Well my patience is exhausted."

"Mine as well," Anselm agrees.

Hausser stands up straight, his cap under his arm. "I am going to send a squad down there. There are only a few places in the Pyrenees where one can escape into Spain. I will have my men explore all of them."

Captain Anselm unfolds his arms. "Yes, surely it is time to inquire about the lady."

"I'm glad you agree. I thought for a bit that the young beauty had bewitched you into total inaction."

14. Movement in the Mountain

"Next Sunday," Marguerite announces, "Tatie Jeanne's daughter, Claire, is marrying the town electrician, Lionel. Afterwards, we are to partake of a feast at her house.

"Sounds like fun, Simone responds. "Are they related?"

"Third cousins," Jean-Luc remarks.

"Lots of fun," Clovis remarks. "We will eat like swine. These feasts are magnificent and tend to go on a while. Endlessly!"

"Don't discourage the girl's curiosity," Marguerite scolds her nephew.

Later that day, upon her return from the sandal factory, as Clovis lounges in the dining room, reading Kierkegaard, the afternoon sun looming over his shoulder, Marguerite suggests to Simone that they visit the orchard together. There, by the house, and in an unusually warm twilight, they face one another on a bench.

"Lots of apples and pears coming in," Marguerite remarks approvingly.

Simone realises that Marguerite has something specific on her mind. And it has little or nothing to do with the fruit orchard.

"Something bothering you?"

A momentary pause.

"I'm concerned about your relationship with Clovis," Marguerite begins. "I've known my nephew from the moment of his birth. He was born down the hill in Pau, and as soon as I saw him, I fell in love," she croons. "My only nephew from this side of the family," she lilts. "When I saw the two of you together, it became apparent that once the war ends, my Clovis might leave France entirely for America. Is that what you have in mind?" she asks, peering intently at Simone.

The question catches Simone at loose ends and she pauses momentarily before replying.

"Look, we haven't talked about what happens at the end of the war. If you are asking me whether I love Clovis, the answer is yes. He is the only man I have ever come to know intensely, and the only man I can say I feel congruent with. My bond with him cannot be overstated. As for Clovis, his feelings for me, you of course can ask him, but I think he will respond in like manner. I know he cares for me. Better, I am sure he loves me. But that love cannot reach total fulfilment until the war is over. France is his first love, and he must stay married to that love until the war has reached a conclusion."

"So, you are not going to wed and run off to America."

Simone smiles, "We have no plans. But I don't want to lie to you. It has crossed my mind. I want to be with Clovis, and if he prefers to stay here, I will stay by his side. So, in a very true sense, it has to do with his preference, his needs."

Marguerite takes Simone in her arms. "I shouldn't be so impertinent," she whispers into Simone's ears. "What you youngsters are planning, only you can decide for yourselves, but if truth be told, you must know I am afraid of losing Clovis forever once the war is finished."

"Forever is a long time," Simone responds. "I can't deal with forever right now, nor can Clovis. Maybe once the war has ended…. But I'm glad we had this talk."

That Sunday, they cross the quarter mile to the other side of the village, past the post office, the little hotel with its half dozen rooms, the mini grocery store and bar and, next to it, the one room box with the drooping Quincaillerie sign that passes for a hardware store. A few moments later, they have arrived at Tatie Jeanne's house in the valley. A low slung, dark affair, yet the home was large enough to encompass some five bedrooms. Tatie Jeanne has been busy producing babies over two decades, and most of these have remained in the same village. Her husband, Arnaud, a carpenter, some fifteen years her senior, is now retired except for an emergency handyman's job which he accepts either for his family or for friends in the village. Around seventy, his hands were gnarled and arthritic, and he was frequently in pain. A man of few words. A man fully devoted to family, but ailing, short of breath as time squeezes his lungs together.

Arnaud sits at the head of an extended table. The children will congregate at a smaller table by the chimney. The bride, Claire, and her husband of but an hour, entwine one next to the other. They are dressed elegantly, in the style of the commune, Claire with a reticulated lace white veil around her forehead over a plain white dress with frilly lace cuffs. The girl has no make-up on her face, but her cheeks are rosy, and her lips pink. Three of Jeanne's adult children, along with two spouses, are already seated. Pierrot arrives and is embraced by Jeanne and seated next to her. Jean-Luc leads Odile, Clovis and Simone to their places. After a blessing offered by one of the youngsters, Jeanne serves mushroom soups, breads, and wine. Afterwards, she brings plates of sole, followed by a cauldron of crayfish accompanied by a green salad and white wine. Next, a pork roast from a pig grilled for more than eighteen hours on a backyard spit. Roast potatoes and a variety of vegetables follow. More wine is brought out.

Pierrot springs a surprise, rare pastries obtained in Oloron, and these are laid out to admiring gasps.

The conversation focuses more on the events of the village than the war. Eventually, someone asks Clovis what he knows about the advancing German army and how they are faring on the eastern front, but Clovis has no more information than anyone else. It is his impression that, for the moment, the Nazis are continuing their assault on Europe which, so far, has proven successful.

"But Russia is another matter," Clovis goes on.

"Yes," Jean-Luc agrees, "This is how Napoleon lost hundreds of thousands of soldiers: by invading in winter."

The luncheon with a series of light conversation, pastries, coffee, and liquors, requires some five hours. No one thinks to leave early. When it is time to return to Marguerite's house, Simone is not certain she can walk all that distance with several added kilos of food weighing down her belly. Clovis laughs. He has paced himself better than Simone and takes her hand as they cross by the fronton. It's a leisurely walk to the house, and then a short flight of stairs, Simone giggling as Clovis pushes her ahead. He lays her down onto their bed upstairs.

"You did better than I expected," he says to her.

"You mean I ate like the pig I ate," she laughs.

"True," he responds, "But also to sit at a table for five hours consuming and imbibing means you have to be in rather spectacular shape."

"I always said I was a strong, fit woman," Simone replies, flexing an arm.

The following Sunday they climb up the mountain to the Pierre Saint-Martin which crowns the top of the mountain. They will be among the first to arrive for the feast. They are high enough so that the tree line has ceased.

Barren, a moonscape, they reach it in the late morning. The air, however, is unearthly clear, light, void of pollution. With them, they have carried food and drinks. Pierrot has driven a car laden with folded tables and chairs up the dusty road. When they reach the top, Simone helps to set up the tables.

"We are expecting Spaniards?" she asks.

"I understand they will be here by noon," Clovis replies.

Jean-Luc has walked up the mountain with them, his wife electing to remain down in the village.

"Have you ever been inside the mountain?" he asks Clovis.

"Never," Clovis says. "I've heard that there is a lake you can lower yourself into."

"It is quite spectacular," Jean-Luc acknowledges with wonder in his voice. "A lake inside the top of a mountain in the Pyrenees. And all you see when you are inside, provided the sunlight peeks through, are stalactites and stalagmites. There must be a million bats there, but since I have never been there in the evening, I haven't seen a single one flying."

"I don't think we will have time for the lake this trip," Clovis says.

Jean-Luc responds. "The lake will still be there when you ask to see it."

Around noon, as they look down the mountain towards the Spanish side, they can hear the rumble of several trucks climbing, and beyond them, discern the figures of hundreds of men and women singing Spanish folksongs as they move up the mountain.

Suddenly, they are all together, perhaps five hundred people from both sides of the border. The mayor of Arette is there with a proclamation which expresses his thanks to the Spaniards for respecting the treaty signed by both countries so many centuries ago.

Two Spaniards are playing classical guitar. In a moment, another has started a flamenco rendition and both men and women begin to dance. Wine is flowing everywhere. It is as if the world were replete with total joy and carefreeness. No one is contemplating the horror of war not so far away.

"I am Manuelo," says a man finding Clovis. "I have brought with me a half dozen men."

The two engage in a lengthy conversation, half in French, half in Spanish as Manuelo reaches for this or that word or expression.

"Come down the mountain with us," Clovis says. We will put you and your men up at the hotel for a few days, and then you will continue your path to Paris. I will take you there myself. Once in town, I will provide you the name and address of someone to contact once you reach the city. He will have a family for each of you. A family you can live with as long as you are in town. Most of them are in the suburbs, but in a real sense, you will be incorporated into the city. And then we shall see how best to use you."

The Spaniards have lugged up the mountain a cooked side of beef. Cut up into steaks, it is roasted over a large fire.

"We shall eat well to commemorate the treaty," Manuelo remarks.

"Enjoy," Clovis retorts, "for this may be your last wonderful meal in quite some time."

Manuelo laughs, "We did not eat so well in Franco's jail," he remarks. "So, anything that is more bountiful than bread and water feels as if we had stumbled into paradise."

15. The War Comes to Arette

Idyllic. Peaceful. Days spent scampering through woods and up and down mountainsides. All is well in the universe, Simone crows, at the end of another day in the fresh air. No rain has fallen for more than ten days. Tatie Rite's garden is beginning to dry out and her attempts to water by hand are not succeeding. She complains about it. She believes that the bombings that have taken place in the port of Bordeaux have interfered with the normal rain clouds that waft their way over Arette. Once the bombings stop, she believes, the weather will revert to normal.

Food is plentiful on the mountain. Certainly, there is rationing and restrictions. Sweets are very hard to find. There is a black market for foodstuffs. What one cannot procure normally in the course of purchase or barter, can be paid for at a heftier price to be sure. Pierrot needs a tire for his truck. It's not possible these days to locate one on the open market. The black market comes to his rescue charging only double. Pierrot is grateful.

Odile has recovered well from the strain of leaving Paris. Once their luggage was picked up from lost and found at the Gare, and driven down to Arette, she felt as if a new day was dawning. True, she had heard from neighbours that their apartment had been looted by soldiers, and that the Germans had seized valuable paintings, silverware, several antique watches that belonged to their ancestors. But these, as Jean-Luc would say, are but things.

"We have our lives and we are in the company of our relatives. We have wonderful air, water, and even more food than one could find in the capitol. So, there is truly little to complain about."

Mornings, Clovis spends an hour or more reading Heidegger or some other philosopher. Without a foil for his questions, his assertions, he often talks aloud to himself in question and answer form. He has brought with him a handful of paperback books on philosophy.

"This is what I will devote my life to," he tells Simone, "Once the war has been won."

"You are sure the war will be won?" she asks.

"Naturally," he says, and states it with such confidence, that perhaps, for the first time, she fosters a new belief. Not that the war effort has been so successful against the Germans. The little wireless radio feeds them information that the Germans are still firmly entrenched. But America is now in it, and this unpredictable but mighty force could change everything. Fingers crossed!

Evenings, Simone helps Tatie Rite clean house. The cauldron which has been simmering with soup for over a month needs scraping. Silver needs polishing. The hanging pig needs slicing. Vegetables are to be picked, cleaned. Simone sits for hours clicking off the ends of green beans, and peeling potatoes. Tatie Rite watches her with interest as she works, the intensity of effort, the commitment. She is slowly showing a fondness for the girl. Despite the threat she poses to the bond between her and her nephew. One evening, as Simone prepares to climb the stairs to go to bed, she takes her and, pulls her closer and embraces her.

"Sleep well," Tatie Rite murmurs in her ear.

"You're winning her over," Clovis clucks in her ear.

Late mornings, Clovis and Jean-Luc head for the fronton with borrowed wicker gloves to play a form of jai alai. But Jean-Luc does not have the stamina to play very long. Breathless, even a bit distraught at how easily his son defeats him, the boy moving effortlessly and striking the ball called the pelota with precision and so cleanly, he withdraws quite early. On his own, Clovis smashes the pelota against the fronton another fifteen minutes.

Evenings, when Clovis and Simone hike along the road that leads towards the village of Aramits where there is a pub to visit, stars above on a cloudless and icy evening glow along their way.

"No flashlights needed here," Clovis remarks. Shooting stars abound cavorting in spectacular arcs in the northern sky. In a distant corner, the remnant tail of a comet which, at one time, would have heralded much superstition, the advent of plague or some similar catastrophe. Instead, the pub offers a stein of beer or a glass of good cheer. They watch the locals throw darts with much enthusiasm, Simone caressing his hand.

One morning everything abruptly changes. An armoured vehicle enters the town. The first time since the occupation that Arette has seen German soldiers. Two of them ride to the town city hall where they are made to wait until the mayor has completed her breakfast. The young German soldiers have been given the task of locating and questioning Simone Valois. Their instructions are that they need to ask her specific questions, but not injure her. If her answers are at variance with the truth, she is to be taken into custody and returned to Paris.

The mayor finishes her breakfast and is smoking a Gitane while she slides into the chair at her desk. Lifting her head, she bids the soldiers enter. They ask her about Simone Valois. To be accurate, they show the mayor a photo.

"Never seen this person," the mayor remarks offhandedly.

"You're sure of this?"

"Quite sure. I know everyone in my village."

"And the young man named Clovis?"

"Yes," the mayor responds surely. "He visits here from time to time, but I have not seen him recently."

"His aunt has a house here."

"Yes."

"Show us the way, please."

"I cannot do so just this moment, I have a meeting."

"Madame Mayor," one of the soldiers says. "I asked you to show us the way. Now. This is not a request."

"Of course," the Mayor responds shakily. "Of course. I just need a moment to confer with my staff so that they will be able to handle work in my absence."

She goes to the back, whispers to a girl. The girl gets up, leaves by the back door, and begins to run up the hill. In the interim, the Mayor is offering the soldiers a cup of coffee. One looks at the other.

"We have not had real coffee in some time," the first soldier admits. They sit contentedly drinking coffee and snacking on sausage with bread. In the interim, the girl reaches Tatie Rite's house.

"Two German soldiers will be coming to the house in a few moments," she advises, out of breath.

Clovis nods his head, thanks the girl, "I think we can welcome these men appropriately," he remarks. Upstairs, under his bed, he keeps a pistol, a Luger PO 8. Checks it, cocks it, and places it securely in his jacket pocket, his finger on the safety. His face is changing as he translates the safety of his village persona into the resistance soldier. His contented vapidity dissolves, to be replaced by a concentrated force, each and every fibre in concert. He descends to the ground floor, settles firmly into an armchair by the fireplace, his body turned towards the front door.

"I'm going out back," Simone says.

"Do you have a gun?"

"No, I have a knife."

"Don't start anything up," Clovis advises. "If they find you, tell them who you are. They're certainly looking for you. Give yourself up. Once they have you, they'll relax. Then we have them."

Simone bristles at the comment. "I'll take care of myself, you can be sure."

"My God," Clovis complains, hearing steel in her voice, "Please be careful."

Simone edges out the back door into the orchard. Checks it. Now retreats to the safety of the door. From there, she can see a piece of the winding road which must be travelled to come to Tatie Rite's house. Clovis's aunt herself is at the sandal factory. Odile and Jean-Luc are upstairs, sitting quietly, waiting nervously.

In a few moments, Clovis can hear the pronounced engine of the armoured vehicle edging slowly up the mountain. He does not move. Pondering Heidegger on death: "Death is not the end of our existence, but rather the internal structure of our existence."

The machine stops in front of the house, engine idling. Both men get out. The mayor remains in the back seat, and once the two men have exited the car, she crouches. Each soldier checks his rifle and now advances towards the front door. Heinrich Glauser is twenty-four, a corporal in the army. The other soldier, Klaus Feinheld, is two years his senior, a sergeant. They are each wearing the

M36 tunic with the dark green collar and shoulder straps with white Waffenfarbe, a colour-coded insignia, and the Wehrmacht Sadler above the right breast pocket. It is Feinheld who comes to the front door, motioning his colleague to check out the garden at the rear of the house. As Glauser stealthily moves towards the back of the house, Feinhold rings the doorbell.

"Come in," Clovis says.

Pause. "Open the door."

"The door is open,' Clovis says pleasantly.

Feinheld turns the doorknob slowly, advancing his Gewehr 43 rifle. When the door opens, he observes Clovis reclining in his armchair.

"We are here on official German business," the man says in a stilted French.

"We're not used to German military in our village."

"I need to see your papers," Feinheld says, his eyes wide open as he scans the remainder of the living room and eyes the steps that lead upwards.

"What have we done?" Clovis asks quietly.

"We are looking for two people," Feinheld says. "One of them is the woman, Simone Valois. We are told she lives in this house. Is this true?"

"She does," Clovis admits.

Feinheld smacks his lips. "Please get up," he says. Clovis gets up slowly. "And take your hand out of your pocket, please."

"Simone is in the orchard out back," Clovis says. "Picking apples from the tree, I can show you."

"No," Feinheld says with a stammer." Don't show me this. I want to see your documents. You are Clovis, aren't you?"

"Yes, I am," Clovis says, his hand reaching into his pocket.

"What the hell are you doing?" Feinheld shouts, pointing his rifle.

"Looking for my papers," Clovis replies. He pulls out his documents carefully and now hands them to the Sergeant.

Sergeant Feinheld begins to scan the documents.

"Yes," he begins, "You are the man we are looking for. We are placing you and Simone Valois under arrest."

Out back, Hauser has made his way through the garden and is now returning to the house. He spies the back door which is closed, opens it. Inside, behind the door, Simone Valois is waiting. Her breathing has ceased. The corporal enters slowly, closing the door behind him. In an instant he senses something is wrong. There is a presence, a body behind him, and he starts to turn towards it just as a thin, feminine hand with red nails curves under his chin raising it forcefully, and in that same moment, a knife travels across the scope of his neck slicing the carotid artery. In an instant, as the soldier faces his murderer, blood fountains out of him, Simone dodging to one side to avoid the spray, and now the corporal is crumpling to the floor, looking beseechingly at the stone-faced woman hovering above him, her knife covered in his blood rising high into the air to strike downwards one final time. As it does, the boy lifts his brown eyes upwards into her direct line of vision. Simone cannot fail to see those eyes, piercingly wide with confusion, a profound instinct announcing to the boy his demise, for he knows that he is fatally wounded, and collapses into death. Before expiring, he lets loose a garbled whistled scream, a sound resembling that of the coyote howling and the train whistle's banshee screech.

At this moment, as Feinheld hears the shriek of his colleague's death rattle, his eyes flitting upward towards the rear door from Clovis but momentarily, Clovis is edging into his pocket and without freeing the pistol, shoots the Luger through his jacket into the stomach of the enemy. In an instant, the man falls onto one knee, attempting to lift his rifle. Clovis kicks it away. Then as the man rests quaking on one knee, Clovis lifts the butt of his Luger and crashes it down onto the head of the soldier, felling him. In an instant, the house is quiet. Jean-Luc and Odile descend the stairs carefully. Clovis has run to the back to see that Simone has dispatched the other soldier.

"Good girl," he beams. But the woman is shaken, standing knife in hand, staring downwards at the limp face and body. A person who, one moment previously, was still breathing, was still fomenting trouble, still had dreams, and is now consigned to oblivion.

"Help me remove the body," Clovis says. She understands none of this. He touches her face splotchy with tension, fear, and excitement. "Shake yourself out of this," he says to her, taking the knife from her hand.

"Yes," she says. "Yes." But she does not move.

"I'm going to get Pierrot's truck, " Jean-Luc says, and we'll dispose of the bodies."

"And their jeep," Clovis advises.

But Simone is standing shaking as if she were frozen. He embraces her with his body.

"Quiet now. It's over," he says calmly. "Quiet now, little one."

Speechless, her eyes darting back and forth, she cradles onto the ground, Clovis holding her as they sink together.

"Sweetheart," he says to her. "You did what you had to do, what you were trained to do."

"Yes," she responds, trembling. "Yes, but I looked into that boy's eyes. His eyes!"

16. Leaving Arette

Jean-Luc and Pierrot drive the truck to the house. They wait until dusk before wrapping the bodies in sheets and carrying them onto the truck. Simone stays behind. The men climb the hill half way to an entrance into the forest. They intend to bury the bodies, one by one, deep into the forest. They begin to dig, Pierrot and Clovis sharing the heavy work. They do not offer a prayer. They simply dump the bodies into the graves, cover them with soil, and cover the soil with autumn leaves, raking them until there is no sign of disturbance. They do not set a cross. They leave without a word. For the moment, there is nothing which can add to the gloom of death and, as importantly, what is to follow.

In the morning, after breakfast, Clovis leads Simone to the fountain. They sit on the stone side by side.

"Are you all right?" he asks her.

"I think so," she answers. "I don't exactly understand what happened to me. But I do know that I killed another man, a young man, and this was very hard."

"It gets easier," Clovis offers.

Simone looks up at him, shaking her head sadly. "I don't believe it."

"But you understand that our time here is done. Once the soldiers do not report back in a day or so, others will follow into the village. We cannot be here when they arrive. Not because we fear fighting the soldiers, but because they will wreak vengeance on the village. I know how they operate. They will kill at least a half dozen villagers at random. One of them may be Tatie Rite or perhaps Tatie Jeanne."

Her head is low. "I do understand this."

"So, we must leave, perhaps as early as tomorrow."

And then, words tumble out of her mouth, words she never thought she would hear herself say. Trembling as she utters them.

"I thought I understood you. I thought we saw life in the same vein. But we do not. Killing for you seems expected, natural. You do it easily. You even dream about it. Not nightmarish dreams. You may even beg for it to happen. You can face a man directly and extract the life out of his soul. I cannot kill this way, this easily. I saw the boy's eyes I slaughtered. Before, when we did the raid at the Lycee, I watched a man's arm ripped off by a grenade, listened to him wail as he witnessed his arm fly into the air followed by a hurricane of blood. Blood followed his body as it collapsed into the ground. Perhaps he survived. I don't know. But you: you are so very cool under fire; so cool, somehow divorced from the deed. You and your body are no longer connected when you are firing a gun. You the philosopher who engages ideas endlessly, but the idea of life seems to have escaped you. This is insane! We cannot be together if this is true, if life is so meaningless."

Clovis turns to her enraged, "What do you know about it?" He asks her. "You think this has been easy for me? I grew up a little boy interested in the play of one idea against the other. I studied at the same Lycee where men died, some who died for us, some who died because of us. I have killed many men; this is true, not because I was born to it, not because killing is innate within me, but because it needed to be done. We take the lives of those who would take ours. I despise such a world. I hate it. I want a world in which ideas flourish where we can debate them, talk about them over steins of beer deep into the night. I want our ideas to blend together and then take you in my arms and make love to you and not worry about the next batch of soldiers who will break into our bedroom and threaten our lives. But this is not possible. You have to evolve into the killer you never thought you would be. I did. Painful growth. It's difficult to justify, for in today's philosophy, the philosophy of torture, mayhem, occupation, one dies a little every day. But you also know my creed: we offer our lives in a meaningful quest. Not random, our lives are not given easily. The quest must be truly valuable. This is what living is about these days in wartime. It is finding the right reason to die."

"I despise this idea," Simone retorts. "Living is what matters, never seeking its end. Death can never be permitted to intervene until it's nature's time to take us. To die for a cause is grand, but how meaningful is this or any other death once we have settled in the tomb? Does it matter then that we perished for France or for America? It matters only for those who remain. Life, only life matters. So, to take another's last breath is much like abandoning my own."

Clovis puts his arm around her, but she moves away. "And love? Does love matter so little?"

Perturbed, Simone's words are issued in a tremolo.

"I can't give myself entirely to someone who cares so little about living."

"You misunderstand me," Clovis says almost casually, "But only time may enable you to see me as I am."

"So, what are we about to do, then?" she asks hopelessly.

"We're going our separate ways," he replies with a steady voice. "I am accompanying the Spanish fighters to

Paris and intend to work with them there. You will guide my parents to Nice where we have a cousin who will welcome you to her apartment. It once belonged to her and her husband. She owned it after their divorce. Once I am free to come to Nice, I will do so, but this may take time. I don't know what we will face once we arrive in Paris. On the other hand, for the time being, Nice is occupied only by Italian soldiers. This means that very little danger exists for you or for my parents. Nonetheless, my cousin understands that we need to hide Jean-Luc and, especially, Odile, in her apartment because she is Jewish, that for the two of them there may be restrictions as to their movements about town. But you will be able to assess the dangers better once you have spoken to our cousin, Kitty. She will be waiting for you."

That evening, in their bedroom, no words are shared between Clovis and Simone. In the depth of her being, she has not lost love for this man, but the ease with which he is able to dismiss life stands immutably in the path of her feelings. As for Clovis, he tries to put Simone out of his mind. More important issues await: how to move a band of some half dozen men to Paris with no papers. He will return to his feelings for Simone once he has achieved this task, he says to himself. He looks at her face which is squarely on the pillow, her eyes open. Breathing is shallow. He waits for her touch, a word, but she is withdrawn, the chrysalis adamant in her silence, in her thoughts.

"I would give you a pistol," Clovis says to her before leaving early in the morning, "If I thought you would actually use it."

She responds to these words scornfully.

"Don't underestimate me," she snaps. "I will take the pistol gratefully and, trust me; I will use it if I have to, but only under that circumstance."

Clovis is embracing Tatie Rite at the door.

"Don't be foolhardy," his aunt cautions him. "Try to save yourself for the family that loves you."

"I will save myself for you," he responds with a smile, kissing her on the cheek.

His parents watch him descend the hill trailed by a half dozen men.

"My God," Odile cries, breathing heavily. "Will he survive this trip?"

"The boy is a magician," Jean-Luc says consoling her. "A wisp of air. You cannot capture such a thing."

Now Pierrot brings the truck by and they climb in.

"God be with you," Tatie Rite says to Simone, Jean-Luc and Odile. She touches Simone's cheek with her hand.

"German soldiers will come to the village," Jean-Luc responds, lighting a cigarette. "Tell them nothing. Nothing about the soldiers who were here. Will you lie to save yourself and others in the village?"

"Who do you think you're talking to?" she spouts at Jean-Luc. "There were no German soldiers in this village....ever."

Within the hour, they find themselves in the rickety train that proceeds southward at a snail's pace along uneven tracks. Benches are hard. The smell of live fowl wafts through the wagon. Someone has brought four caged hens with him. No one dares open the window due to the onslaught of black smoke that would cover everyone and everything preventing normal breathing. It's sweltering in the compartment. After a time, Jean-Luc and Odile nod off. Simone is watching them, envious of their bond. They have been together for forty years. Not that they don't have a cross word now and then. Not that they don't explode in protest or disgust at something the other has said or done. But these disagreements last a minute, an hour, and never more than a day. Their bond is so powerful that it overcomes the disarray even of war. But if she were to ask Odile about the arguments, Odile would respond gently that this is a part, perhaps a necessary part, of two people living intimately as lovers and friends. Nobody is immune to opposition.

In a while, Simone nods off, but is snapped out of her doze by her vision of the boy she has killed a few days ago, his face rising into consciousness, his eyes visibly brown with a green tint looking upwards beseechingly as if Simone could arrest the death she is delivering, for in fact, this is hardly more than a child. He has not lived intimately with a woman or fulfilled his promise in life other than in his soldiering. Never to father a child or to attend to his ailing mother, Simone thinks. And so much else. She has taken all of that from him by the deftness of her blade slashing the boy's artery. She cannot put his face aside. The eyes! The blood! The vacuum of sound as the boy descended into the last instants of life and into the throes of death.

In a moment, she forces herself out this. Quaking, she banishes his image from her thoughts and settles on the comforting one of Clovis. In her mind, she is looking at her lover's ringlets, the curls that surround the boy's head, the lips pursed as he studies Schopenhauer, the intensity of his gaze as he speaks about the resistance, about Combat and Camus. And still, there has now developed a league of distance between them, for Clovis is all consumed with the horror of war, has abandoned the brilliance of living. The boy cannot eat anymore, cannot breathe, and cannot conjecture without deliberating the necessity of armed combat. Her last sight of him: checking his pistol, shepherding his Spanish men to fight to the death against the Nazis. Despite her approval of his commitment, she finds his total attention to his goal overwhelming, it dominates the life force she feels within her, that energy she has seen in the Nazis boys she has snuffed out. Can they overcome this barrier? Doubtful, she believes. This is fundamental. Sure, Clovis is ready to connect permanently, but can she, Simone, overcome the brutal philosophic distance between herself and this man whom she loves? Perhaps once the war is over they can try to reconnect in peace, meet in some garden looking over their shoulders at flowers, a fountain, a cinder path with children running. Perhaps.

The trip to Nice proves virtually uneventful. German troops occupy the north of the country leaving Vichy police to maintain order southward. In Nice, the Axis allies, the Italians are supposed to continue the work of the Germans. They seem, however, to have forgotten their duties. They do not turn in Jews, nor arrest them, nor send them to concentration camps for extermination. They don't even look for them. As a result, no French resistance is mounted against them. Many Italian soldiers have relatives on the French side of the border. Weekend afternoons and evenings are spent en famille eating and drinking. Italians in the north of their country have access to certain foods unavailable to the French which they bring over and share with friends. Smuggling abounds. When smugglers are caught, however infrequently, they are adept at bribing the police or the judges to gain their release. They share ill-gotten goods willingly. In the meanwhile, the German high command, hearing of questionable camaraderie, is becoming increasingly anxious with regards to the lack of military disciple on the Riviera.

At the station in Nice, after an arduous, waterless voyage, hungry and exhausted, the trio are met by Kitty Panousse. Kitty is a cousin to Odile, some twenty years Odile's junior. Kitty was married to Philippe Panousse, the manager of an electric power station in Beaune. They had children together. They were once happy together. But Philippe's mother, Marie-Anne, never accepted her daughter-in-law, even when she delivered two precious grandchildren. Over a period of years, she concocted suspicions and concerns, insisted on injecting her criticisms into her son's marriage until he relented and sued for divorce. Kitty could not look after the children. She had little money of her own. Philippe refused to pay child support. Instead, after a lengthy consultation with her son, Marie-Anne would act as a surrogate mother to raise the children. One the divorce was finalised, Kitty marched her children to the shed outside their home, her arms around their shoulders. She hugged and kissed each of them and told them to be kind to everyone, and above all to remember their manners. Then she turned, picked up a rather skimpy suitcase, and hiked the half mile to the bus station to undertake the next chapter in her life.

Kitty had been raised as a linguist. Of course, she spoke French, but her mother was German. A German who never truly accepted her French adopted land and always preferred to speak her native tongue. As a result, Kitty learned German and spoke it fluently. Her grand-father born in Lucca, preferred to speak to her in Italian and, over the years, this language also became ingrained. Finally, in school, she learned passable English. There were two reasons to go to Nice. First of all, the apartment that she and her ex had bought together on the Marechal Joffre and which he relinquished to her as part of the divorce. Secondly, there were always many foreigners in the south of France, to visit this spectacular jewel of a city on the Mediterranean, and somehow Kitty with her four languages, would make her way among them. She quickly found a job working as a tour guide on the tour bus that took either the road to Menton, Monte Carlo and Ventimiglia, or the road to Vence, Antibes and Cannes. Before the war, her company's busses were full of tourists, Germans, French, Brits, Americans, Italians who came for the warm winters and the tepid waters of Nice. Once the war began, German soldiers on leave, and many Italians crossing the nearby border took their place.

At the train station, Kitty lifts Simone's suitcase despite Simone's protestations.

"I'm used to carrying suitcases," Kitty says with a smile.

They board a bus which takes them along the Promenade des Anglais, the walkway that borders the Mediterranean. To their left, hotels flanked by palm trees. It is a warm, but not hot, day in Nice. As the bus rolls along, they can make out swimmers on the beach. Several German soldiers who have doffed their suits are swimming in skivvies in the water, cavorting with a beach ball. A female admirer is standing on the shore whistling at them.

"Don't they know a war is going on?" Odile asks, amazed at the sight.

"Playtime away from the front," Jean-Luc advises.

"It just looks so trivial with so many on both sides hurt and dying every day."

"Nobody cares here," Kitty responds. "They come here to forget the trenches, the blood, the planes, the machine guns. Leave everything behind for a few days."

Off the bus, they still have a quarter mile hike up the hill to the apartment. It is a building constructed in the 20s. The front has art deco motifs sculpted into marble adornments, the figure of a silver half-clad sea nymph above the front door.

"My apartment is on the third floor," Kitty says. "But we do have an elevator and when there is electricity it works."

"Why wouldn't you have electricity?" Simone asks.

Kitty shrugs. "I think it is simply a reminder to us of the lack everyone is experiencing throughout France. There is no good mechanical reason for it. My ex says that the Italians who are running the plants have no idea how to make repairs. When power is short they call him or one of his colleagues to learn how to fix it."

The apartment is large by French standards: three bedrooms, one and a half baths. It has a balcony that looks out over the avenue Marechal Joffre. From the balcony, they can look down on a tobacconist shop, a small convenience store with crates of fruit crowding its outside.

Odile shakes her head. "My God," she laughs, "This is paradise."

Kitty laughs. "Not quite. While you are with me," she says addressing her words to everyone, "You must stay inside at all times. If you were caught outside, even the Italians might detain you. It's too risky to take a chance."

"But this beautiful weather will go to waste…" Simone says, brooding.

"Afraid so," Kitty responds. "But if you are caught, then I may be as well. Harbouring fugitives, harbouring a Jew," she adds," Is an act of treason. I would be sent to jail or to a camp."

"Then we will be good children and do as we're told," Jean-Luc says with a smile. He and Odile find comfort in their room. It is rather large with two windows offering a morning breeze overlooking a garden to the back of the building.

"Now that we are settled in here," Odile says to her husband, "We need to have a chat."

Jean-Luc recognises the tone, settles back into a chair, and lights up a cigarette. "You do know that it is entirely possible for us to be discovered, captured," Odile begins.

"Yes."

"And even possible for us to be caught separately," Odile continues.

He smiles. "Not likely. We are always together."

"Life likes to throw the dice at our certainties," she says. "In case you hadn't noticed."

"Go on."

"Let's agree on a convention If either of us is caught, we will say to our captor that we just came into town that very day, that we know nobody in Nice or even in the area."

"Ok," he agrees.

"Be more assertive about this," Odile says. "Because if one is caught, the other may not be far behind, and then our stories have to match. Otherwise, if one tells one tale, and the other another story, we may put Kitty and Simone into jeopardy."

"You are right, of course."

"So, you will remember our agreement?"

"Perfectly," he says, "But I do believe that we will always be together."

Simone's room is smaller but well decorated. There are paintings on the walls of various exotic birds, none of which she can identify. But she thinks them pretty. The bed is exquisite, she thinks, bouncing on it. Firm but not rigid. I will sleep well on this. Her window also looks out to the rear of the garden, but she can also make out a section of road to the right. Delivery trucks pass by noisily, stretching their gears as they climb up the hill.

"The trucks stop after seven normally," Kitty says to her, as if catching her thought. "The town is generally noise free as long as you are not on the Promenade, the main avenue to Cannes and other towns. The avenue can be quite turbulent. Also, drunks abound on the Promenade at night. Mainly soldiers on leave. They too have nothing pleasant to add to the atmosphere."

Later, Kitty shows them the kitchen. "We should take turns cooking," she suggests. "If you tell me what you plan to make, I can usually obtain the ingredients. We all need to chip in to make this work," she adds.

She is an energetic forty-year-old woman with blondish hair veering on the brown. A pretty face. Except for her lips, which tend to meet into something like a pout. When her face is in repose, it can be quite striking.

"I have heard about Kitty's adventures," Odile says, looking at her husband. "We both have. Not from Tatie Rite who would be too gentile to mention it, but Jeanne told us stories one afternoon. She claims her sources are reliable. Quite reliable."

The following morning after breakfast, Kitty leaves for work. Simone is in the kitchen cleaning dishes while Odile is drying them.

"Tell me about her adventures," Simone asks Odile.

Odile has been waiting for this request. She continues drying as she speaks:

"I think you know that Kitty came here after her husband divorced her. For almost twenty years, she had been living intimately with a man and then, quite suddenly, she found herself alone. Unattached until she started work on the tour bus. The driver, a man named Antoine, some fifteen years her senior, had been driving for the company a good part of his life. Married he was, with five or six children. His hobbies included working on the bus, keeping it running in tip top shape. He had always fancied himself a mechanic. The bus was already weary when Kitty began her work. After several years, it was in constant danger of breaking down. So, at every stop along the tour, Antoine would stay behind and labour over the engine, coaxing it, pleading with it to remain running throughout the tour. This went on every day. At lunch, when the bus stopped before some hotel, Antoine brought with him a baguette filed with ham and cheese, along with a bottle of red wine. He never followed the tourists into the restaurant. Couldn't afford it. One day, he invited Kitty to remain behind. He told her that he had enough of a sandwich for both of them and that while the tourists were feasting, they could also partake of lunch followed, if she wished, by a pastry from the patisserie next to the hotel restaurant.

So, they took their lunch and walked down the path along the forsythia bushes to a secluded spot and ate their lunch. No sooner was lunch over, no sooner had Antoine consumed most of the bottle of red he had brought with him, he reached over for Kitty's hand. Pulled her over to him and kissed her fully on the mouth. Kitty, who had been untouched by any man for quite some time, became like a jade autumn leaf turned into red gold. In a word, she became inflamed. And the next thing you know, they are rolling down the hill entwined as lovers. Kitty knew of course that Antoine was married. She had seen pictures of his brood in his wallet. But this did not impede her for a moment. Having sex with Antoine felt good. Furthermore, it felt right, and so most days thereafter, when the bus stopped, the two of them would take a half hour to secrete themselves in an isolated spot, strip themselves naked or nearly so, and make love. As far as I know, this pattern continues to this day."

"And Kitty never asked Antoine why a married man was doing this?"

"She's afraid to pursue the issue, I think. She may have expressed a little surprise about it at first, but Antoine just shrugged it off. After all, my dear Simone, we are not in a puritanical country. We're in France, where many men have a mistress.

"I wonder whether she would take me on one of her tours."

"Ask her," Odile responds. "But undoubtedly she would not want to take the chance."

In fact, Odile refuses to do so, concerned as she is by the possibility, however slim, that someone may uncover Simone's identity.

In this fashion, months pass. In Simone's mind, she is certain that Captain Anselm has by now clearly grasped the fact of her treachery and is doing everything in his power to find her. Careful as she has been, she told nobody in Arette where she and Clovis's parents were going. Clearly, she imagines, Anselm would send a contingent of troops to Arette to find out what happened to his men.

And not finding them there, he would assume that they have been killed. And following this line of reasoning, someone in Arette would be made to pay for those murders.

In fact, Anselm has sent down a fairly large contingent of men to scour the countryside for his two lost soldiers. When Simone and Clovis weren't found nor could anyone in the village account for their disappearance, Anselm lined several civilians at random against the fronton and had his troops execute them.

Simone learned of this indirectly. Clovis had communicated with a member of the local Maquis in Nice, and had that person make a telephone call to Simone that he and his Spanish fighters had made the trip back to Paris safely, but also, to convey the news in Arette. One of the men murdered in revenge by the Nazis was Pierrot, she was told. Once she had re-established her equilibrium, she asked the man on the other end of the line to get word to Clovis that they were all safe, that all was well, and that she wished that the two of them had not had bitter words before parting. The man indicated that Clovis wished he could speak with Simone directly, but was reluctant to take the chance that the line from Paris might be compromised.

In the capitol, Captain Anselm was pleased to learn of the resolve of the Wehrmacht to take over command of the Riviera from the Italians. Ribbentrop had personally communicated to Mussolini his concern that Italian soldiers were not ferreting out Jews. Nor were they sending Jews they had identified to Drancy, the processing station in France before eventual removal to Auschwitz or some other labour camp. Furthermore, Ribbentrop had heard many stories of lax Italian leadership and command, of ribaldry, of lewd behaviour between these soldiers and

French girls. Italian soldiers were known even to dance with Jewish girls at local celebrations. This was simply too much for Ribbentrop. This was no way to promote the final solution of the Jewish question. As a result, as the war began to turn against the Nazis, he sent down troops to Cannes and Nice to take over the region from the Italians. It was said that many Italian soldiers slunk back to Italy wearing women's clothing so that they would not be seen scurrying away from the country which they had agreed to govern. One of the soldiers in Paris who requested and received permission to transfer to Nice was Captain Anselm.

As these measures are being contemplated, Simone could no longer stand confinement. She determines one fine morning to leave the apartment and take a walk along the Promenade. Nothing said to her by either Odile or Jean-Luc could deter her. Kitty had already left for work when Simone opens the door to the apartment and quietly descends the stairs on tiptoes. The massive glass door of the entrance swings open and suddenly the rush of morning air strikes her in the face. Stunned, she is breathing air, fresh air. The Nice sun is bathing her with radiance. Simone starts down the street, down the hill. When she strides by the Hotel Negresco, perhaps the most famous hotel of the region, she sees no Italian soldiers. She walks by the front door, which opens as several women exit accompanied by a man in a fine leather coat, an unlit cigar in his mouth. Across the street is the Promenade, and farther beyond the beach in that direction, the waters of the Mediterranean. There is a bench directly in front of the water. She sits. Simone has left the remains of a baguette on the bench next to her. Looking out upon distant ships curling up smoke as they ply through the Mediterranean, she cannot tell whether these ships are warships or perhaps freighters. Flocks of seagulls shriek in the air as they swoop down upon the sands. As she holds up a piece of the baguette, a gull swoops down and takes it from her fingers with his beak. Others follow in a consistent parade until the baguette has been whittled down. Then they stop their cries and settle into the sand. Curiously, they all face in the same direction. The air is still cool as the morning wears on. She lapses into a kind of dream state; her face warmed by the sun and wishes she had sunglasses. She remembers Clovis holding her face under a tree in the hills above Arette, and how warm were his fingers. A piece of mint under his nose. The man's face, smiling and tender, waxes and wanes in her memory. She wonders whether she has been a fool.

A man walks by, looks out of the corner of his eye, and settles in next to her. He engages her in conversation, wondering whether she has today's newspaper, Nice Matin. She does not. He is a young man with a trench coat, too warm for the day. Gray fleecing his blond hair. His nose is short, nostrils widening when he speaks. Unbuttoning the coat, he reveals a jacket worn by German soldiers. His French is amazingly fluent. He says he learned it in school. Now he is sitting closer, pressing against her. She is not wearing make-up. She wonders why anyone would want to be close to her. She is not yet frightened by the situation. Just another man, she thinks, among the many she has had to handle in time.

"Let's have lunch," he says, smiling at her. "There is a hotel nearby which has quite a lovely menu," he continues. My name is Ardal."

"I'm sorry," she says, her eyes straight ahead. "I have another appointment."

"Perhaps afterwards…perhaps for dinner," he continues.

"I am married," she says.

"But I don't see your ring."

"I left it at home because I have swelling in my fingers," she continues somewhat awkwardly. "It's the time of month for me."

"I'm just looking for some company," the man protests. "Je me sens tout seul."

"Sorry that you are feeling alone. I imagine that many soldiers on leave are without companionship. But I'm afraid I cannot help you."

"Pity," he remarks.

Simone arises. He takes her arm. His hand is firm.

"You're hurting me," she complains.

But he does not relax his grip. "There are thousands of you sluts in Nice these days," he says with a smirk. "Thousands of Jews. You have been able to evade our justice," he continues. "But the least you can do for a German soldier is to make his time here more agreeable. What am I asking for? Just a moment for two in an alleyway, just the two of us. I think you would like it," he goes on.

She turns her face away. "Look at me, you tramp," he says loudly. Pedestrians walking by are staring at them. "More of your kind," he indicates with a wave of his hand. "But you are a different little girl. Prettier than the others. I could make your life a bit easier here while I'm on leave."

"Let me go."

"I don't think so," Ardal retorts. "I really don't think so. We are going arm in arm to the alley behind the Negresco across the street. And there, I am going to lower your panties and for once, my little Jewess, you are going to feel the might of the German Army bulldoze your body." Roughly, he seizes her and pushes her across the street.

Simone has stopped thinking. She reacts exactly as she was trained, with calm. She is looking at the brutal eyes of the soldier, eyes that are dilating with confidence and desire. Breathing forcefully, unevenly. When they reach the alleyway, as he bends down to reach under her skirt for her panties, she drives her left knee hard into his face. Stunned, falling backwards, conscious, but in pain, blood streaming from one nostril, she is upon him. She remembers in fine detail where to thrust the middle finger of her left hand with its curved, pink nail. She drives it just below his Adam's apple into the soft spot of his neck where there is no resistance. Ardal's eyes are clouding over. Blood is spurting from his neck like a fountain. Unable to speak, his breathing has been arrested. For an instant, she stands over him, waiting for his life force to evanesce. It is as if she perceived a fog seeping from his body into the ether.

"Isn't this the fuck of a lifetime?" she derides him, as he falls first on one knee, his head striking into the concrete. Immediately, she hikes her clothing, quits the alleyway, moving swiftly but without panic back along the Promenade and turns towards her apartment.

"So how was your outing? "Jean-Luc asks her, as he lights a Gitane.

"Uneventful," she answers. "Just a short walk along the sea."

17. September 1943

Frustrated with the lack of control by the Italian Army in the Riviera, the German Army decides to take over. They send down several battalions of soldiers. The Italian Army retreats under cover of night and, it is said, in women's clothing to spare themselves the embarrassment of retreat. Many Frenchmen and women are truly disappointed, even sad to see them go. As an occupying army, they have been more friend than foe.

The Germans immediately send a clear and resounding message to the Cote d'Azur. In bright daylight in the middle of the principal square, Place Massena, they hang two civilians for all to see, and leave the corpses swaying in the Mediterranean breeze for several days. Days and nights of relative safety have ended. The Jewish population, once numbering some thirty thousand on the Riviera virtually disappears overnight. Some are trapped by Nazi patrols and shipped by rail to Drancy from where they will be herded into cattle cars to concentration camps. Others scurry into Italy, while others attempt to pass the Spanish frontier. Anything to flee occupied France.

Almost simultaneously, the food situation becomes fragile and, within a few months, dire. Foodstuffs are seized and sent to the front lines. Little is left for towns like Nice.

The German high command appropriates several hotels, the most famous the luxury hotel, Le Negresco. The hotel provides lodgings for highly placed officers. But rooms once meant for meetings and conferences are transformed into torture chambers. Anselm, now a Major, moves into a suite overlooking the Mediterranean. The once teeming Promenade des Anglais is mainly vacant save for German soldiers, a few delivery trucks and vans, and seagulls.

Only the deep blue light of the sky remains unchanged, unfazed by the events below. The beauty of the setting, the Alps on one side, the Mediterranean Sea on the other, its warmth, and brilliant sky makes the arrival of the Nazis even more appalling.

Anselm and the SS fuehrer Hausser are dining on a lunch of quail, rice and squash. Two bottles of the finest French wine grace the table. The restaurant is virtually empty. It is now reserved only for the highest placed officers of the Wehrmacht. The army will make certain that the Negresco does not run out of food.

"So, you believe that your friend, Dawn, has made her way down here," Hausser says, wiping his mouth.

"That is the rumour," Anselm replies. "We caught several of the new recruits, a couple of Spaniards recently arrived in Paris, and they had heard this. Of course, they did not reveal this information at once. We had to ply them with appropriate inducements."

"I am aware that your inducements can be quite effective," Hausser chuckles. "This white Beaujolais is quite excellent," he adds.

"She will reveal herself eventually," Anselm says. "I am confident of it, and when she does, we will have her."

"To do what with?"

"First of all, she has quite a bit of information which will be useful," Anselm says, his lips narrowing inwards, "And I believe I know the proper method to draw this out of her."

"You would like to kill the bitch," Hausser laughs.

Anselm covers his mouth as he begins to yawn. "I don't appreciate her form of betrayal," he says. "Yes, I will kill her, but only very slowly. I want to see her torn to pieces bit by bit before she dies."

"Let's drink to it," Hausser laughs, raising his glass.

In the apartment, Kitty lets it be known that she is worried.

"I count on this job," she says. "Now that the Germans are here as an occupying army, I don't know how well we will be able to continue. I myself have Jewish roots. Well-hidden roots, since my husband is Catholic, and my parents are as well. But if they dig deeply enough, they will find that my grandparents were Jewish. It is enough for them. And if I go, they will find everyone in the apartment as well. On the other hand, the war is beginning to go badly for them and they may be consumed with their losses. At least for a time, as they settle in to Nice and along the Mediterranean, we are probably safe."

Jean-Luc and Odile have become concerned about Simone. Their worry stems from the bitter parting with Clovis, which has settled her into a state of gloom. Clearly, she is in love with the man, but she rarely hears from him. Simone believes he has lost all feeling for her after their argument and separation. Something else is pestering her, but she will not reveal it. They think it is her isolation in an apartment day after day, month after month.

"It is wearing on all of us," Jean-Luc says to Odile, "But it must be all the more difficult for a young woman like Simone." In fact, Simone is mentally replaying the murder of the young German soldier on the Promenade. At the time she killed him, it seemed like a reflex action for her. A form of self-defense. That made it different from other killings. And yet, she shudders as, involuntarily, she revisits in grim detail every fibre of her body moving in deadly fashion against the man. She recalls how her finger targeted the man's neck, how he attempted to fight back while blood gushed from him, Simone jumping backwards to avoid the tide, and how in less than a minute, his life force ebbed, and he slumped onto the concrete ground. Unavoidable, she convinces herself. And yet she wonders whether she should not have handled this situation differently. Still, he was not just some persistent suitor, she argues to herself. He was the enemy. Nonetheless, the event remains a fresh and daily irritation preying heavily on her mind.

Several weeks pass. One day, while Kitty is out working, a knock on the door. Nobody will answer it. They all freeze in their tracks. Quiet. Breathing subsides. Simone ventures to the window, carefully pulling back a slip of cloth so that she can see the front door. There's a man knocking on the front door. She recognises him as one of the Spaniards she met in Arette. She opens the door.

The man has been wounded, shot in the arm.

"A roadblock I tumbled into," he says to her. "I started to run, and somebody fired. I made my way through the woods." He pauses. "I was asked to come here to deliver a message." He has badly applied a compress to the wound, and it is still bleeding. Odile staunches the wound

"Later," she says, "We need to extract the bullet from your arm."

"I am so looking forward to this," the man replies with the slip of a grin.

Just then, Kitty opens the door. When she sees the Spaniard, she becomes extremely nervous.

"You are going to get us all killed," she says to them all. "A resistance fighter we are harbouring who has been wounded by the Germans! A recipe for a catastrophe," she adds. But she is the one with the most medical experience, and she extracts the bullet with a pair of kitchen forceps.

"At least he didn't scream to the sky," Kitty remarks admiringly, dropping the bullet into a waste paper basket. After a moment, she reaches into the basket, picks up the bullet and slides it into a pocket. "I better get rid of this elsewhere."

But now she wants to know what Simone intends to do with the Spaniard. His name is Raul, she learns. He does speak French with a Spanish accent. Just passable French, but when he cannot make himself understood he lapses into Spanish which Jean-Luc understands fairly well.

"He was sent here by our son," Jean-Luc says. "He needs Simone to go with him to Menton on the coast and deliver a message to a professor there."

"Impossible," Kitty cries out. "The roads now are speckled with Nazis just waiting to net our Simone and, wouldn't it be wonderful for them, if they also caught a Maquisard?"

"There must be ways to get around the road blocks," Simone says.

"Perhaps," Kitty says, calming somewhat, "But I would not advise it. You would have to walk along one of the corniches, and you could not use a car, if that is what you were thinking. A distance of some twenty miles. Everything and everyone is subject to being stopped, to being interrogated. We have done so well for so long here. I hate to think what could happen if either or both of you are caught. To make matters worse, nothing prevents the

Nazis from a house to house search for a wounded man. If they come here, I have no way of hiding everyone."

"How important is what you have been asked to do?" Odile asks Raul.

"I have memorised a formula. It is for a rocket which the Germans are perfecting. The professor can code the formula and send it off to London."

"A rocket!" Kitty sniffs.

"You know the Germans have been bombarding England night after night. This new rocket can be sent over the English Channel. No pilot is needed. Much deadlier. The formula I am to transmit has to do with the accuracy of the rocket."

"I just don't want to be involved," Kitty retorts.

"But we have to do this," Simone responds quietly. "How quickly must it be done?"

"In the next week," Raul says.

"Tell us about Clovis. How is he? What is he doing?"

Raul smiles. He is a swarthy man in his late forties with an abundant nose and red, puffy cheeks.

"Clovis is in good health. He sends his love to everyone. The resistance is ten times greater than before, and he is one of the leaders. Every night they meet to make plans. The Nazis are scouring the city looking for him. But a smart boy, he never spends more than one night in any location. He is truly a needle in a haystack."

"Did he give you a personal message for me?" Simone asks.

"No," Raul responds. "Only to send his love to everyone."

Kitty is rethinking her earlier objection.

"I think I may have a way for you to get to Menton. Not that I like any of this. It is dangerous. The best way for you to go to Menton is as a tourist on my bus. The bus itself is known to everyone and has only been stopped once or twice. You have a decent chance of making it. Menton is one of our stops, just before the Italian frontier."

"But you would be taking a hell of a chance," Jean-Luc remarks, if the bus is stopped."

"I don't think so," Kitty smiles. "I would simply say I don't know these tourists. They paid me and got on the bus. I'm not saying I like any of this. But chances of surviving are probably better on my bus than on foot. At least for me. Am I being selfish?"

"We all need to look out for ourselves," Odile answers.

Kitty examines the address off the rue Pasteur and says the bus will stop nearby.

The following morning, Raul and Simone walk with Kitty down to the Place Massena. Antoine, the bus driver, is waiting for them. He kisses Kitty on the cheek but asks no questions about the others. They board the bus.

"We wait for another ten minutes," Kitty says.

Twelve other passengers board the bus. They are all male. They appear to be German soldiers on leave, perhaps a tourist or two from Italy. Kitty welcomes them in French, asks whether other languages are required. One of the males raises his hand and says he prefers German. From then on, Kitty divides her description of the tour between two languages. She stands just behind the bus driver's post and fields questions from the tourists, a small microphone in her hand. The bus sets out, passing Villefranche-sur-Mer, then on to Beaulieu, Cap d'Ail, and stopping at Monte Carlo where everyone gets out briefly to stretch their legs and to examine the entrance to the famous Casino at a short distance. After a rest stop, they continue. They drive directly to Menton. The plan there is for Kitty to lead the tourists through the commercial part of the town for perhaps a half hour's walk, and then to stop for lunch at a restaurant near the train station.

While the others are following the guided tour through the streets of town, Simone and Raul head for the rue Pasteur. They easily find the correct address, a small villa with a metal gate entrance. A bell. A curtain opens inside the villa then slides slowly. In a moment, an aproned woman with her hair in a bun comes out quickly and opens the gate.

"Suivez-moi," she says. "Follow me."

They are led into a salon replete with damask coverings, seventeenth and eighteenth-century furnishings. The walls are layered with books dating from the sixteenth and seventeenth centuries. A massive gilded, walnut desk squats in the middle of the room, and behind the desk framing a large plate glass window onto a garden, sits a gentleman. He rises as they enter.

"I have been waiting for you," he says. "My name is Frederic Pornant…but you must already know this." He bids them sit in leather chairs before the desk.

"We don't have a great deal of time," Raul begins. "I have some information I have been asked to transmit to you."

"You have written it down?"

Raul smiles. "No, sir. I have memorised it."

"Then speak the information and I will transcribe it," Pornant replies taking out a pen as well as a blotter from the middle drawer. He dips the pen into an inkstand.

Raul tells him the formula.

"And what is the formula for?" Pornant says, raising his head.

"Surely, you must know what use this formula has."

"Of course," Pornant responds with a stammer in his voice. "But I needed to understand if there was additional information you were transmitting."

"None," Raul says.

Simone is looking at Raul piercingly now.

"Repeat the formula once more. Just as a guarantee I have written it down correctly."

Raul repeats the formula.

Pornant lays down his pen and opens another drawer in his desk.

"I have something for you in return," he says.

From the drawer, he pulls out a Luger and points it at them. Simone and Raul jump up. He tells them to sit.

"I'm afraid I have not been entirely forthcoming," Pornant clucks. "My real name is Wisscher, Lieutenant Wisscher of the SS. Professor Pornant was arrested three days ago and, under a bit of persuasion, indicated that he was expecting the visit of a Simone Valois, known to us simply as Dawn. We are so pleased to welcome you, Mademoiselle. The only one missing from your coven is Clovis, but I am certain you will tell us his whereabouts in the next day or so. In the meanwhile, I trust you will appreciate our accommodations. Now get up and turn around."

He searches each of them. Simone has carried with her a pistol which he seizes.

"Late model," he says admiringly. "I did not know these were available yet." His search of Raul finds nothing.

"We are going to take a little walk," he says to them, "Down the street to the headquarters of the German command. It's only five minutes away. They will be so delighted to welcome you. By the way, the formula you have given me is used for what?"

"Didn't Professor Pornant tell you that?"

"Not yet," Wisscher admits. "You can save some of his skin if you were to tell us about it now."

Raul laughs, his jowls shaking up and down.

"Hmm," Pornant says. "I never permitted you to laugh. I don't like it. Now walk directly out of the gate you entered and turn right."

As they enter the garden, Simone and Raul precede Wisscher who has now replaced the gun into his pocket. As they reach the gate, Raul trips and falls. Wisscher looks down in the same moment as he extracts his pistol. In this instant, Simone reaches Wisscher, pulls him forward over Raul's body. In one movement they have seized his gun.

"Kill him," Raul says. "Kill this bastard."

Simone lifts the pistol, and cracks Wisscher's head with the butt.

"We need to get out of here," she says, breathing hard. "If we hurry we can rejoin the bus at the train station."

"Just as soon as I find the formula our German friends has written down." Once located, Raul tears it into small pieces and then swallows each one quickly. "Not very tasty," he remarks.

"What do we do with the woman who let us in?"

"We don't have time to find her," Raul says. "On to the bus."

Kitty has been holding the bus.

"We had a quick lunch," she says. "Antoine has to get home. He has a sick boy. Measles he thinks."

"Sorry we are late. We were walking around the town on our own."

"No matter. You are here now, she responds with relief showing on her face." And with that, they enter the bus and begin its return journey to Nice.

Later, Simone says to Raul. "They know now that I am on the Riviera. Not good for any of us, I'm afraid. You need to return to Paris and inform Clovis exactly what has happened."

"I will leave early in the morning," Raul answers, "But one thing which disturbs me. You should have killed the imposter. Instead, you knocked him out. I'm surprised, that's all."

Simone shrugs. "It was enough."

"It was shoddy," Raul replies. "If he awakened while we were escaping, he could perhaps have alerted other troops."

"I'm afraid I have to agree with Raul," Kitty remarks.

"He did not awaken. I made sure of that," Simone responds.

"You should have killed him. You took a chance not only with your life but with mine. He now knows that you, Simone, are in the area. You have put this entire family and yourself in jeopardy. Unacceptable!" Raul repeats, shaking his head.

"This is unlike you," Jean-Luc says looking at her not without sympathy.

"I can no longer just kill like that," Simone admits, her voice frail. "The killing must stop."

"It's the fucking Germans who have to stop," Raul cries out. "Don't you see that?"

"I did what I thought was right," Simone replies.

"I will report this failing to Clovis, you understand."

"Yes," Simone replies through closed teeth. "I understand he will be disappointed. He is someone like you who can kill at a moment's notice and not give it another thought."

"That's unfair," Raul remarks, his eyes wide open. "Totally unfair. You seem to have forgotten that we are in the middle of a war!"

In the early hours, before morning has unfurled, lampposts still flickering with the remnant of night, Raul leaves for Paris.

18. Jean-Luc Wants a Smoke

Several months pass. The situation on the coast has deteriorated further. Food is even harder to negotiate. Fortunately, Kitty has contacts in Italy, and they provide her with provisions when her bus enters Ventimiglia crossing the Italian border.

One day, while Kitty is out, the phone rings. Unusual for the phone to ring during the day, Simone thinks. Sometimes she can hear the phone at night, but it is usually Antoine conferring with Kitty either about the bus schedule or about their relationship.

"Pick it up," Jean-Luc urges.

"Allo!" she says into the receiver.

"Simone," the voice responds softly. "This is Clovis."

Simone is defensive at once, "You are crazy to risk calling. You don't know how advanced the German's listening devices may be."

"I had to take the chance," Clovis replies. His voice continues soft, caring. "I needed to know how you are. Raul told me about the episode with the Professor."

"Don't be angry with me," Simone pleads. "I did what I could do."

"But Raul was right," Clovis says, his voice still in a soothing tone. "You could have jeopardised everyone's life."

"Yes," she admits. "I'm sorry about it."

"Look," he continues. "I'm so sorry that we had a disagreement. It is true that we view some things differently. But don't we basically look at life the same? We both want to live, and I for one, want desperately to be with you once this is over."

"I want that too," Simone says. She begins to sob.

Silence.

"I hoped my call would create a happier effect," Clovis remarks after a pause.

"Sorry," Simone says. "I thought our bridges were completely destroyed. But I love you, and I know it is right for us to be together."

"I needed to hear you say that," Clovis remarks. "How are you holding up in that apartment every day?"

She has a short laugh. "We hate it. We are so needy to breathe in fresh air, especially your mother and father, but they have restrained themselves. They're better than I have been."

She has decided long ago not to tell Clovis or, for that matter anybody else, about her encounter with the German soldier on the Promenade.

"But we hear that the war is turning against the Germans, and we hope our prison will release us very, very soon."

"Be careful," Clovis says. "Have to hang up now. I love you. Tell my parents I think of them often."

"I love you," she answers. The line clicks off. Sits by the phone quietly, the receiver against her ear, eyes moist, but her soul revived. She feels as if she can withstand anything as long as Clovis has life, substance, hope. She turns to Jean-Luc and Odile.

"He sends his love," she says. "He sounds good."

"Did he say what he was doing? When we might see him?"

"No," she says. "But the war seems finally to be heading in the right direction."

Jean-Luc pours himself a drink of vodka.

"Perhaps," he reminds them, "But not down here. The thousands of Jews who walked the streets of Nice and Cannes have disappeared, seized by the Germans. Sent to labour in Poland and elsewhere we hear. We also hear that these are extermination camps, their sole purpose to murder as many Jews as possible in the shortest amount of time. I look out my window each morning and orthodox Jews who used to stroll down the Promenade reading from the Talmud have disappeared. So, if the war is advancing in our favour, it cannot happen quickly enough."

Three weeks pass. One morning, Jean-Luc awakens and reaches over to the nightstand for his pack of Gitanes. The pack is empty. When he arises, he searches where he may have laid another pack, but to his dismay, they are all gone. Kitty tells him that she will buy cigarettes for him when she goes back to Ventimiglia in three days' time. She claims that she can even buy blond tobacco, American cigarettes there. But this means that Jean-Luc will be without smokes for that entire period.

He looks out the window mid-morning, on a fresh but warming day. The flowers on the window sill are blooming and are moist with dew. He cannot remember when last, he was out of the apartment to take even a short walk. It is driving him crazy. His legs are tingling with the energy of a much younger man. He puts on a jacket and a scarf about his neck.

"I'm going to the tobacconist on the corner," he remarks casually to Odile, "To buy some Gitanes."

Odile takes his hand. "You can't live without them?"

He laughs. "You're kidding. But you know as well as I that the store is but a block and a half away. As soon as I buy a couple of packs, I will return. Look out the window," he adds. "The day is spectacular."

"Then hurry,' Odile says to him. "And if you see any candy at the tobacconist, especially chocolates, bring some back for me."

Out the front door, the sun massages him full in the face. He cannot move. The warmth of the sun has transfixed him in place. He stands there a full five minutes with the sun caressing his face. After that, he re-opens his eyes, and begins to amble down towards the Promenade. One block. Hardly a soul walking, he notices. Then the half block to the tobacco store. It is a small store with an American cigarette pack sign outside the front. Pall Mall. The store sells newspapers, candy, a few household items, but mainly tobacco. As he enters the store, he gives the French greeting to the woman behind the counter and the man in front of it.

"Bonjour, Monsieur, Dame." They respond with a perfunctory 'Bonjour'. The girl behind the counter is young, perhaps twenty years old.

"Can I help you?" she asks.

"After this gentleman," Jean-Luc responds.

"He has been helped," the young woman replies.

"Then I would like two packs of Gitanes."

The woman grimaces slightly, "I'm so sorry, sir. But we have no Gitanes left. I do have some Gauloises and some brown tobacco from Turkey."

"I'll take the Gauloises," Jean-Luc says. "I'd also like a Nice Matin, as well as some candy. Just a little assortment."

At this point, the man at the counter turns. Brown hair, soft brown eyes, lips that curl upwards. He is looking at Jean-Luc in what amounts to a stare.

Suddenly, Jean-Luc is becoming nervous, his skin crawling. The air is thickening for him. The girl is squinting behind the counter as he reaches into his pocket for money. She is handing him a package of newspaper, cigarettes, and candy when the man looks him in the eye.

"Papers," he demands.

Jean-Luc's breathing ceases. "And you are?"

"With the Wehrmacht," the man says curtly, "Papers. Now."

Jean-Luc reaches into his pocket. He has left his identification papers at the apartment. Reddens.

"I have left them," he says. "How stupid of me."

"Quite," the man replies, taking his arm. "You will come with me."

"And where are we going?" Jean-Luc asks, his mind in turmoil.

"To verify your identity," the man responds.

The man has a vehicle outside, sleek, long, and black. Jean-Luc is handcuffed to a post in the rear of the car. They drive a short distance to the Hotel Excelsior along the Promenade. For some reason, Jean-Luc is astonished that the sun continues to shine unabashedly, as if in the past half hour nothing had changed.

"But I don't need a hotel tonight," Jean-Luc jokes lamely.

"Nonetheless," the man retorts, "This will be your lodgings for the time being."

They tread through the lobby, floors of shiny, coloured porcelain in pastels. Patterns of half-moons and comets. The walls are painted in red and mauve. There's a desk, with a soldier behind it. He looks up from his book, prickly about this interruption. Nonetheless, he straightens, and salutes the man holding on to Jean-Luc's arm.

"I have a prisoner for you," the man says.

"Something new!" the soldier responds drolly. "Your name?" the soldier asks.

Jean-Luc does not answer.

"What is his offense?"

"He has no papers."

"Probably just another Jew on the run," the soldier responds casually. "Is that what you are, a Jew on the run?"

"Not at all," Jean-Luc says.

On the first floor, a room virtually empty save for a chair and manacles dropping from the ceiling.

"Sit," the man says.

Jean-Luc sits. "Listen," he says, "My name is Jean-Luc Rastine. I was a professor in Paris. I am not Jewish. I am not running. I have no reason to run."

"We can verify this," the man says. He undoes his coat, unbuttons a sweater. Then, he turns and leaves without another word locking the door behind him. Jean-Luc knows what is coming. He wishes he had a cigarette, then laughs because it was his uncontrolled hunger for a cigarette that caused him to be arrested. There is some irony in this, he chides himself. He also realises that these fleeting moments of irony, of grinning, are soon to end. If he is worried, it is because he fears that he will not be able to withstand torture and will reveal where his wife and cousin are living. Jean-Luc steels himself. A nostril is running red with a little blood. Tension, he knows.

In a half hour, the man returns. He says his name is Schtellar.

"I work with the SS," he says by way of introduction, "So we have verified this information, and apparently, you are Jean-Luc Rastine of the Sorbonne. The description given us from Paris suits you quite well. So, what are you doing here in Nice?"

"On holiday," Jean-Luc replies, shifting his feet.

"A splendid place for a holiday." Schtellar agrees. "And your wife? Is the Jewess on holiday with you in this special place?"

"My wife and I separated in Paris," Jean-Luc says.

"Oh, what a pity…a marital dispute?"

"We agreed to divorce."

"Aah," Schtellar says with a grin. "Somehow, Professor, I don't quite believe you. I think because your wife is a Jew that you are hiding her from us. Would that be a fair assessment?"

"She was picked up in Paris after I left," he retorts, "And sent to Drancy for processing."

"We can find out in a day or so whether you are telling us the truth. But if this proves to be a fabrication, then, dear Professor, your quiet dignified life may take quite a serious turn for the worse.

In Jean-Luc's mind, he needs to play for time. When Odile sees that he does not return to the apartment, she will understand what has happened to him. And if she understands the effectiveness of torture, that eventually her husband will divulge her address. As a result, she must leave. Simone must leave. And, sadly, even Kitty will have to go.

"Check it out," Jean-Luc remarks quietly. "I think you will find that I am telling the truth."

In the apartment, Odile is fidgeting with sheets.

"You have already replaced the old sheets," Simone says to her.

"Yes, of course, you are right. I'm terribly concerned," Odile responds, her hands quaking.

"Yes," Simone responds. "It has been more than an hour since he left. It does not take that long to find the tobacco store, to buy cigarettes and to return. Something has happened."

"Maybe he fell," Odile posits almost as a question.

"Maybe."

But when Kitty returns three hours later, it is clear to her that Jean-Luc has been arrested. Odile has already discovered his identity papers in his vest.

"My God," Kitty says. "This is the end of everything. Your husband has killed every one of us."

"Please," Simone responds. "Let's not bury one another before the fact. Let's say that he has been arrested. We still have enough time to decide what to do."

"There is but one thing to do," Kitty replies. "I can take the bus into Italy where I have friends who will put me up. But I dare not bring you with me. Too dangerous now," she adds. "You must find a way to escape or to locate another place to live."

"I think I may have found a way to help," Odile says quietly.

"Please," Kitty thunders, "Let's hear it."

I am going to find out where my husband is imprisoned. I intend to give myself up. If they send him away, then I want to be with him."

Kitty frowns. "The height of stupidity! They will kill you."

"Perhaps, but if so, then I will be with the man whose life I swore to share."

"You cannot do this," Simone adds. "You did not agree to share death. It is suicide."

"I prefer to think of it as devotion," Odile answers with serenity. "But once I give myself up, I will say that

Jean-Luc and I have just come down to Nice from Paris, that we knew nobody in town. In this fashion I will be able to protect the two of you."

Kitty ponders this answer. "She does have a point."

"If you consider suicide a reasonable alternative," Simone scoffs. "Provided, of course, that Jean-Luc has the same narrative."

"We agreed on this story months ago. Anyway, I have made up my mind," Odile says with steel in her voice, her hands flashing with renewed vigour. "I know that they are keeping him in one of two hotels, either the Negresco or the Excelsior. And I know where both of them are." And as she is saying these words, she dons her jacket. Embraces both Kitty and Simone with clear eyes, and leaves without another word.

"This is wrong," Simone says forcefully to Kitty.

"Yes, I know, but it is her husband's mistake that put us all in jeopardy. Look," Kitty adds. "I am going to follow her and see where she ends up. I can walk the streets without problem. Wait for me here." And with that, Kitty descends the stairs to the street, spies Odile walking steadily if slowly down towards the Negresco. At the entrance to the hotel, she sees Odile converse with a guard who tells her to address the man at the reception. In a moment, Odile exits the hotel, and moves in her determined, if dawdling, walk towards the Excelsior.

At the entrance to the hotel, she addresses an armed guard. He responds animatedly. Kitty watches intently from her perch some fifty yards away. Odile lifts up both her arms for the guard to search her. After a time, she lowers her arms, then puts them behind her back. The guard snaps on handcuffs and leads her into the hotel.

A soldier comes out of a room quickly to speak to Odile.

"You are surrendering? He demands incredulously.

"Yes. I understand that my husband has been arrested, and I want to be with him."

"You know you are a fool," the solider says sneering at her.

"I do know that," she responds simply.

"Your husband's name?"

"Jean-Luc Rastine."

"Yes," the soldier says. "He was captured earlier today. So, you are his wife."

"Yes."

The soldier steps over to the counter and pulls out a book, examines it carefully.

"You are a Jew?"

"Yes."

"But you are not wearing the Star of David which is required."

"That is true."

"Odile Rastine," the solider says. "I am arresting you in the name of the German Republic."

"Thank you," Odile responds softly, eyes moist but voice firm. "May I see my husband?"

"Better than that," the soldier answers. "You may share his cell."

In a few moments, Odile is led, still handcuffed, down a flight of stairs into a room marked 'Nine'. The door is unlocked. No light in this room. When the soldier illuminates the room, Odile sees her husband asleep on the floor, his head raising as he awakens. Odile looks around for an instant. There is no furniture in this room. The walls, which once were beige are scraped and marked. There are huge gouges and blood stains in the wall. She looks down.

"Odile," her husband gasps.

"Quiet," she motions to him as the soldier is undoing her handcuffs.

"What are you doing here?"

"I gave myself up," she says.

"Oh no," Jean-Luc replies, a long sigh escaping from his lips. "Oh no."

"Whatever happens to you will happen to me as well," she continues.

The soldier leaves locking the door behind him.

"They think we have information about our son."

"Yes."

"And they will do anything to obtain that information."

"Yes," she answers, now slipping onto the floor besides her husband.

"I wish I believed in God," Jean-Luc says angrily.

The following morning the interrogations begin. Separately. Alois Brunner, Hauptsturmfuehrer, has looked over the dossier and assigns Major Anselm to the case.

"You know this story better than anyone," he says to Anselm. Obtain the information we need to find their son. And use any device at your disposal to do so."

Major Anselm Baer and his dog, Wotan, enter their room. Odile is hustled out. A soldier has brought one chair for the major. Jean-Luc remains on the floor.

"So, Monsieur," the Major begins not unpleasantly, "How long have you been in Nice?"

"My wife and I just arrived."

"Pity that you were caught so quickly. You could at least have enjoyed some of the sunny days here."

"Yes, I thought so as well."

"Is it possible that you are not telling me the truth?" the voice raises. "That perhaps you have been on the Riviera for a longer period of time? You do know that we will ask your wife the same question."

"We are not liars," Jean-Luc says firmly.

"Good. Then tell me where we can find your son."

"In Paris,' Jean-Luc replies.

"Where in Paris? Give me his address."

"You know as well as I do Major, that my son never stays in one spot more than a short time. I have no idea where you would find him."

"Convenient," Major Anselm remarks, without changing expression. He goes to the door, calls in the soldier standing guard outside. "Come in and shoot this man in the arm," he commands. The soldier looks up questioningly as if he did not understand the order. "I repeat. Shoot him, but not fatally. At least not yet, he adds casually."

The solider reaches into his holster, pulls out his pistol, cocks it and aims at Jean-Luc's left shoulder and fires. The impact revolves Jean-Luc about so that he is spinning onto the floor gasping, the pain rippling through his body, blood beginning to course out of his arm.

"Give him a handkerchief," Anselm says. "So that he won't bleed to death right away."

The handkerchief is applied to Jean-Luc's arm.

"So, I ask you again, Monsieur. Where can we find your son?"

"I told you I don't know," Jean-Luc responds through his teeth, grimacing.

Anselm turns to the soldier. "Shoot him in the other arm."

"Wait," Jean-Luc says. "You can shoot me until I bleed to death, but I simply do not know where my son is. I can give you an address, if you wish, the last address I am aware of, but I doubt that he will be there."

"Now you are cooperating. Quite sensible of you."

"15, rue Napoleon."

Major Anselm stands. "We will verify this right away. If we find that you are misleading us, you can imagine what will happen next."

And then, he visits Odile in another room. Her back to the wall, she is holding her head in her hands. She does not look up when the Major enters.

"Good afternoon, Madame," The Major says. He is slipping off his leather gloves, deposits them in his pocket. "Can I get you a chair?"

She looks up wordlessly, her eyes cowled.

He shrugs. "I've just had a visit with your husband," the Major continues. "But he has not been very cooperative. We need to know where your son is hiding. He has been a lance in our side for a very long time. Quite a gaping wound your young man has dealt us."

Odile's eyes become blank.

"Look," the Major continues, almost whispering now. "My mother whom I loved dearly is dead now. You quite remind me of her. I don't believe in inflicting injury upon older women. This makes me feel guilty. I don't care for the feeling. Am I speaking too much?"

"What do you intend to do with us?"

"This depends entirely on you. I may not injure you physically, but there are other ways I can get you to confide in me. If I don't obtain the information I need, I am going to kill your husband. And kill him slowly!"

Odile cannot suppress a gasp.

"But if you cooperate, then of course, things will be better for both of you."

"You mean, "Odile says, I should give up my son in order to save my husband."

"Something like that," The major avows, his lips parting in the beginning of a smile. "And you have one day to decide. I should tell you that already your husband has not been entirely likeable, so we have shot him."

Odile blanches. She cannot bring herself to say anything. Her eyes roll up, and the fingers of hands reach upwards as if they were straining towards the sky.

"He is all right. He was wounded in the arm. So," the Major continues, "I am going to have my men bring you some dinner, perhaps a cup of coffee and we shall revisit the issue again in the morning." And with that, Major Baer leaves.

The following morning, he returns to visit Odile.

"So, what will it be, then? If you tell me what I want to know, you and your husband will be sent to a camp for the duration of the war. If not, your husband will be shot on the spot. As for you, I will turn you over to someone with less compunction than I have. No, dear lady, I could not bring myself to murder you, but I see nothing wrong in asking someone else to do it on behalf of the Wehrmacht."

Odile collects herself. "I have nothing to add."

"Your husband gave us an address on the left bank. Can you corroborate it?"

"You mean the rue Napoleon," Odile retorts. "Yes, Clovis has been known to live there."

"That's all I needed to hear," the Major says. "So, this afternoon, you and your husband will take a short walk to the train station and from there; you will be loaded with several others into a freight train to Paris."

"And from there?"

"I cannot tell you."

"We have heard that Drancy is a processing stage for those you send on to death camps."

The Major shrugs. "I wouldn't know about that. I have my orders. I send Jews as well as political prisoners to Drancy. What happens to them afterwards is none of my business."

19. A Visit from Clovis

Late that same afternoon, a phone call. Alone in the house, Simone picks up the receiver. Clovis!

"Quickly," he remarks. "I plan to see you early tomorrow morning."

"You know that your parents have been arrested," she says.

"Yes," he responds, his voice unaltered, "And that is why I will be coming with a few friends to see what can be done about it."

"I will be waiting for you."

"You will not return to the apartment afterwards whatever happens," Clovis continues. "You need to prepare to leave it permanently. So, say your goodbyes tonight."

"Your cousin will be happy," Simone replies. "She is in a dead fright about all of this."

"I have to hang up now, can't take the chance that we are being taped."

She cannot sleep that night. Every time the calm of slumber lures her towards oblivion, the sense that Clovis arrives in the morning snaps her into full awareness. Simone realises that a bit of sleep will calm her nerves, make the burgeoning day more tolerable. She has no idea what Clovis intends. But knowing him, it will involve some action. She washes in the middle of the night, and wears clothing that should be appropriate for virtually any activity. No high heels this day, she says ruefully. She is so tired of conflict, so very tired and wishes that the goddamned war would end.

Unable to catch a wink, she decides to take the chance, steps out around four in the morning, and walks down to the Promenade des Anglais. Nobody is on the streets. There is a curfew but no soldiers visible to enforce it. Anyway, she no longer cares. She simply needs to move, to take some action, to feel the throb of blood in her veins, the pulse of feet treading on pavement. The Promenade has completely changed. Where once there was an extended curve of beach that went on for a mile or more, the beach is now partially obscured by massive razor wire. The Germans must think that the Allies are going to invade from the Mediterranean. Below the sand, landmines have been placed everywhere. She has heard that gulls alighting haphazardly on one of them have been blown to bits. This is not the final image of the Cote d'Azur she wants implanted in her brain, but it is the one that prevails, that reiterates uninterruptedly how perilous life has become. She turns and quickly walks back to the apartment. Kitty is not yet up, but they have already said their goodbyes the night before. Tearful goodbyes. They do not know when they will see one another again. Fear is redolent in Kitty's throat as she wishes Simone Godspeed. Around five thirty, as the first glimmer of dawn casts a halo, a truck pulls up before the apartment house. Clovis! Her first reaction is to fix her hair. She rushes to the bathroom to find a comb and applies a bit of lipstick.

At the door she opens it and falls into his arms.

"Are you all right?" he asks.

"Better now," she says. They are embracing, kissing. The men behind Clovis are clamouring to enter. They do not want to be seen in the street.

"I so wanted to see you,' Simone murmurs. "But this is the wrong reason for us to connect."

A grim expression on his face. "We have much to do," he says simply, sidestepping her need to hear him say how much he has missed her. Instead, he is moving forcefully. The men take seats around the dining room table. Simone is offering coffee. A baguette is passed around. Kitty has found a pound of butter. The delighted men are eating spoonfuls of it. Out in the street, a siren sounds. A fire truck passes. The siren halts.

"My parents. How were they?"

"They were fine. But your dad was desperate to get out for a walk and equally desperate for cigarettes. And that is how he was arrested."

"Fucking smokes," he says lighting up. "I told him years ago they would do him in."

"And then your mother wouldn't hear of staying here alone. She said she had to be with him whatever happens. So, she left. They are being held at the Exelsior Hotel. That is, they were being held there. Eventually, they would be transported up to Drancy, and from there to another camp, probably somewhere in Poland."

Clovis nods. "We are going to find them and free them," he says simply. He is looking at Simone. "You've changed," he remarks softly. "Not only older, but more serious. You were always intense, but now it is in the service of something."

She laughs. "Survival."

He grins.

"And you look the same. Still the philosopher with curly hair who prefers to read Leibniz rather than kill Germans."

"Simply an order of priority," he replies. Now he turns his attention to the group. "All of us will leave here in a few moments. The truck will take us up to Cimiez. It is on the hill above Nice. There are Roman ruins there, even a monastery. Nearby, a Nazi building that houses armaments for soldiers in the area. That is where we need to stop first. We need to pick up ammunition for Sten guns and, preferably, find either grenades or Molotov cocktails. Then we continue to the hotel. By then it should be midday. Time for lunch. And as the soldiers are eating, we will pay them a surprise visit."

Boarding the truck. A canvas covers them in the back. Simone is in front with Clovis driving.

"There is a road block along the Promenade," she says.

"We can avoid that. I will go along the avenue Victor Hugo, and then turn left up the mountain to Cimiez."

"So, you know where the dump is?"

"I have never seen it, but I have been told exactly where to find it," he answers. The truck roars to life and moves slowly along the avenue Victor Hugo. "Nice hotels on this road," he remarks as if to inject something routine into what they are imagining.

"The Splendide is supposed to be quite lovely," she replies, her eyes on the road.

For a time, he says nothing. The truck is moving slowly, evenly up the mountain, past the train station and into the hills above town. There is virtually no traffic. It's too early for businessmen and too early for most soldiers. And then, just as they are congratulating themselves on finding the optimum path to Cimiez, a roadblock appears ahead. Clovis slows the truck.

"Tell them in the back that I intend to run through it. We have no choice."

Simone opens the window to the back. A corner of the canvas lifts. She relays the message. She can hear metal, weapons checked and loading.

Nearing the roadblock, a three-man affair without physical impediments, Clovis picks up speed. The truck, climbing up a steep grade, is struggling to meet the demands of its driver, but begins to advance more quickly. A soldier mosies into the street ahead, has his arm raised to halt the truck. Clovis pretends to slow the vehicle, and then as he nears, guns the truck, striking the soldier's arm and thrusting him through the air and into a building. Commotion. Men shrieking. The two other soldiers pick up their rifles and begin to fire. From the back of the truck a steady stream of machine gun bullets strikes them, hurtles them backwards. And then there is silence. The truck slows and continues its rise.

As Clovis is driving up the mountain, his mother and father are being marched from the hotel to the train station. Jean-Luc's arm has been bandaged and they have been fed a breakfast of cereal and water. Major Anselm has a farewell for them.

"We are checking on the information you gave us with regards to your son. Either we find him there or we do not. As for the two of you, we are sending you after one short stop to a concentration camp in Poland where I fear life will be exceedingly difficult for two old people. Had you been more cooperative, we would have found a nicer place for you to rest your weary bones for the duration of the war."

At the train station, there are perhaps three hundred people standing silently guarded by a dozen men with arms. A train lumbers into the station, grates down to nothing, and stops. It is a freight train with one wagon after the other perhaps used at one time to transport grain, coal, or animals. This day, fifty or more standing individuals will be compressed into each wagon. The trip to Drancy will take some ten hours. There will be no stops along the way, no food, no water, no place for the ill or elderly to lie down. Within a half hour, the train is crammed with people, mainly elderly Jews, a few gypsies and, it is said, homosexuals. As the train departs, chugging slowly towards the west before turning north, a fearsome explosion rocks the morning. Up the hill, an enormous firestorm is taking place. Jean-Luc and Odile cannot see the explosions. Nobody knows what is causing this. Nobody dares even guess.

Clovis and his men reach the armoury. They park a discreet block away. Clamber out of the truck.

"Stay with me, "Clovis says to Simone. He hands her a pistol. "If they wound me seriously, you will know what to do," he says to her quickly, but without drama. She nods without the slightest idea whether she would be able to carry this out. Below, sirens have started to saturate the morning quiet. The sound of metal, of heavy vehicles fills their ears.

"We don't have a lot of time," Clovis remarks. And with that, with hand signals, he sends two men to the left, two to the right while he and Simone walk up to the guard gate, Clovis firing at the single guard, striking him in the chest before the man has a chance to lift up from his stool. Front door locked. Clovis fires into the lock, the heavy door flying open. He enters. A half dozen men are facing him. From the left, through a side door, two of his men are firing. German soldiers are falling at their feet, bloodied, eyes open. Cries echo throughout the building. A siren is set off. Clovis finds an electric box and fires into it, quieting the sound. A few more men appear with rifles and pistols. A gunfight ensues. One of Clovis's men is shot in the face. His buddy, seeing that the man is mortally wounded but still alive, kills him mercifully on the spot. Simone is standing there, the pistol in her hand without firing. She is seeing the scene around her as if through a mist. But not panicky, not angry, nor irritated. Simply an isolated figure in the melee taking place as if she were a statue in white.

In a few moments, the hall has been cleared of German soldiers. Several have run off. The rest are either grievously wounded or dead. Their guns have been kicked to one side or carried off. The Maquis enter the armoury. They find crates of machine guns and take several. Plus lots of ammunition. Then a case filled with grenades is passed to all.

"One more thing," Clovis says with determination to one of the men. "Give me the detonator." He attaches a plastic explosive, sets a timer for three minutes. And as quickly as they have entered the armoury, they leave with their spoils, run to the truck, and begin the ride down the road towards the sea. As they descend the hill, behind them an enormous explosion resounds, rifling palpable shock waves through the air. The late morning sky flashes into a hundred suns. The light proves so bright that the men in back of the truck are forced to avert their eyes. And then, the fire craters up into the mountain as if it had been fired upwards from hell. The sound is a deafening cacophony of crashing metal, shards of glass, ammunition combusting, a roof blown sky high into the bristling air.

"They will know we are up here," Clovis says to Simone. "They'll be sending troops as we speak. We will take a different route to go down the hill, perhaps through neighbourhoods. This will take somewhat longer but is safer."

The Hotel Excelsior is near the train station on the avenue Durante. Slowing down as they approach. Parking at the Gare Thiers, the main train station, is close by. A freight train is leaving at this moment crammed with humans. Unaware of the train, the Maquis move forward with weapons under their coats.

"Maybe you should stay here," Clovis cautions Simone.

"No," she nods vigorously. "I am going with you."

Now as the men turn the corner, the hotel is looming in front of them, an exquisite Belle Epoque edifice with concrete balconies and wrought iron fences protecting the balcony of each room. The hotel is on full alert. Soldiers are milling outside everywhere. Snipers positioned under the roof and on several balconies. A machine gun emplacement to one side of the hotel.

"To do this," Clovis says with determined clarity, "We need to throw bunches of hand grenades: first at the machine gun, then at the front door where many of the soldiers are congregating. Once we enter, expect many more soldiers to greet us firing. Be ready! On my signal!"

In an instant, Clovis waves them forward, and they begin to run towards the hotel. Snipers are already firing down at them. The first grenades destroy the machine gun emplacement. The second and third smash into the heavy glass door of the hotel and the explosion hurtles men into the air screaming. Uniformed men are rushing from the hotel into the vacuum, the gunpowder smoke delaying them a few seconds, long enough for Clovis to begin firing his Sten gun into the crowd of animated soldiers. Simone looks down and finds a pistol in her hand. Looks up and begins to fire straight ahead. She follows Clovis as he lurches from one column to the next his shooting uninterrupted, the hail of bullets whizzing around and near them. Suddenly, Simone sees that he has the throat of a German soldier in his hand.

"Simone," he shouts. "Here. Ask the man where they keep the political prisoners. Ask him in German." She does so. The man whistles out an answer along with blood swelling out of his throat.

"Downstairs," he says. Clovis nods. "Danke," he says to the man who drops onto the floor. Two of Clovis's men have been shot, but they are still advancing. A new round of fighting breaks out ahead of them as German soldiers fly, tripping down the stairs. A killing field as one after the other emerges into a field of bullets and collapses into a heap mortally wounded or dead. Clovis is exulting, waving everyone forward towards the staircase, when suddenly a soldier flying out of a staircase like some avenging demon, still airborne, fires at close range. Simone turns to the man still in midair, lifts her pistol in his direction, but fails to pull the trigger. A shot fells Clovis. At once, Simone is by him. She reaches for his face and turns it to her. His eyes are vacant, mouth still. Flowing blood is pumping out of his chest where the heart has ceased expanding and retracting. Dead! Clovis is dead. It is as if all life ceased as the sight seeps into her brain. And yet, for an instant, she will not believe. Surely, this crazy, defiant, superb life cannot be brought to an end by such puny people. Simone kisses each of his eyes.

A Maquisard pulls her up and drags her towards the front door but as he is pulling her with him, he is fatally shot and also tumbles. And suddenly, as if it were a nightmarish ballet move, a body is flying through the air at and into her body, knocking her down. The body remains on top of her breathing hard weighing her down, her mind suffused with the sight of so much blood, still witnessing the last vestige of Clovis's life force escaping from his body. She turns her head to see the last of the Maquisards gunned down. And suddenly, the action is finished. A stillness emerges from the mist of spent gunfire. The smell of carbon and death! Quiet. Death remains, it always triumphs. The lives Clovis and Simone have come for have vanished, are elsewhere, gone. Those lives have been given over to the cause, she thinks bitterly. Clovis has died for his ideals. Happy boy! She cannot stomach the thought, rolls over to vomit and, as her body moves out from under the soldier still pressing on top of her, he smashes her head with the butt of his rifle.

20.   A Season in Hell

Simone wakes up in restraints, shackles on one ankle. Bleary-eyed, she notices the stains on her dress. Brown stains: dried blood. Now she recalls what has happened. An open wound on her skull. Damp, blood-stained hair. She recalls Clovis dying just as she catches his last breath. The curls on his head dampened by exertion, by perspiration, his forehead wrinkled in a virtual scowl, lips unmoving, stilled. She tries to sidestep the image but does not succeed. His face forefront in her mind as a reminder of how incredible, how stupid, how unearthly the event. This young man, her lover, has died, but there is no rhyme or reason to his death. He expected to live the philosopher's life reading and lecturing to students. At war's end, he would marry Simone Valois. They would have children together, perhaps in America, perhaps in France, he the professor, she the government employee still labouring in the vineyards of spy craft decades after the war had been won. Yet, here's the truth of it. He will never have children. I will never bear his children. I will never again hold him in my arms, and he will never touch my cheek the way he was wont to do when he became sentimental.

Looks around, Simone realised she was in a small room of the hotel. There is a window which she will not be able to reach. The shackles allow her movement within two feet of the window. She will be able to see light in the morning, pale shadows in the afternoon, a sliver of sharper light now and then. But no breeze. No grasp of the outdoors. It is warm in the room. Summertime on the coast. The walls are of a beige which have been gouged by implements, perhaps hands. Scraped paint. Even bloodstains. A pen marking on one side perhaps calculating days interned. Next to her two buckets. One is large and empty. The other is smaller but filled with water. She picks up the small bucket, cups her hands together, and drinks.

Her mind refuses to cease. Bullets are blazing in crisscross patterns through scenes she remembers. She recalls the young man side by side with Clovis, the Maquis one by one, falling to the ground, their faces blending surprise, amazement, perhaps even doubt as their life evanesces. She even remembers the soldier flying towards her, his face a comical contortion as he squarely lands pinning her to the hard porcelain ground. He looks up in her mind's eye to see his rifle butt raised.

The door opens. Major Anselm comes in followed by Wotan. Wotan immediately runs to her and licks her face.

"You have returned to us," the Major says with pleasure. She has never before seen the face of the man as it is in this moment. A face which has debated doubt and conviction for many months. In its place a pale likeness of the face she knew in Paris. She has never before heard the tone which he clearly tries to restrain as he speaks. Still wearing his trench coat, he stands with his hands in his pockets, the harelip a trifle red.

"Wotan!" he commands, and the dog retreats to his side.

She looks into eyes which are narrower than she recalls. The fierce pupils scan her, dodging in and out of his skull.

"Do you recall what happened yesterday?"
"It is already tomorrow?" she asks.
"Yes."

"I recall," she responds.

"So, you now know you have lost!" he exults.

She lowers her head. "Yes. Lost." How painful to hear this man rejoicing.

"I asked you several times in Paris to help me arrest Clovis. It has taken years, but finally you have brought him to my doorstep. Sweet of you. Pity he won't rise again!"

He opens the door. A soldier stands there with a gramophone. He winds it up, places it on the floor. Turns it on, sets the needle to the recording, a record of Strauss is playing. Ein Heldenleben.

"The music is heroic," he sighs. "So heroic. Your Clovis was also heroic. I give him that. I wished he had fought for us. So damn heroic. So utterly foolish. But once he blew up the weapons depot in Cimiez, it was just a matter of time before he assailed the hotel. We were waiting for him. Like a mother duck awaiting the return of her duckling. We knew it had to be Clovis who wrought such damage. Only he could have carried it off. Such swagger!"

"I wish you would not speak of him," she says.

He grins. "Of course! Two young people spilling blood together! You must have fallen in love with him. He was about your age. Not bad looking. Not a good sign, of course, that his mother was Jewish. But it could have been worse."

"What do you want from me?" she asks.

"I want to hurt you," he says placidly.

"I thought you might," she says, her breathing accelerating. "Thought you might want to hurt a woman."

The Major sits on the floor, sliding along the wall to slip into a resting position.

"Clovis's parents were in this very room," he muses. "I had every opportunity to injure Odile, but I decided against it. My sense of courtesy obliged me to restrain myself. She is an old woman. She reminded me of my mother. I would never have hurt my mother, so I let her go."

"You mean she is alive?"

"Yes."

"And Jean-Luc?"

"Also. On their way to Drancy."

"Still," Simone says bitterly, "you have managed to save them only for a few days or weeks. For once they reach the concentration camp, they will be murdered."

"Not right way, perhaps not necessarily," the Major considers. "Odile, probably, because she is a Jewess. We would like to clean up Jewish debris once and for all. But if Jean-Luc is strong enough to work, then he may survive. Fortunately for him, he is no Jew. You know that Auschwitz has its motto: Arbeit macht frei. Work makes you free."

She stifles a giggle. "A likely fairy tale!" Simone says. "We have heard too many stories of rail cars filled with Jews sent to their death."

"Some of it is simply Allied propaganda," the Major says, yawning. He gets up. "But I think you have a bit more information which we would like you to provide. I am assigning you two guards. They have my permission to make you talk in whatever way they wish. They are not allowed, however, to put you to death," he adds. "No need to thank me." He picks up the phonograph, closes the top. "Perhaps you would like to keep this here," he offers. "Music might assuage some of the pain which I thrill in thinking you are about to experience."

She waves him way.

An hour later, Gottfried and Helmuth enter the room. They do not knock. They bluster the door open so that it cracks into the back wall. They are lower level soldiers. Gottfried is older, perhaps forty-five to fifty, heavy, his belly wiggles when he moves his torso. He wears an unkempt handlebar moustache, hair is greying. He says he is from Nuremberg. His face is rosy. He does not often smile. Helmuth is thin, lanky, and quite a bit taller than his colleague. His face looks sad, cheeks narrow as if they had been tweaked together, but he laughs often, especially when he is nervous. They explain to Simone that the larger pail is for her bodily functions, that she will be allowed twice a week to take the bucket outside, dump it, as well as rinse it. Water will be provided every third day.

"And will I be able to take a walk?" she asks. "Or exercise?"

The soldiers look at each other.

"You think this is a gym!" Helmuth exclaims loudly and contains a giggle.

"So,' Gottfried begins. "We would like to know where you stayed when you were in Nice. Was it a hotel? Perhaps an apartment? You are not the sort to sleep out on the beach. And who did you stay with?"

"We never had to find a place," Simone responds. "We came into Nice yesterday morning from Bordeaux. We drove all night."

"I don't believe you," Gottfried says flatly.

"Nonetheless, that is what happened."

Gottfried approaches and with his left-hand smacks Simone cross the mouth, driving her back into the wall.

"Now once again, where did you stay?"

I have told you the truth," Simone retorts, wiping a small stream of blood from her mouth.

Gottfried hits her again, this time with his fist.

"You know, Gottfried," Helmuth cautions. "Maybe we shouldn't mark up her pretty face right away. Why don't we just beat the shit out of her body?"

"That is a lovely idea," Gottfried says. He is not smiling.

For the next half hour, the soldiers take turns beating Simone. Barely conscious, she is spitting blood. A tooth is coming loose. She would like to snarl, but her face us unable to perform the gesture. Before they leave, Helmuth has some information for Simone. "I suppose you know that Americans and others landed on Normandy beach a month ago. Now there is talk of a similar invasion on the coast here. So, we don't have a great deal of time to drag information out of you. Tell us where you stayed, and also provide us with all the names of the men you worked with in the Maquis. If you do this, you may live long enough for the Americans to rescue you."

"Vive la France!" Simone responds through clenched teeth. In dire pain from body blows, punches to the abdomen, she vomits into the large pail, then stretches out on the floor and slips into a scattered, painful unconsciousness.

From time to time, a young man who is not a soldier and who is clothed in the white uniform of a hotel server, stops by with a tray. He bears a piece of bread and a cup of broth. Sometimes, Simone is hungry and consumes the bread and broth in what seems like one gulp, but most of the time, she simply allows it to grow old. Normally within the hour, the young man in white returns to take the tray away. His name is Thierry.

"You should tell them what they want to know, he whispers to her. "They are ruthless, and they eventually will kill you."

"I know," Simone says defiantly.

"You are being stubborn."

"I was in love with a man who did not want to die, but when he did, it was in the way he wished it to be."

"You don't have to die for any reason," the boy remarks almost vehemently.

"Thank you," she says, closing her eyes. "Thank you for being kind."

Every morning after breakfast, Gottfried, and Helmuth return. Simone prepares herself for what is about to come. Then she remembers the best way to steel herself is not to tense up herself. On the contrary, she must relax as the blows reign down upon her. She must absorb them one after the other. The pain will not last forever, she knows. She wonders whether she has the fortitude of a Clovis to give up her life for a cause. She does not think so. She may want to die, but only because life has become unbearable. That is different than surrendering oneself to an ideal.

This day, the soldiers strip. They have decided to rape her. They are chattering with one another believing that Simone does not understand German. They speak to her always in broken French. Of course, she understands them totally. Before they have unclothed, she is already sinking her consciousness into a secret, hazy state, a place where these men, or for that matter, any man, can ever touch her. They can rape me, they can kill me, but they cannot reach my core. And with this in the forefront of her mind, she looks up to see the heavy, sweating Gottfried whose belly is jiggling to and for lowering himself onto her. Instead of resisting, she lies still. Perhaps they like necrophilia, she thinks. Gottfried comes almost at once. He dismounts, leers, and says that the girl is pretty but not otherwise appealing. His partner disrobes, considers slipping on a condom, but decides against it. He takes more time, his leering face against hers, his tongue caressing her cheeks, reaching between her closed lips into her mouth and into the recesses of her throat, spittle dripping from the corner of his mouth.

"That was fun,' Helmuth says.

"Enjoyable," Gottfried agrees, looking down onto the naked, impassive body of the woman he has just violated.

"But it would be better if she encouraged us, don't you think?" Gottfried says. "She's not much fun to fuck. When I fuck my wife, she is reaching for my cock and stroking it."

"Yes," Helmuth agrees. "Mine likes to stick a finger in my ass. It's quite pleasant."

"I think you told me that you come from Heidelberg." Gottfried says, putting on his pants.

"A village nearby, yes," Helmuth responds. "I have a wife and three children there."

"Really," Gottfried remarks with interest, stepping on the inert figure of the woman in the room. "I knew you were married. Your job?"

"Bookkeeper," Helmuth remarks. "I worked for a company in Aachen for many years."

"How interesting," Gottfried says. He moves over to the girl on the floor and steps on her neck. "Can you imagine?" he asks of his friend. "I am causing pain to this woman and she doesn't even register it. A worthless cunt, this one."

"So," Helmuth says, bending over Simone, "Why don't you cooperate a little with us? We could make life so much easier for you in the hotel Excelsior."

Simone says nothing. She does not open her eyes. Her very breathing appears to have stopped.

Helmuth reaches for her throat, finds a pulse.

"For a moment, I thought I had killed her with my massive love," he says, chuckling. "The Major would not think this funny."

The following day, Thierry escorts Simone to the rear of the property. Another fifty yards, and they come to a ravine. "This is where you empty the bucket," he says.

Later, he takes her to the rear of the hotel and flushes out the bucket himself with a hose. I'm not supposed to do this," he confides, "But I don't know if you yourself are up to it." For her part, Simone, despite physical agony, is thrilled to step outside into the open, into the sunlight.

"Thank you," she says, content that this young man has charity in his heart. For a time, she had thought it had totally disappeared from the face of the earth.

Escorting her back, Thierry slips a piece of Sachertorte into her hands.

"Eat this right away," he says to her. "If I was caught giving this to you, I might be chained to the wall in your place."

Two weeks elapse in this fashion, with Simone losing weight. Her period has stopped completely. The punches to her belly have left her black and blue. Her insides feel aflame, irritated, and often splintered as if someone had lit a fire inside of her. Simone becomes wracked with pain day and night. From time to time, the soldiers rape her again, but each time they arise unsatisfied.

"Did you cum?" Hellmuth asks Gottfried.

"Of course, I always cum," he answers. "But it does not feel right. Like fucking a dead person. I might as well jerk off."

"Exactly the way I feel," Hellmuth replies. "She's a total stiff."

"And yet, we are just having a bit of fun with her. She must enjoy this more than the beating we give her other days."

"If she just gave us a little information, we would leave her alone. I wasn't brought up to punch women in the chest," Hellmuth says.

"We're only following orders."

"Didn't you tell me that you worked for a munitions factory in Hamburg?" Hellmuth asks his colleague.

"Yes, for many years," Gottfried remarks. "That's where I met my wife. Before her, I met several women who worked there. One of them became my mistress. I tell you this. When I fucked her, she always came. She made it a point for us to cum together. Sex was lovely. Not like this piece of female garbage. You put your dick in her and you might as well be sticking it into a kilo of pork loin."

"A pity that she does not enjoy sex more," Hellmuth says. He undoes his condom and throws it into Simone's pail.

Once a week, the Major visits with his dog in tow. Wotan is always eager to see his friend, Simone, and often curls around her legs as the Major pulls up a chair and sits down for a chat.

"Your army is almost here," the Major acknowledges. "They're moving up the coast. We have perhaps a week before they arrive in Nice. A Panzer division is being sent down here to stop them, but I have no illusions that we will prevail. So quite soon, I shall be leaving town. No point returning to Germany. Apparently, there is not much left of my country. The bombings have been fierce and indiscriminate. So, I may travel to Denmark and mix in with the people. Thus, I have the thorny question as to what to do with you. You are unfortunately quite well known to the Allies. Simone Valois, one of the few women who acted valiantly in the war against us. So, if I kill you, they will hunt me down like a dog." With these words, he reaches over to pet Wotan. "I suppose I will simply leave you here in the hotel. I don't expect to extract any information from you. It's too late to do any good, even if you gave it. So, what do you think about all of this?"

"Vive la France," Simone says whistling her words.

Anselm laughs. "I can hardly understand you these days. The boys have been overzealous and have knocked out a few of your teeth. Must be hard to chew or talk."

She says nothing.

"Come, Wotan. Time to pack our suitcases."

21. The War Comes to an End

And then, from one day to the next, the thrashings cease. Gottfried and Hellmuth beat a retreat into the Alps with their unit. Anselm has disappeared. It is said he has fled to Scandinavia.

"The Allies are on the beach," Thierry beams. Joyously, he hacks away Simone's chain with an axe.

"Americans?" she asks, rubbing her ankle.

"Yes, and others too." He is smiling at her. "Can you get up?"

She tries, but is unable, too weak, too hurt, legs rubbery underneath her. "The hotel is empty," Thierry goes on. "Even the director of the hotel has disappeared. So, I am putting myself in charge. Thus, I shall take you to the fourth floor and put you into a suite. Would you like that?"

She looks at him uncomprehendingly. Thierry leaves the door open. She can hear him clattering down the stairs. After an hour, he returns. He has a wheelchair.

"I borrowed it from the hospital," he says. He helps her settle into the chair, then wheels her to the elevator. "You will be on the top floor," he says to her.

Simone is wheeled to a suite. Into a salon decorated in the belle époque style, a large bathroom with both shower and tub. The bedroom is spacious and decorated with art nouveau paintings and etchings. A Tiffany style lamp rests on the bedside table. A mammoth crystal lamp adorns the ceiling. The bed has a backing in mahogany. There are at least twelve pillows. The bathroom contains a tub twice her size.

"Put me in the bed, please."

He reaches underneath her and is able to pick her up rather easily.

"You have lost a lot of weight," he scolds. She is grimacing from the pain of touch. "I am going to call a doctor for you," Thierry declares. "I can't take you to the hospital. I inquired but was told that there are already too many soldiers and civilians suffering from gunshot and shrapnel wounds there. But tonight, I promise you the visit of a doctor. A neighbour."

"Can you open the window?" she asks in a whisper.

He pulls open the French doors. Through them Simone sees a balcony and beyond that, a deep blue sky. A robin is circling and lands on the balustrade, chanting a song momentarily. She looks at him curiously, almost as if she has never before seen a bird. In an instant, the robin flies away.

Later, Thierry brings up a tray of food.

"You can thank the Americans for this," he says. "They have brought all sorts of rations. Spam. Canned potatoes. Simone can eat but a little of it. She picks at it. She has no appetite.

That night, the doctor arrives and examines her carefully, painstakingly. He takes blood. The following evening, he returns.

"My dear, you really ought to be in hospital. Sadly, we have no room for you. So, I shall treat you here to the best of my ability. First, you need pain killers. I know you are in severe distress. You have some damaged ribs. One arm is broken; your collar bone is a mess. Your private parts are severely lacerated. The beatings have left an irremediable mark. Nor will you be able to bear children." He pauses, but Simone has no reply, unable to process all of this. "Lacerations on your left leg," the doctor continues.

"We will have to operate first opportunity to save it. It's gangrening. For the rest, I don't know what they have done to your brain. We don't have a competent neurologist right now, but clearly, you need a dentist. I will send one to you after our surgery. Your face is swollen, badly swollen, from the savagery of the attacks. I am starting you on morphine," he goes on. Injects her. In a moment, her face which has been taut relaxes into a repose she has forgotten is possible.

"Bless you," she says with difficulty, taking the doctor's hand.

Two days later, she is ferried to the hospital before dawn and undergoes surgery, successfully. Her leg is wrapped carefully. Wires are pulled out of her hand. When she awakens she feels nothing and thinks even less. No thought has been in her head for weeks, perhaps months. She does not know how long her captors have held her, how long the beatings took place. She did everything she could to render her mind blank, to uncoil her muscles and, in this way, to survive the savage assaults.

The following morning, Thierry lifts her into the chair and rolls her onto the balcony. From there, she can view the Promenade and the beach as well as the sea. Simone hears the rumble of massive machinery. She watches machines pulling razor wire down, men following in protective suits scooping the wire into huge balls and depositing the rolls into trucks. Behind them, a dozen soldiers are on their bellies crawling inch by inch along the beach searching for landmines. From her distance, they resemble cockroaches. She watches one soldier lift his hand to indicate that he has found a live one. Another soldier crawls over to him. The two of them disarm the mine, pull it out of the sand, then sit back and light up a smoke. The scene is repeated fifty times that day. Seagulls reappear on the beach. In the distance, there are warships, presumably American, off the coast wafting up and down on the waters. This is Simone's preferred spot in the suite. The air feels soothing, the sun warmly enveloping and inviting. Below, she can observe cars halting before the hotel, either picking up guests or depositing them. Many military uniforms. Hardly any women. Besides a brief exchange with Thierry and the doctor, she realises that has not spoken a word in many weeks.

But she is perennially tired, exhausted. Every bone in her body aches. The painkillers are unable to assuage the pain entirely. No longer on morphine, she begins to ingest daily aspirin. It helps, but it does not obliterate either pain or memory.

"I'd like a glass of wine," she says to Thierry one day. "Red wine. Can you bring one with dinner?"

That evening, he opens a bottle of wine. She downs a glass quickly.

"Slowly," he cautions her. "You haven't had any alcohol in quite a while."

The taste is foreign to her, even exotic.

"I'd like one more." She drinks a second glass which cradles her into a zone of relaxation, of numbness.

"No more," he says to her after she demands a third. "You are also taking medication."

She smiles at this young lad reprimanding her. A caring smile. Relaxing now, she turns to Thierry, examines his little face, the straight blondish hair and mauvish eyes.

"You seem to have escaped the Germans," she remarks.

"Yes, I did," he says. Then adds, "But others did not. Many of my friends did not. The hotel hired several immigrant young men to serve as valets, busboys, elevator operators and assistants to the concierges. A dozen or so. When the Germans took over the hotel, they demanded that all the male help appear in the ballroom one morning. And then they required that we all lower our drawers. Those who were circumcised were partitioned to one side of the room. One boy called out to the German Major who had orchestrated the meeting. He yelled he was not Jewish, but had been circumcised due to an infection, The Major shrugged, said it was impossible in a short period of time to distinguish between Jews and non-Jews. Then his men took him as well as the circumcised boys to the ravine and executed them one after the other with a bullet to the back of the head." The boy finishes his story shuddering.

"A terrible story," Simone commiserates. "But I am so glad that you were spared."

In the bathroom, she stares intently at her face, the clump of wires on her head which she identifies as hair. She tries to comb it, sees the black eye that will not heal. The nose, broken, apparently shifting to the right. She opens her mouth. Lacerated gums, and a broken tooth. She closes her eyes.

Thus, continues the transitional period. Simone learns that she can live with constant pain. Medication helps. But even without the painkillers, she can manage. What she cannot control, however, is memory. Her mind brutalises her with images she cannot flee. Slowly, the vision of her last moments with Clovis surface. The useless gun in her hand. Suffocating memory breaches as if she had lifted a thick but fiery, opaque veil, a smouldering remnant of their love for each other. Weeks pass with the violence of this image in the forefront of her mind. Still, no German soldiers every morning to abuse her. Thanks her lucky stars. She wonders why she is not vindictive, why she is not howling for the capture and torture of Major Anselm and his men. In the recesses of her soul, she feels contempt for them. Yet also triumphant. For they failed to break her. And this must rankle these supermen, that a little, damaged woman could withstand their beatings. And then, from one day to the next, the quiet period ceases.

The Americans are in town, many of them taking rooms in the hotel. Just as they are settling in, Kitty returns from Ventimiglia to Nice.

"I heard that you were here," Kitty says, opening the door and seeing Simone in the wheelchair. Simone turns. Her face is still heavily bandaged. One tooth still missing. Her leg has been stiffened with two boards splinted together. Her stomach girded with bandages.

"Oh, my dear! What did they do to you?"

"I don't know whether I have words to describe it," Simone answers thoughtfully. "They showed me a cultured people when their decency dies."

"It's a miracle that you are still alive," Kitty wonders.

There was no way that Kitty could be aware of all the events that took place.

"You know that Clovis is dead."

"I did not know," Kitty says mournfully. Sits on the corner of the bed and holds Simone's hands. "And his parents?"

"We don't know yet. They were sent to Drancy and presumably to a concentration camp, but nobody has any record of them."

"Let's hope they survived," Kitty intones. Then in a foggy voice straining out of her throat: "I'm so sorry for leaving. I was a coward. But I was certain that the Nazis would find out who and where I was, and that my end was near. I panicked."

"Poor Kitty,' Simone sympathises. "You did what anybody in your shoes would have done. Running from murderers is no sin."

"Thank you for understanding," Kitty sighs. "But I still don't feel right about it."

"You put us up for a very long period of time. Any day, one of those stool pigeons or a Nazi sympathiser could have found out about us and arrested us all. So, you think you acted with cowardice, but in fact, what you did was quite remarkable."

This observation leaves Kitty in tears, her head bent over Simone's hand. After a time, she lifts up, drying her eyes.

"The brand-new newspaper, Nice Matin, has been in touch with me. They want to interview you, take some photos. They asked me to talk to you for your permission."

Simone is quiet.

"What do you think?"

"I don't know what they want with me," she concludes, finally.

"They have questions to ask about your participation in resisting the Nazis."

"I don't know whether I am up to it," Simone says. "Look at me. Photos of the lovely Simone Valois? Please!"

"I'll tell them not to bother."

"Tell them to forget about the pictures, but if they want to chat for a short period of time, have them come someday after breakfast. Give me another few mornings to continue my recovery, please."

Four days later, a reporter and photographer from Nice Matin are ushered into Simone's apartment. Several of the hotel staff come in as well intrigued by what is about to happen.

"I'm not sure what you want with me," Simone says.

"You are the woman the Germans call Dawn, isn't that so?" a young reporter asks.

"Yes."

"A double agent. You convinced them that you were working on their side."

"Yes."

"How did you do that?"

Simone shrugs. "I lied a lot."

"That is already exceptional," the reporter laughs. "But you also participated, it is said, in raids on German installations, German trains and depots. Is this true?"

"I helped where I could."

"So, you knew the young leader of the Maquis, Clovis Rastine?"

"I did. Yes."

"Well?"

"Yes," she says, her throat tightening.

"And what kind of a man was he?"

"A fine man, completely devoted to his country."

"He gave up his life standing next to you, it is said, attempting to liberate his parents from this hotel."

"That is accurate," she answers, "But his parents had already been sent to Drancy."

"So, you saw him die." The reporter continues.

"Please," Simone says, uncomfortable with these questions. "I won't say anything further about Clovis or his family."

The reporter shrugs. "The rumour, however, is that you held a pistol in your hand which remained unfired despite a gun battle in the lobby of the hotel."

"I would not know about that," Simone answers, flustered. Pleading fatigue, and feeling nauseous, she ends the interview.

Mornings, Thierry takes Simone into the elevator to the rez-de-chaussee, and pushes her into the gardens that abut the hotel. In a few days, they venture out further, down to the Promenade, which now is cleared of razor wire, mines, and debris. In fact, some American soldiers are sun bathing on the beach, their uniforms hanging on poles. Simone sits on a bench facing the gentle waters. People are returning to the Promenade, walking by the Mediterranean. One woman is carrying her Schnauzer in her arms, speaking to it as she strolls. Thierry has brought pieces of stale bread, and now Simone feeds one gull after the other by holding a crumb in her right hand, gull after gull swooping down to take it from her.

"Feels right to feed the gulls," she says, almost triumphantly.

A week has passed since the article appeared in Nice Matin. The article portrays her as a once young, beautiful double agent ravaged by the Nazis, and so traumatised by the death of her mentor and friend, Clovis Rastine, that she could not fire her pistol in the battle which ended his life. Is that the sum total of what happened? She asks herself. Maybe it is just so simple. Sinks into a reverie, her agitated mind replaying the events of that late morning, the entry into the lobby, Clovis shooting with deadly accuracy, she next to him, a warrior who refused to engage.

She recalls a conversation she shared with Clovis in the hills above Arette. Often, he opened himself to a universe of intimate thought. That afternoon, as they lay in the grass, he was chewing on mint leaves and blades of grass: "All these people perishing. In the most personal sense, their death is inexcusable, taken by thugs who simply want a world excised of the people they fear, are jealous of, or can't stand."

"That's unusual coming from you,' she had remarked. "That you choose to understand the common dilemma of the war, of the world as it is now."

"You portray me sometimes as an idiot," he told her, "Or an insensitive clod. Maybe the truth is that I'm simply a fool like everyone else. Humour me. I want to go the next step," he said. "We all die eventually, isn't that so? Yet none of us asked to be born. So, none of us asked for the beatings, the torture, the hanging, the drowning, our lives seized and destroyed by stupid people whose only claim to virtue is that they, for a moment, hold a weapon in hand or perhaps a secret in mind. How many of us, had we a choice, would have asked to enter life knowing how we would leave it?"

That had made her laugh, "You make it seem as if that is all we have, only final moments of fear."

"It's a con game," Clovis continued scornfully. "Born, creating a life for oneself, only to have it taken away by nature or a Nazi or a Communist or some other thug. The truth is that we didn't ask for life, but since we had no ability to plead our case, we exist and for what? Finally, to disappear. To become dust particles in an indifferent universe. Isn't that maddening?"

Her train of thought was interrupted by a knock on her door. She bids the person come in. A French officer enters with several soldiers and a woman whose job it is apparently to transcribe the events about to take place. A woman identified as Mayor of Nice wears a tricolor banner around her chest.

"Mlle Simone Valois," the French officer says. Straight as an arrow, only his eyes lower to look at her."

"Oui, C'est moi."

"I have been sent from the Free French Forces and by order of General De Gaulle to present you with this medal." He holds it up for everyone to see. "It is the Croix de Guerre. For services to the Nation in the face of danger and peril. Congratulations, Mlle Valois".

Simone is stunned. This is the last thing she expected. She does not feel that she deserves such an honour. In fact, she doesn't think herself deserving of any honour.

"I did what I thought was right," she says. "I did what I could," she exclaims, almost in defence.

The Mayor of Nice reads a proclamation in her honour. Simone pulls the covers up to her eyes. She feels less honoured and completely embarrassed.

The French officer lowers himself to place the cross around her neck, and then to apply the customary kiss on both cheeks, but she holds him at bay.

"It hurts too much. Perhaps we could just shake hands?"

Simone shakes hands with everyone in the room. It leaves her exhausted, almost sorrowful. Such an honour, she says to herself, and yet they don't know the full truth about her. It is possible that her lover's death was caused by her inability, her cowardly unwillingness, to fire the gun she held pointlessly in her hand.

Fortunately, sleep gains on her dismissing the thought. Another ten days elapse. Simone is now able now to stand and walk several yards. Day after day, she is accumulating strength. Her ability to move increases. And yet, lagging behind the achievement of her body, her mind feels sunk in mud. She takes no joy in little daily conversations, the voyage of the sun as it dances its way from one side of the earth to the other. Days pass in this fashion. An American consul visits bringing with him a brand-new passport and offering to transport her back to America in a state department plane. She declines for the moment on the grounds that she is not ready. Ready? Not ready to leave France. Not able to leave the past. Not capable of putting aside all that has been done to her, the savagery, the uselessness of the violence perpetrated against her, the stupidity of war. Just because some half-crazed soldier convinced a country that his group was more perfect than others, that they were superhuman.

Dead days. Sitting on the balcony observing the gulls, the bathers, the sea in the distance sparkling like a diamond field. The door opens, and Grace enters.

"Simone," Grace whispers, seeing her sister in a state of half sleep. Simone awakens and stretches. Sits up.

"What an illusion I have right now," she says mainly to herself. "I actually believe that my sister is here with me in Nice."

Grace chuckles, takes Simone's hand. "I've come for you," she announces. "Look at you," she clucks. "Those hoodlums! But you can forget about all that. I've come to take you home."

"Of course, you have," Simone says, and for the first time in many days musters a weak smile.

"I have been reading about you," Grace grins.

"All lies," Simone interrupts.

"You have become a peculiar person of note. Any man doing what you did…well that's one thing. But the fact that you are a woman is striking everyone as unprecedented, at least unusual, and maybe even peculiar. People are fascinated by you, a member of the Maquis, you as gunfighter. And now there is a story circulating that you and one of the chief Maquisards were in love with each other, but knowing you, I doubt you would ever allow yourself such a thing."

Simone sits up. "Give me a cigarette, please. They are on the table."

Grace lights one for her. "I fell in love with Clovis," Simone says. "He loved me as well. We had a stupid argument, a philosophical argument about dying which separated us for a time, but I knew he still loved me. And then I allowed him, caused him, to die."

"This is nonsense," Grace says. She appears older to Simone, more confident, no longer a child. She seems in control.

Simone details the last minutes of his life, how she failed to act, and what happened.

"But" Grace immediately jumps in, "Even if you shot the pistol a thousand times, it may not have saved his life. You cannot blame yourself."

Simone says nothing in rebuttal. She cannot argue. She won't get into it with Grace.

"Tell me about you, your life."

"You're asking about Faron?"

"Well, yes."

"We are still together, but not entirely. I discovered that he had a girlfriend on the side. So, I confronted him. He denied it of course. But after I wouldn't speak to him for ten days, he telephoned, admitted it, and promised that this was simply a little fling, the kind that men have, and which are meaningless."

"Not meaningless to me, I told him," Grace says. "But he promised then to mend his ways. I said: OK, but you will have to win back my trust. Years later, he is still trying."

"And do you really trust him now?"

"As long as I hold him at bay, I think I do. But if he were he living with me, then I think he would take advantage. So, we go out. We make love, we share a great deal, but we don't live together."

Three days later, Simone and Grace are preparing to take a state department flight to Washington, D.C. Simone looks out the porthole. At the front, the sputter of propellers revving, a small cloud of dust spewing from each engine. I have lived a lifetime here, Simone reckons. Is it possible to leave this life, to leave Clovis behind in his death? And yet, a certain relief that the extraordinary tension of war is now receding. It is time to live, she thinks. At the airport in Washington, a car picks them up and drives them to Atlanta.

22. Simone Comes Home

The vestiges of ferocious heat and humidity have wafted out of Atlanta. In their place, cooler breezes from the north and west ushering in fall. After considerable urging form her sister, Simone has decided to move into Grace's apartment. There she will have a room of her own. A small space painted in gold. Meant, she thinks, for the future Grace, Jr. if and when that tyke appears. Simple furniture and rudimentary sketches adorn the walls; it has a clock and a radio. Two green ferns sit in tall copper vases.

"I hope you like this room."

"You are kind to offer it," Simone says. "I'm still pretty tired and need a bit more time to recover from my ailments."

Grace hugs her gently. "Take the time you need."

The first night, with the window open, the rustle of leaves on a pine tree outside lulls her into a deep sleep. Only once in the middle of the night does she awaken as shadows of limbs outside scurry across her ceiling. She covers herself with a blanket.

The first days pass uneventfully. Simone is wondering about a new beginning, wondering about a new way of life, to leave behind, memory, sinew, blood. Somehow to deal with the uncontrolled emotions which still rail within her against the human condition.

She sees a specialist at Grady Hospital; an older gentleman who examines her delicately.

"What they told you is correct. You will not bear children," he says, lifting his gray mane. "And it is possible that you may always walk with a slight limp. The leg is healing but scars remain and internally the leg has been terribly afflicted."

Simone looks at him helplessly. "So, then what am I supposed to do?"

He has no brilliant answer, but the one that trips out of his mouth in such instances.

"Live your life. Others limp. Others can't have children. Everyone has something extraordinary to offer. Find the courage you showed in France, and now use it here."

The physical restrictions pose but a small difficulty blocking the way forward. There are intimate explosions within Simone's mind. Images of gunfire, of shards of concrete, of metal ripping men asunder, men looking down as their lives pour out of their bodies and eyes that have been emptied of their light. Clovis's gaze, imbued with energy suddenly drained, dimmed, now gone. And try as she may, Simone cannot shut off completely these visions that rise up like carousel lights in a dizzying display of despair.

Ten days have elapsed.

"Would you like to go out for a walk?" Grace asks. "Faron and I want to see Gone with the Wind at the Fox. We missed it when it came here years ago. I don't know how we missed it. There was such a to-do about it, and even Clark Gable and Vivien Leigh were in town. Maybe we just couldn't get tickets. But it's back now."

"It covers the war between the states, right?" Simone asks.

"Well, it's mainly a love story."

"But fighting and gore are part of it."

"Yes, I think so."

Simone shades her mouth with her hand.

"Then I think you and Faron ought to go alone."

Faron comes to the house carrying a grocery bag, strides up the stairs and boisterously says hello to Simone. He has not changed, she thinks. He still has the same Mediterranean look about him. Something off-putting but she cannot quite name it.

"I was so happy when Grace told me you were going to stay here. Imagine, a true hero in our house."

"Yes," Simone repeats, "In your house."

"I mean of course Grace's house, but you know Grace and I have been seeing one another now for several years." He continues somewhat sheepishly. "I think to marry her, but she is not ready for this step."

"You have to be trustworthy," Simone says without monitoring herself. "You have to be her hero before she marries you."

"Aah, I see that she has spoken of me. I have been sorry for disturbing her peace," Faron replies. "I brought new toilet rolls at the grocery store as she requested," he adds. With that, he backs out of the room, forcing a tiny, crude smile.

Later that same afternoon, there is another visitor. This time it's Anderson. Simone is downstairs in the parlour aimlessly rifling through old magazines when the doorbell rings.

"Anderson!" she exclaims almost in a shout. He enters and takes Simone in his arms and squeezes gently. He has aged a bit, she thinks. Still the red suspenders are in evidence, the spectacles, the friendly smile.

"I wasn't sure for a time," he says, "That we would ever see one another again. I had heard that the Nazis had captured you. A Major Anselm, the same man you were in contact with in Paris."

"Yes," she answers. "He turned me over to two goons who worked me over for a very long period of time."

"But to your credit, you survived. Look at you. Years older, but I have trouble seeing any difference."

Simone grins. "You're too kind." The restored teeth irritate her. Irregular, spaced badly, they hurt her mouth. Furthermore, she knows that the shape of her mouth has been altered, that it subtracts from her looks.

"I wanted," he continues, "To thank you on behalf of the OSS. I cannot fathom the adventures you undertook, the work you did on our behalf, even hand-to-hand fighting you engaged in on behalf of the French. On behalf of all of us. It's remarkable for a woman, well, for anybody! We're being reconstituted into something called the Central Intelligence Agency. I will have a role in it, and I hope you will as well."

"I don't believe so," she answers, lighting a Chesterfield. "My time as a spy is over."

"Not as a spy," he answers quickly. "You can do work for us in an office. There is always intelligence to be deciphered by a good mind."

She has no response to this. Now she offers him coffee. She pours him a cup.

"I came for another reason as well," he continues, sipping from the cup. "Not bad coffee for instant."

"Go on."

"I have received news about the parents of Clovis Rastine. These are people you lived with for some time, I know."

Simone feels her brain stiffening. "Yes. Go on."

"We learned that they were sent to Auschwitz. Two months after their arrival, they were both gassed there. If only they had been able to hold out. The liberation of the camp was to take place shortly thereafter. They were simply unlucky."

"Yes, unlucky," Simone remarks crestfallen.

"You knew them well, didn't you?"

"Yes."

"I'm sorry to burden you with such bad news."

"You do what you have to," she says. But after this exchange, the conversation slows into tepid chatting, diminishes into monosyllabia. Anderson arises. He understands full well that this young protégé of his has suffered enormously and requires time and space to recover.

"When you are feeling better call me. We'll get together. Maybe we can talk then about your future with the CIA. Oh, and one other thing." He says, rising. "You'll be happy about this. You have earned a disability pension which will be paid out to you every month by the government. Actually, you won't ever need to work again, but knowing you, I am certain you won't just want to sit at home reading the Ladies Home Journal."

So, Jean-Luc and Odile are also gone, she thinks, as Anderson departs. That night, her restless mind wanders endlessly through the Pyrenees, through the forests and up into the hills as if she was still searching for girolles and cepes. Down in the valley, at home, Odile and Jean-Luc reading the morning papers as if nothing would ever disturb their concentration. Simone forces her mind into the forest, to the foot of trees where cepes abound. But there are no mushrooms to be found. In a powerful dream, she is running wildly through the forest searching for something which she cannot find.

The next days, she remains at home. She does not read the Atlanta Constitution, the local paper. Nor does she peruse the magazines except to rifle through them. The radio remains silent. Grace is often at work. When Grace returns at the end of the day, she cooks for the two of them. Simone has no appetite and often eats only at the bidding, the cajoling of her sister. Occasionally, Faron comes over. Unable to participate in the conversation, he straightens the tissue boxes in the bedrooms or the paintings on the wall. Simone says virtually nothing to him. She is exquisitely tired and sleeps fifteen hours a day. She has neck pains, but when a doctor is called, he can find nothing wrong. Headaches pursue her day and night. Aspirin has little effect.

One afternoon she unearths a bottle of gin in a cupboard and begins to drink. Alcohol knocks her out. When she awakens, she drinks some more. Grace comes home to find her sister giddy, morbidly giddy, speaking nonsense about eternity and the ether, but with more spirit than she has heard in a while.

Still, Grace removes the gin.

Suddenly, after weeks of self-confinement, Simone gets up one day and steps out. She waits for the bus to Piedmont Park under a shelter. When the bus arrives, she boards it, pays, and finds a seat. She watches as two older men enter the bus, lurch by her. She turns her head slightly to see where they are sitting. They find seats in the rear, and chat to each other. She is certain that they are speaking about her. When she disembarks, however, the men do not follow. She finds this odd, wonders what kind of spy training doesn't require them to follow their prey. She finds a bench and sits. It is a cool, misty morning. She closes up her coat around her neck. Simone observes men and women walking, dogs playing with one another and a woman tossing a ball for her toddler.

Across the way, a red-haired man is standing, one leg crossed over the other leg, smoking a cigarette. He would appear in his thirties. She cannot quite make out the features of his face. But Simone is certain that he is observing her, examining her at a distance. He snuffs out his cigarette, lights another one. They are now staring at one another. The man begins to cross the distance between the two of them shuffling between dogs and running children on the path. Simone is paralyzed, her throat constricted. The man is smiling as he approaches. She feels faint. Then he is by her side and sits next to her on the bench. She is looking straight ahead.

"Nice morning," he says. He speaks with a foreign accent. Maybe Spanish. She says nothing. "I often bring my dog here to walk," he says, "But I walked him earlier this morning in the neighbourhood."

"What do you want?" Simone says, turning to him quickly and speaking shrilly.

"Want? Just to say hello."

"Who do you work for?"

"Work for?" he asks uncomprehendingly.

"Wehrmacht?"

"I don't follow."

"You want something from me. Yes? You have a message to transmit?"

The man stands up. "Look, I've upset you. That was not my intention. I have nothing for you except a cheery good morning. I thought you looked interesting and I wanted to make your acquaintance, but I see this is the wrong day."

"Don't follow me," she says sternly.

"You are a funny one," the man responds quietly and leaves.

In the bus back to her neighbourhood, Simone realises that she is making a fool of herself, that the men she believed tailing her are simply men living their lives without reference to her. She sits, giggling in her seat. What a fool I've become, she ponders, and both hands slap her face gently to emphasise the point.

A few days elapse, days in which Simone sits by the window observing the people passing by.

"I've made an appointment for you at the dentist," Grace remarks, taking off her coat.

Simone looks up concerned. "Dentist?"

"Yes, you told me that your teeth hurt. Whatever they failed to do in France during wartime conditions can be remedied here."

"I don't need to go."

"Damn it," Grace responds, dropping a scarf on a chair. "You are going to the dentist, and I am taking you."

"I don't feel well leaving the house," Simone retorts. "Why do you want to make me do this?"

"Because you need to have your teeth fixed."

"I don't like being forced to do anything."

But when she looks up into Grace's frowning face, she realises that she has gone too far.

"All right," Simone relents. "I'll go."

The dentist's office is within walking distance.

"Five to seven minutes from here," Grace prompts. She is concerned by her sister's unwillingness to engage. But she has no idea how she can help to remedy the problem. She cannot even identify the specific scab although it is clearly related to Simone's wartime experiences abroad.

The dentist outlines a course of treatment.

"You will have to come here once a week for perhaps seven weeks to take care of everything," he says, retracting a tool from her mouth. Simone nods, but once she returns home, she tells Grace that she is thinking about living with her teeth as they presently sit.

Grace is losing patience with her.

"Impossible."

"All right," Simone relents, seeing the glare in her sister's eye. "I'll do it for you," she says, thinking that Grace may well forget about the dentist in the next weeks.

"I so appreciate it," Grace responds with sarcasm.

Repeatedly, Grace accompanies her sister to the dentist, usually after a fierce argument. But at the end of seven weeks, Simone refuses to leave the house. She is bewildered. The first check from the government has arrived, and she needs to deposit it in some bank. She asks Grace to do this, but Grace refuses.

Later that day, Simone opens the front door, looks out and immediately closes it in a panic. She feels faint, her heart thumping madly. She slams the door and sits.

"I'm not well," she says to Grace.

"I know," Grace says taking her hand. "I get that you are not well. But you have to make an effort. There is nothing physically stopping you from walking to the bank, the grocery store, anywhere."

Simone blinks hard. "I'm afraid to go out."

"I see that."

"Deposit the check for me, please."

"Not on your life,' Grace answers. "I work all day, and when I come home, I cook for us and try to look after your needs, but I cannot also run your errands. That's not reasonable."

Simone is consternated, feels bad.

"I should not have asked you to do this," she says to her sister. Later, after Grace has quit the house, Simone approaches the front door. She opens it a peep, peers out. The street is empty. Simone opens the door wider. Now she ventures out one foot after the other. There are three steps down. One. Two. Three. On the sidewalk, her nostrils heave, searching for air. Then she begins to move and the weight of the moment eases. Suddenly, she is walking freely, arms swinging. Feels good. Great. The moment is delicious.

At the bank now. She completes the paperwork, hands it to a woman behind a glass panel.

"Is this for deposit?"

"Yes."

"You can cash it, you know."

"Yes."

"Yes, you want to cash it?"

"I told you I want to deposit it."

The woman looks up askance. "No need to get huffy about it."

"Please handle it. I'm in a hurry."

An officer stands at the door. He has a pistol in a holster, she notices. "Is there a gun store nearby?"

Somewhat taken aback by the question, the officer composes his answer carefully.

"Certainly, miss. Two blocks straight ahead, one block to the left."

Simone strides confidently to the gunstore. There, she handles several weapons. She picks up an Astra 400."

A salesman approaches her.

"Good gun," he says. "Brought back from Germany. Very accurate at short distances."

"That's fine," Simone responds, checking it out. Cocks it. Looks into the barrel. "Fine. I'll take it and fifty rounds of ammunition. Nine-millimeter, right?"

"You know your ammunition," the salesman says. "Any reason you're buying a gun, miss? It's a little unusual to have a woman purchasing an Astra."

"For protection, of course," she responds.

"Somebody after you, miss?"

Simone looks up with tight lips.

"If you feel threatened, you ought to call the cops."

"That's why I'm getting the gun," she responds with determination, her voice straining. Simone drops the pistol into her purse.

Now she walks to the pharmacy in her neighbourhood. There is a short line. She waits. A man comes up behind her. A large man. She moves a bit closer to the person in front of her. The man behind her follows her in. She turns.

"You're standing too close to me," she says shrilly. "Please move back."

The man looks astonished. "I haven't touched you," he remarks with a stammer.

"I didn't say you had. But you were too close. I could hear you breathing."

The woman in front of her is at the counter speaking with the pharmacist.

"I always stand behind people at a respectable distance," the man stammers askance. "I wasn't close to you. You must be crazy."

Simone is outraged. She reaches into her purse and takes out the gun. At once, the man behind her steps back, his hands shielding his face. The pharmacist has stopped speaking but does not move. He wants to intervene, but his mouth does not issue words. The woman slides away from the counter on bent knees towards the front door. The pharmacist's wife in the office above is on the phone.

"Look," the man says to Simone. "I didn't mean to offend you."

"You were standing too close," Simone repeats.

The man, who for one moment was cowering, now stands up straight.

"I fought in the war," he says. "In Okinawa. I know when a gun is loaded and when it ain't. This gun ain't loaded. I can see into the barrel." And with that, he grabs Simone and tries to knock her down. Simone trips him, swings him into a cosmetic tray. Bottles go flying. The pharmacist has come around and seeks to restrain Simone. A teen-ager entering the pharmacy at that moment runs forward, tackles Simone. On the ground, squirming, shouting, biting, kicking. It takes all three men to restrain her. The police arrive and cart her downtown.

Processed, she finds herself in a jail cell. Calming down, she looks around. Her breathing reverts to normal. The cell feels familiar, almost cosy. The bars are limitations on freedom. She thinks that is both necessary and fine. It's comfy in the cell, despite the lack of a window. There is a bench with a pillow on it. She stretches out, fluffs the pillow behind her head, and looks up at the ceiling. Relaxes a little. A pale light bulb reminds her of something in her past. She has no feeling about anything now. What has just happened anyway? She cannot entirely recall. There was some kerfuffle about a man too close to her. He pulled a gun on her, did he?

Four hours later, an officer walks down the corridor to her cell, searches for the right key, cannot find it at once in the plethora of jumbled metal clustered on his chain, swears that he must remember to colour-code it, at last finds the correct key, opens the cell, and tells her that she is free.

"Bail has been posted," he says.

Simone gets up, smoothes down her skirt and walks out. She stops at the bathroom. An officer at the front desk hands her purse over without the gun. She has to sign for the purse. The ammunition is also gone. She says nothing but turns to see Anderson waiting for her.

"I heard you were arrested," he says with concern engraved on his face. "I'm springing you."

Simone says nothing. Anderson drives her home silently. She opens the door.

"You need help," Anderson says at last. "I have someone who can help you."

Simone closes the car door.

Three days later, Simone is riding the bus downtown. It is a Saturday early in the morning and the streets are virtually empty. She is looking for the Equitable Building, the high-rise on Edgewood Avenue. She has never been to this building before, but she knows of it. She read about it. Can't miss it.

Enters. No guard. Lobby is empty. In front of her is a bank of elevators. Instead, she locates the stairs. Concrete stairs with metal railings, they lead up to the second floor. Images of her childhood resonate. A swing. Her mother frowning, her father reading the papers, Simone sat at his side handing him a pipe. She holds onto the railing as she ascends to the third floor. Her brain is filling with scents of the past, a barbeque in the back yard, a pig roasting overnight on a spit. She continues to climb. Grace at her bedside when she suffered from the flu, a bad flu. It made her vomit, gave her a high fever. She remembers Grace swabbing her cheeks with a cold cloth, but Simone cannot continue to think about her sister.

Simone is passing the fifth floor now. She stops to stabilise her breath. Only a few more steps, she knows. Transported to France. The first time she sees Clovis, he wearing his glasses below curly hair, reading a book intently. A frisson. There was a bridge that they were asked by the Free French to blow up. Yes, they did it. Or perhaps he did it and told her about it. Yes, that was likely for she can remember neither the explosion nor the bridge. She wishes her mind were less of a jumble as she climbs up to the seventh-floor landing. I ought to be perfectly clear, she says to herself. Pauses. The scent of mint Clovis hands her. She has a bit of an allergy to it and sneezes lightly as she presses it to her nose. He laughs and stuffs a clove in his nostrils. Just like the Arabs do, he reminds her, smiling. It refreshes. She grins at the memory of his pleasure.

The final landing. A heavy metallic, brown door she pushes open with some difficulty. Succeeds at last and squeezes through. The roof. She steps out into it, into the fresh air. The chill rocks her for a moment. She wishes she could sit, but there is little to sit on. On the Edgewood Avenue side, there's a concrete border. She walks over to it and sits down, legs dangling into space.

So, what is this all about? That question permeates her being. What is this all about? For Clovis, very little. Even the journey is secondary to the end. The end is pointless except for our meaning and that, Lord knows, is fleeting and may, in and of itself, be worthless. Yet, Simone always responded to this dark side of Clovis in the same manner. The life force triumphed over despair. No concept alone could bring it to its knees. She experienced it within her, exulted in it. In this moment, however, it is no longer clear whether that force survives. Ravaged by loss, by blood, by pain, by anguish, Simone is abandoning it. Instead, she wishes to lie with her lover, whether in his forever dark place, or in the last vestige of imagination.

She stands on the border, looks below. A couple on the street crane their necks up. They're pointing to her. Simone looks beyond them to a park at a short distance. Birds are cavorting, cawing. Squirrels chase one another up and down trees. Simone feels that she lacks the will to claw herself back to desire. What once spurred her to become a spy, to love another human being, to belong to someone else, is now lost in a spate of horrific images....that singular moment that Clovis, crouching next to her in surreal isolation from the rest of the fiery eruptions surrounding them, fire emitting from his weapon, falls. She, the beloved warrior, holding a pistol which she does not fire. Did she enable his death? An empty vessel sans soul shuddering. Her body positions itself shakily on the border. Her soul feels departed.

She is keen, inclined. In an instant. She will not jump. She intends simply to allow the corpse to fall forward towards the couple pointing upwards. One moment passes. Another. The third arrives with a new welter of images.

What about the voyage to Arette? What about the sun playing on her back on a cool morning as she climbed the mountain? The feast at Tatie Jeanne's? What about the gulls on the Promenade screeching with delight as they seize a morsel of bread? What about a sprig of mint on a hot afternoon? A cacophony of scents, of colours, of faces, of ideas grappling one with the other assaults her. Simone looks down. Gracious fear stirs through her, afraid of this absurd end.

Simone steps back trembling, her face and arms glistening with sweat. Later that day, she dials Anderson's number.